Praise for the previous novels of Jodi Thomas

"Will warm readers with its huge heart and gentle souls."
—*Library Journal*

"Thomas's memorable, refreshingly candid characters are sure to resonate, especially the strong female protagonists. Series fans will be delighted."
—*Publishers Weekly*

"Highly recommended."
—*Library Journal* (Starred Review)

"Compelling and beautifully written, it is exactly the kind of heart-wrenching, emotional story one has come to expect from Jodi Thomas."
—DEBBIE MACOMBER, #1 *New York Times* bestselling author

"A beautiful love letter to the power of female friendship, and when you read it, you'll feel like you've come home. Perfect for fans of Debbie Macomber and Nina George."
—ROBYN CARR, #1 *New York Times* bestselling author

"Tender, heartfelt, and wonderful. Jodi Thomas's beautiful writing and her compelling, vivid characters will work their way straight into your heart and stay there forever. I loved every word."
—RAEANNE THAYNE, *New York Times* bestselling author

"You can count on Jodi Thomas to give you a satisfying and memorial read."
—CATHERINE ANDERSON, *New York Times* bestselling author

DINNER
on
PRIMROSE HILL

JODI THOMAS

ZEBRA BOOKS
KENSINGTON PUBLISHING CORP.
www.kensingtonbooks.com

ZEBRA BOOKS are published by

Kensington Publishing Corp.
119 West 40th Street
New York, NY 10018

All Kensington titles, imprints, and distributed lines are available at special quantity discounts for bulk purchases for sales promotion, premiums, fund-raising, and educational or institutional use.

Special book excerpts or customized printings can also be created to fit specific needs. For details, write or phone the office of the Kensington Sales Manager: Kensington Publishing Corp., 119 West 40th Street, New York, NY 10018. Attn. Sales Department. Phone: 1-800-221-2647.

ZEBRA BOOKS and the Z logo Reg. U.S. Pat. & TM Off.

First Zebra Books trade paperback printing: November 2021
First Zebra Books mass market paperback printing: November 2022

ISBN-13: 978-1-4201-5135-0
ISBN-13: 978-1-4201-5136-7 (eBook)

10 9 8 7 6 5 4 3 2 1

Printed in the United States of America

For my sons, who are always there to help me

Prologue

Friday

Professor Virginia Clark stared out the third-floor window of her office on a campus so small it seemed more like a set for a Hallmark movie than a college.

Tomorrow would be the start of spring break, and at forty-three years old she no longer cared. In her college days she'd loved the break. A time to travel, have fun, and maybe go wild, but now it was only a time to clean her office and catch up on paperwork.

If she could turn back time, she'd live one more wild spring break.

But she had a survey to conduct and a paper to write and an office to organize. No fun in that.

Mischief crawled up her spine. Maybe, even at forty-three, she might enjoy the break of another kind.

After all, you're not dead until you're dead.

Friday

Chapter 1

Benjamin

Dr. Benjamin Monroe folded his notes and placed them in the worn leather briefcase he'd carried since graduate school. His lecture room at Clifton College was empty now. Peaceful. He always liked the stillness after class. He'd done his job, and he took pride in that.

As he often did, he turned to the long, narrow windows behind his podium and looked out over his hometown. From the third floor he could see east all the way to the river and north to where the land rose in rolling hills. There was a balance here that calmed his soul. A wide valley that nestled three small towns, but his town, Clifton Bend, was the best because the college rested in its center.

Benjamin hadn't missed a class in twelve years. At forty-two he always came on time and well prepared. Routine ruled his life. He liked working with his dad on their farm every weekend and loved biking through the valley on sunny afternoons. The exercise kept him lean and tanned, just as his work kept him sharp.

What he didn't like was spring break. It interrupted his routine. A worthless holiday, but he'd help his father on their little farm and manage to keep busy.

"Dr. Monroe?" A nervous, high-pitched voice bombarded his thoughts. "May I speak to you about something? It's important."

A creature with auburn hair, glasses too big for her face, and huge blue eyes leaned around the door. Professor Virginia Clark.

He plowed his long fingers through his straight, mud-colored hair. If teachers were allowed a nemesis, Miss Clark, the biology instructor, would be his. As far as he was concerned, all they had in common was age.

Benjamin was tempted to say, "No, you can't speak to me," but that would be unprofessional.

To her credit, Miss Virginia Clark was bubbly on a down day. Her voice was too high, her manner of dress was in no way appropriate, and her legs were too short. On a good day she was exuberant and misguidedly thought they were not only colleagues but friends.

He'd always hated bubbly people; they made him nervous. But she taught two doors down in the biology lab and officed next to him. Some days he swore he could hear her laughing or running around her tiny workplace like a squirrel in a box.

Right now, she was charging toward his podium like Grant taking Richmond. Too late to say no or run, so all he could do was watch her approach.

Another observation—professors should never bounce.

Miss Clark bounced. She was a bit on the chubby side, a head shorter than he was, and the white lab coat did not conceal her curves. Her corkscrew hair seemed to be dancing to a hard rock beat, and her breasts . . . well, never mind them. Unprofessional, he thought as he watched her coming down the steps row by row, breasts moving to their own beat.

"I need your help, Dr. Monroe." She stopped one foot too close to him.

He fought the urge to step back.

"Of course, Miss Clark, I'm at your service," he offered. Maybe she needed a ride or she was locked out of her office, again. He could make time to be kind. After all, they were colleagues. "I'd be happy to help any way I can."

"Good. I was afraid you'd say no. It's a great opportunity and we can split the work and the money."

Benjamin raised an eyebrow. "What work?"

"My research paper entry for the *Westwin Research Journal* has been approved as one of five finalists. The winner's findings will be published in the journal as well as winning the ten-thousand-dollar prize." She smiled. "Just think, we'll be famous. Last year's subject was how aging relates to location. The winner was interviewed on the *Today* show."

She was bouncing again. This time with excitement. "I might finally get to go to New York City. I've always dreamed of seeing plays and walking through Central Park. They say you can hear the heartbeat of the whole world in the streets of New York."

Benjamin fell into her pipe dream for a second. "If I had money to blow, I'd go to Paris and see Marie Curie's office and lab. I've read every book about her dedication, her work, her life. Imagine walking the streets she walked."

He didn't mention that he'd also find his mother, if she was still alive. She'd left him when he was four years old, saying she must paint in Paris for a few months, but she never came back. He had only one question for her. Was the life she'd given him up for worth it?

Miss Clark frowned at him as if measuring his sanity. "Paris, really Benjamin, sometimes you surprise me."

When he frowned at the use of his first name, she sighed, obviously reading his thoughts.

"Dr. Monroe," she corrected. "We could split the research and the writing. I've already obtained the president's approval for a small survey. All we have is a month to get this done, but we've got spring break to kick off our project with a bang."

He nodded slowly, not willing to jump in, but willing to listen. "What is our topic of research?"

Blushing, she added, "Redefining sexual attractions in today's world."

Benjamin straightened slightly.

Miss Clark giggled. "We could call it, 'The Chemistry of Mating.'"

He swallowed hard as she turned and bounced out of the room.

For a few moments, Benjamin forgot to breathe. Calamity had blown in on a tornado with red hair.

The only good news. Spring break wasn't going to be boring.

Chapter 2

Ketch

When his Friday night class ended, Ketch Kincaid marched down the sleeping streets of Clifton in fast military steps. Peaceful shadows rested between houses and the melody of a spring night did nothing to calm him as he stormed toward what the locals called Low Street.

As he neared neon blinking lights, his surroundings darkened with caution and the melody of the night changed to a raging heartbeat. Trash rattled in the roughly paved street, echoing the rush of water from the river a few hundred yards away. This was a street, he thought, where dreams go to die, and his just had taken their last breath.

The barn-of-a-bar that backed against old train tracks wasn't much to look at in daylight. Now, lit only by a sliver of moon, the COME ON IN, PARTNER sign seemed more an order than an invitation.

A hungry wind suddenly howled through the valley. The old bar seemed morose, as if the building was rotting from the inside out.

Just the kind of place Ketch was looking for.

His worn steel-toed boots throbbed against the plank

sidewalk like a ragging heartbeat as he rushed toward his own personal implosion.

After fighting his way through the army for four years and then working two jobs while taking a full load in college for the past three years, tonight his world was crumbling.

Every dream, every plan, every goal was crashing around him, dissolving into rubble.

Thanks to one letter.

Crystal had broken up with him from half a world away with one page.

The six-year-old version of him standing outside his third foster home with all his possessions in a trash bag flashed through Ketch's mind. He was the kid no one wanted. The soldier who made enemies because he pushed too hard. The student a few years too old to fit in at college.

"Alone Again" would be the theme song of his life, if he had one.

Kincaid's big frame hit the door of the bar so hard it slammed the inside wall and sifted dust from the rafters. Not that anyone noticed. A country band played at full volume and everyone crammed inside was screaming above the music.

The smell of stale beer and sweaty bodies hit him in waves as he stomped across the floor. The lights were low enough to make every drunk look handsome and every wilted flower perk up. Glasses and longnecks clanked in applause at every stupid joke.

At six-five Ketch had no trouble looking over the crowd. The smell of sweat and mud seemed to grow thicker as he moved. This was just the kind of place he hated. No one was real; they were all pretending. He'd seen hangouts all over the world just like this. Different music. Different drinks. Same action.

Right now it was what he needed. He planned to do

damage to as many brain cells as possible before dawn, maybe get in a fight or get arrested. Nothing mattered. Crystal had dumped him in a damn letter and scratched out all his dreams with her pen.

They'd served together, both Army Rangers. Spent a thousand hours planning their future and sometimes flying halfway around the world to spend their leave wrapped up in each other. Crystal was his only friend, his one love, his today and his tomorrow.

They had decided he'd muster out first and start college. She promised she would follow in a year. Crystal would complete her tour of duty, leave the army, and start teaching wherever he was, maybe get a master's while he finished up. By the time he graduated, they would have saved enough for a house in any state that offered them both jobs. They had it all planned out. A home. A life together.

But she'd hesitated when it was time for her to leave the army. After all, it meant a promotion if she stayed one more year. Then another year passed. She said she wanted to travel, and her military assignments gave her the chance. She would serve another year. By then they could start grad school together.

Only now his graduation was less than two months away. He'd been expecting any day to hear when she'd be back to the States and out of the army. But her call never arrived.

Their texts and calls had grown more sporadic the last few months. He'd figured they were both just busy. While overseas she took online classes in programing, and he tried to get thirty hours of construction work in each week while studying, attending classes, and sometimes taking on programing jobs for some of the faculty. Some weekends, when he'd laid bricks or roofed a house for twelve hours, he'd been too tired even to check his email.

Then there were the times Crystal would move from one

location to another with her team and he wouldn't hear from her for a few weeks. But it never bothered him. They had a plan. They'd known it would be hard for a few years, but it would be worth the struggle. Once they were out of the army and out of school, they'd have a great life. That was the plan.

Until today. Time 17:57. He'd opened the letter.

Ketch had stopped thinking at 17:58. He'd stopped believing in dreams. He simply sat through his night class in a daze and now pushed through the drunken crowd cussing to himself.

She'd written him a damn letter. A real letter. Her first. Her last.

No fast text sent off in anger, but a letter. She'd had to think about it. Walk over and mail it. It was sent six days ago, meaning she'd had six days and nights to change her mind. Six days to send an email to tell him not to read the letter. She'd made a mistake. Nothing had changed. She still loved him.

But she hadn't. The letter said it all. It took Crystal just one page to say goodbye. She'd even listed why it wouldn't work between them, like she'd been keeping a list since the day they met, and finally she had one too many reasons to leave him.

He'd thought she really loved him. He should have learned that lesson at six years old. No one would ever bother to care about him. Never. And he swore he'd never expect it again.

Crystal had loved her job. He'd been searching all his life to find where he belonged. A home, a real place to call his own. You'd think at twenty-six he'd give up on dreaming. He'd wasted a third of his life looking for something that didn't exist.

His only plan tonight was to prove he wasn't good

enough for her. He'd erase her memory if it took half the alcohol in the bar.

Wynn Henry Wills yelled his name and Ketch started navigating across the crowded room to his lab partner in chemistry. Wills wasn't his friend even though they'd had several classes together, and as a lab partner he was about as much help as a cracked beaker.

Ketch was at the top of the grading curve and Wynn was balanced at the other end. Two sides of the seesaw. The only reason WW hadn't been kicked out of school was simple: a building on campus was named after his grandfather. He was trying to pack six or seven years into getting a four-year degree. Partying was his major and bragging his minor.

Ketch didn't need anyone to try and reason with tonight. He needed someone to drink with and Wynn Wills was just the man.

Another plus about the guy was that Crystal had hated him the one time she'd visited Ketch here last Christmas. She'd even embarrassed Wynn several times by calling him Ketch's "bad influence" friend.

Ketch smiled grimly. Tonight, Wynn would probably prove Crystal right.

"About time you got here, Ketch, my man. You're three drinks behind." Wynn slapped Ketch on the back.

"I'll catch up." Kincaid lifted Wynn's full bottle of Coors and downed it.

Wynn laughed. "So the rumor is true. The blonde bitch dumped you."

"Yep." Kincaid held up four fingers to the waitress.

She nodded back. For a moment, Ketch saw the small barmaid; really saw her, in a room full of people who never noticed the help. She was slender, with long black hair tied up in a ponytail, no makeup, T-shirt a bit too low-cut, but what startled him was the fact that her beautiful green eyes looked sadder than he felt.

He'd thought he'd cornered the market on sorrow tonight, but maybe he was wrong.

Ketch turned away. The last thing he needed was being around someone who was worse off than he was.

When she delivered the drinks, he thanked her but avoided eye contact. Her hand shook a bit when she set the beers down.

"Who is that girl?" he asked WW as she walked away.

"Tuesday Raine." Ketch took a long drink while Wynn added, "Some of the guys call her Mattress Tuesday 'cause she'll go home with anyone. Only, from what I hear, she never talks. She just lays there and lets the guy do what he wants."

"You ever sleep with her?" Ketch watched the waitress moving gracefully through the crowd, reminding him of a willow swaying in the wind. Probably about five foot four, which would be too short to date in his book. Not that he'd ever date again.

"No." Wynn pulled Ketch back to the conversation. "I must have caught her on an off night. She turned me down." WW grinned. "Besides, I like my women to participate. If I'm drunk, I want a wild roller-coaster ride, not a dead fish."

Ketch wouldn't be surprised if WW was a virgin. He was always bragging, but in three years Ketch had never seen a girl look interested in him. Even with his granddad's oil money, he couldn't find a date.

Three girls wearing sorority sweatshirts neared their table. They started talking to WW, but they kept glancing at Kincaid. Wynn introduced him as the smartest guy in the class, and all three blondes smiled as if WW had said, "He's richer than me and available."

Ketch raised his beer in salute but didn't smile. They

were probably barely twenty-one, five years younger than he was. He was too old to fit in with students who graduated from high school a few years ago. Or maybe he'd seen too much of life to talk about nothing.

"You want to dance?" the tall blonde nearest him asked.

"With all three of you?" Ketch noticed her makeup more than her face.

"Why not?" The blonde with curly hair said, "You look big enough to take us all on."

The third girl didn't say a word, but she looked at him like she was hungry and he was the entrée.

Before Ketch could answer, Wynn jumped in. "We'll dance with you ladies." When Ketch frowned, WW added, "How about I take these two and you take the tall one, Kincaid?"

Wynn pulled the shorter two out onto the dance floor. His dance moves reminded Ketch of an out-of-control garden hose. Makeup-girl acted like she was dancing by herself, but the curly-headed one started trying to teach Wynn. He looked ecstatic and tried to follow every move.

Ketch didn't want to dance, but he couldn't very well just stand there. He knew he'd embarrass the third girl if he walked away, so he took her hand. "One dance. That's all. I'm here to drink tonight."

"OK," she answered as if she'd lost all interest in him. Or maybe she decided to start playing hard to get.

Ketch didn't care either way. His boots made dancing impossible, so he just held on to her and swayed. She locked her fingers behind his neck, leaned back and closed her eyes.

Holding this stranger felt awkward. Mixed feelings rumbled through him. He had no interest in any woman right now. Now that Crystal had dropped him, he hated the whole gender.

The tall blonde seemed to forget about him. He might as well have been a pole she was hanging on to.

Maybe he should sleep with this wayward sorority girl first, then swear off the entire female side of humanity. He could act nice. Pay her a few compliments. Offer to take her home. Hell, he could tell her he thought he was falling in love. Lots of guys slept with women they didn't know. He could do that. What did it matter? The whole love thing was all a lie anyway.

Ketch had never done a one-night stand. Not in the army. Not in school. He'd met Crystal the second week of boot camp. They'd been friends for a few years before they'd started dating and sleeping together. He always thought, even from the first, that he was her makeover project, but he'd believed she'd loved him too.

Hell, he almost said aloud. *He wouldn't know love if it body-slammed him to the floor.*

Looking back, he realized he'd been the one falling in love, while Crystal was just working on training him. Sex was the treat she gave him when he performed. Apparently, he'd been the only one thinking of forever. He'd been the one making plans while she always said there would be time to get serious later. With his graduation close, he must have pushed too hard at the forever plan. He doubted she'd even filed paperwork to muster out, or even applied to grad school. All the signs were there; he just hadn't wanted to see them.

What hurt the most was that letter. Sure, they'd been arguing, but that was nothing new.

The letter had mapped out her new plan, one that didn't include him. She'd finish school online, stay in the army, and retire in her forties. She'd see the world and make it better for all somehow, while he'd be teaching chemistry to high school kids who didn't even care about learning. She loved her job in the army and was never going to leave it to live in some little town.

Ketch closed his eyes as he moved across the crowded floor with a stranger in his arms. He could almost pretend he was dancing with Crystal. Almost. But the tall blonde didn't feel right against him. Maybe no one ever would again.

When the dance ended, he thanked the girl and went back to his beers. After several more bottles, his brain seemed to slow down and Ketch watched the world as if he were underwater. Nothing seemed real.

When Wynn asked one of the blondes to join them at the table, Ketch saw his chance to leave. It was almost closing time and he knew he'd be going home alone.

As he walked out of the bar, his head started pounding and he felt like he was on a boat rocking with the waves. He stumbled and fell hard onto the gravel parking lot. Rolling to a sitting position, he waited a moment, wondering if he could stand without tumbling again. The ground didn't seem steady. His head was square dancing and his stomach was a stoned rocker. Two or three drinks was his limit usually and tonight he'd quit counting at eight.

It took all his concentration to stand and try to figure out which way was home.

Something wet trickled over his eye and he looked up to see if it was raining, then he sobered enough to recognize blood. He felt the gash across his forehead, just deep enough to drip. "Damn, what next?" he mumbled, feeling like he was in a fight with fate.

"You all right?" came a voice from the darkness.

"No," he answered. "I'm leaking."

The waitress with the sad jade eyes moved out of the corner blackness.

"Here." She pulled a small towel from where she'd looped

it over her apron. "It's not clean. I wiped up beer with it, but then half your blood is probably beer anyway."

"Thanks." He patted his forehead. "Good night, Tuesday." The last thing he wanted to do was talk to someone gloomier than he was.

She didn't look surprised that he knew her name. "You sure you're steady enough to walk?"

"Sure." If the parking lot would stop bucking, he'd have no trouble.

She stepped away. "Well, good night, Ketch Kincaid." She'd obviously taken the time to learn his name as well.

He was ten feet away when the bar door banged open, streaming a dull light across the parking lot. Out of instinct more than interest, he glanced back.

The door closed, leaving him in the shadows. The one bulb over the entrance showed three men who didn't look like college kids. Too old, too rough. Probably oil workers or cowboys passing through town looking to pick up a local date for the night.

Not his problem, Ketch decided. If they were leaving, they hadn't found a midnight date.

One caught Tuesday's arm before she could vanish back into her corner.

"There you are," the last man out the door said as he captured her wrist with his big hand. "How about you come home with me tonight, honey? I promise you'll have a good time."

"No," she gritted out as she tried to pull away.

Ketch barely heard her, but her body language made it plain she was not interested.

"Oh, come on, Tuesday. It's Friday night. You need to have a little fun. You keep turning me down and one day I'll stop asking."

"No, Jack, the answer is always going to be no." Her

voice came a bit louder. "I've told you before. I'm not interested. I don't go home with anyone anymore."

The drunk didn't let go of her wrist. "It ain't like you got
any other plans. You don't have anything in common with
those kids in there. You're just a local. Homegrown. This
time I won't take no for an answer. You think you're too
good for me?"

"I said no." She didn't sound scared, just annoyed. "Don't
ask me again. The answer will always be no."

"Not this time." Jack pulled her arm like it was a lead
rope. "Come along now. You'll be glad you did, come
morning."

Ketch moved forward, letting his boots crunch the gravel
to announce his presence. He stayed just outside the circle
of light. "Tuesday, you ready for me to drive you home?"

She looked toward his shadow. Ketch saw no fear in her
eyes, just an emptiness, like she'd given up her soul long
ago and all that was left was a shell lined in sorrow. "I'm
ready, Ketch. Let's go."

Jack turned loose of her arm. "Your loss, honey. If you'd
let me, I'd make you smile, sad Tuesday. Maybe next time."
He hurried to catch up with his friends.

Without a word, Ketch watched as she hesitantly moved
toward him. He offered his hand. Slender fingers touched
his palm. They walked a few feet, then he turned to watch
the three men drive away.

She slipped her hand from his. "You don't have to give
me a ride. That guy was harmless, but you did make it
easier."

"So, you don't want a ride home?"

"No. I have a bike."

"Good." Ketch laughed. "'Cause I don't have my car."
He dabbed at his forehead. "I'm too drunk to drive anyway.
It seems I'm probably too drunk to walk as well."

To his surprise she looped her arm in his and said, "How about I walk you home?"

"You don't know where I live."

"It doesn't matter. Nowhere is far in this town."

"I'd turn down your offer, but my knee and elbow are also bleeding. The way my luck is going I'd bleed out before I make it three blocks. Would you be my guardian angel tonight?"

"Sure. I'll walk you to your door." She paused. "But I'm no angel."

Ketch smiled but didn't argue. A bit of his loneliness seemed to fade. More to himself than to Tuesday he added, "I don't need an angel, but maybe you can help me find one good reason to go on fighting my way through this world. I lost my compass today."

Chapter 3

Tuesday's World

Midnight

Tuesday Raine held on to the big man's arm. He probably out-weighed her almost double, but he wasn't steady on his feet. She'd watched him drink more than any man in the bar and still manage to look sober. If he tumbled now, he'd take her down too, but she didn't care. He'd been nice to her and that put him ahead of most folks. He'd said thank you every time she brought him another round and he'd left a twenty for the tip. Then, even drunk, he'd stepped in to help her when he thought she was in trouble.

It had been so long since anyone had even noticed her as a real person, much less offered her a lifeline. Since rumors had started about her, the only attention she got was the kind no woman would want. Some of the guys felt free to whisper suggestions about what they'd like to do with her. It was never a date. Their plan was usually to meet in the bathroom or a car outside. Even though she never agreed to their plans, somehow stories circled and boys who thought they were men lied about what they'd done with her.

"That's my place." Ketch pointed to what looked like a warehouse at the end of the street. The last building in town.

Her eyes widened. "No way. You don't live there. It's a warehouse."

All she saw was a big building and a poorly lit sign that said RANDALL BROTHERS' CONSTRUCTION AND ROOFING.

He laughed as if she'd made a joke. "It's more than that. I live in the apartment in the back. The upstairs corner was just a storage room for years, but I plumbed it, built a few walls, and moved in. I guess you could say the overhaul was my interview for a job." Ketch's words were slightly slurred, but he kept on going. "I work for the Randall brothers most days, and at night, I'm their watchdog. Renting me this place cheap costs less than feeding dogs."

She helped him navigate first the winding street and then the small trail to the back of the second-floor apartment stairway. "I'll say good night here. Thanks again for helping me back at the bar."

"Anytime, Tuesday. To tell the truth, you've been the only one worth talking to tonight."

To her shock, he leaned down and kissed her cheek, then started up the steps. One, two, three. She let out a little cry as he fell backward like a tree that had tried to stand against the wind.

Tuesday jumped out of the way, then panicked as he hit the dirt. He lay stone-still on the ground. It was far too dark to see if he was alive or dead.

Then, like a whisper in the darkness she heard him begin to chuckle. First a small sound, then growing like rolling thunder.

Slowly he sat up. "I guess I'll try that again. Trying to kill myself by falling over isn't funny anymore."

She steadied him as he stood. "I'll help this time. Walking you home isn't as easy a job as I thought it would be."

With both hands on the railing, he leaned forward as he climbed. She followed with her palms on his lower back.

Finally, they made it to the landing. When he couldn't get the key into the lock, she took it and opened his door, then stepped inside and felt for the switch.

When a line of overhead bulbs blinked on, Tuesday was shocked at the size of his apartment. One huge room, fifteen feet high with long floor-to-ceiling windows facing the river. As she turned around, she saw a messy desk the size of a bed, with two computers blinking at her. Along one brick wall were huge sheets of what looked like house plans taped in layers over more huge drawings.

His place reminded her of what a New York loft might look like. Gray and white. Clean. Nothing personal.

In a back corner, she noticed workout equipment, weights and barbells. The bay of the room was lean of furniture other than the desk, a bed, and a few stools.

"You really live here?" she asked as Ketch stumbled into the room. Lightning flashed across the windows as if putting on a show just for them.

"I did, but tonight I feel like I might die here." He managed to make it a few feet, lean over a kitchen sink and turn on the water, then he soaked his head. When he straightened back up, he shook his sandy-brown hair like a dog might, sending water flying several feet.

For the first time, Tuesday saw him in full light. Blood was still dripping from his forehead. But his face, if not handsome, was strong, just like his body.

Dirt and chunks of mud covered his clothes. One leg was bleeding through his jeans. His elbow was dirty and bloody with crimson drops dripping from his fingers.

He was one mess of a man, but he had that stray-dog look that drew her to him. His eyes held a sorrow far deeper than his wounds. A strong man lost in a tempest of his own making, she thought.

"I need to get you to a hospital. I didn't know you were hurt so bad." The trip down the stairs would probably kill them both, but he needed a doctor.

Shaking his head, he slung blood along with water. "How do you think you'll get me there? I left my truck at the library earlier. I was planning to be too drunk to drive home." He took a step closer to her. "And I completed my mission. I was too drunk to even walk home. Thank you for helping me out, but I'll be fine." He staggered forward, making his words void.

He forced his body to move toward the door as if he had the energy to see her out. She looped her arm in his and changed directions toward the bed beneath the long windows. "You need to lie down. I'll get some towels and clean you up."

He didn't argue. When he fell across the tangled covers, he was out cold and still dripping.

Tuesday found the bathroom and the first-aid kit under the sink. She also found a stack of clean towels and went to work. This wasn't the first wounded drunk she'd taped up and it probably wouldn't be the last.

First his forehead. Cleaning, closing wounds with strips of tape, then wrapping gauze around his sandy hair that held not a wave or curl. When she'd first gotten out of high school, she'd wanted to study to be a nurse. She'd even worked at the little hospital near campus and taken a few classes.

This guy reminded her of a practice dummy in the nursing lab. Only he was twice as big, four times heavier, and smelled of beer and blood.

When she checked his elbow, his flesh was almost scraped raw. She put cream on it and wrapped it up. It wasn't a professional job, but it would keep one wound from getting infected. No bones felt broken, but if he moved his arm he might start bleeding again.

Last, she had to pull off his boots and jeans to get to his knee. This one part of his body was not hurt as badly as she'd thought it might be. Not one wound but a series of scrapes running up his hairy leg.

As she worked, she noticed his socks didn't match. Tuesday smiled. If she'd known him better, she would tease him about that. Here was a man who keeps an organized house and yet couldn't match his socks.

He moaned now and then but never opened his eyes as she used a handful of Band-Aids.

Tuesday wondered what she was doing here with a stranger. She didn't owe him all this. She could have just left him once he was inside. If he was too drunk to take care of himself that wasn't her problem.

But Ketch seemed more like a lost knight without his armor than a drunk.

He'd tried to help her in the parking lot, he'd been polite in a bar where most just leered at her, and he seemed totally unaware of how hot he was. All three of the blondes at Wynn's table had studied him like he was a class assignment.

Maybe all he needed for once was a guardian angel. He'd lost his North Star.

It took her half an hour to clean up all the scrapes and bumps. When she covered him with a sheet, she decided he'd live to drink another day.

As she stood to leave, she wished he'd open his eyes just once. When she'd first seen him, she sensed a loss and sorrow in his light blue eyes so deep it might never wash away. For just a moment she thought she'd met a kindred soul.

But the more he drank, the more he turned into just another drunk at the bar on a Friday night.

"Good night," she whispered as she gave him back the kiss he'd placed on her cheek.

"Don't go." His words were soft as a prayer as she moved away. "I don't want to be alone."

She looked back. His eyes were closed and she doubted she was the one he was talking to.

"Don't leave yet," he mumbled as if the pain in his dream was far deeper than the scrapes on his body. "Stay with me for a little longer. Let me sleep thinking you're near."

Tuesday fought back a sob as she remembered so many times she'd had the same wish. Not for the lover who left her bed, but for the one she wished had been there instead of the stranger. No man who ever made promises at midnight remembered them come morning.

Silently she tugged off her shoes and climbed into his bed. She sat with her back against the headboard and cradled his bandaged head in her lap. Slowly, softly, she combed her fingers through his hair.

He rolled closer, warming her with his body. Tuesday looked out the tall windows. The back of the warehouse faced a black river and a shadowy valley beyond. She couldn't see Honey Creek thirty miles away, but she could see tiny lights blinking through the trees along the hillsides. Farms and small ranches were no more than a firefly's light in the distance.

His breathing slowed. His arm rested around her almost like a kid holding his stuffed animal.

Tuesday drifted into sleep.

Saturday

Chapter 4

Benjamin

Dr. Benjamin Monroe preferred to spend his Saturdays working on his father's farm. It was spring after all, and the farmer blood that ran through him told him it was time to put his hands in dirt.

But Miss Clark insisted they start on their project. "The Chemistry of Mating" was about the dumbest title for a research paper that he'd ever heard. He was sure she'd never be easy to work with. Since the day they'd been introduced, he'd had a vague feeling he'd seen her before. They'd both gone to the University of Texas years ago. Maybe that was it. Maybe they'd had a class together or met at a party, though except for a few crazy weeks before his second semester at grad school, Benjamin had spent his days studying.

When he'd graduated with a 4.0 GPA, he could have gone anywhere to teach, but he wanted to come back home. His roots were here and they grew deep.

Yet the feeling that he'd met Virginia Clark somewhere before haunted him. Maybe she simply reminded him of someone. Today, as summoned, he was in his office at nine, the pot of coffee made, the door leading from his office to her office stood open and, no surprise, she was late.

This definitely wasn't a good idea. He'd spent the fall semester avoiding her. She was chatty, she laughed too loud, and she was popular with the students. Which was good, he guessed, but it hurt a bit when a student walked down the hallway and yelled hello to her while they passed him with little more than a nod.

Benjamin closed his eyes when he heard her coming. The sound of her practical shoes tapping on the wooden floor echoed in the empty hallway.

When he opened his eyes, she was in his doorway, huffing slightly.

"Morning, Benjamin. I brought donuts." She charged into his space waving a white bakery bag like it was a white flag.

"Dr. Monroe," he corrected her softly.

"Oh, good grief. We're on the third floor of an empty campus on a Saturday. Surely we can be on a first-name standing."

He wasn't sure where to start. Addressing the fact that she was late, or reminding her that they were professionals, or announcing he didn't eat sweets. When he glanced down below her double chins at her clothes, he saw she was wearing a crop top. Two inches of her very bare midriff pushed out above her jeans.

It might be Saturday, but they were on campus and she was a professor. Wearing jeans was bad enough, but showing off skin at her waist was even worse.

Ben hated sounding like an old man. He'd simply ignore what she wore.

And if he mentioned the improper things about her, it would just take longer to start their research. "Good morning,

Miss Clark. Would you like a cup of coffee before we begin?"

"Nope. I brought a Diet Coke." She shoved her rolling briefcase to the side of his desk, set her Coke on a stack of papers, and reached into the paper bag for a donut. "I got you a chocolate cake donut with chocolate icing. Everyone likes those."

When she thrust the bag at him, Benjamin automatically took it. Now that he had it, he might as well look inside to see what a chocolate cake donut with chocolate icing looked like. "I thought we might work in here since my desk is bigger and uncluttered."

"Good idea." She took the chair across from him and began to build her nest. Coke and donut to the left, laptop directly in front. Papers, books, pencils, her phone, and a box of tissues came out of the rolling case.

The woman was a traveling circus. He wouldn't have been surprised if she'd brought lab rats.

He drank his coffee and nibbled on his donut as he watched her organize her chaos. By the time she finished, half of the desk was completely full and encroaching on his half of the space.

She leaned back and smiled as she handed him a sheet of paper. "I took the liberty of creating our calendar. If we are going to get this in on time, we need to stick to the outline and hire at least one intern immediately to help with the research."

Benjamin was impressed. But then, she must have some skills or she never would have gotten her master's degree.

She pointed her half-eaten donut at him. "I figured since we're both single, we can work weekends and maybe a few nights. I'm fine with hiring an intern to help, but it'll have to come out of your budget. I've already spent my research allotment."

"I agree. The sooner we get the data, the sooner we can begin." He glanced down at his donut and realized it was half gone. "I know just the man to intern. I'll call him this morning. He's about to graduate and this will look good on his résumé. He's a few years older than most students, so if he has time to take the work on he'll be dependable, and he has no family, so he can probably work this week."

She smiled. "So, we begin." She wiggled her eyebrows up and down as if they were starting something illicit.

He shook his head. "I can't work most Saturdays." They didn't know each other well enough for him to explain. "But weeknights and Sundays are open."

"Nights are fine with me." She winked at him. "I've always liked the night."

"Fine, Miss Clark," he said, having no idea what she was referring to.

"Call me Jenny." She looked up from her notes and gave him a quick smile.

"Call me Benjamin, Jenny." She had a bit of chocolate on her lip, but he didn't plan to mention it.

She nodded as she shuffled through her notes and began handing him pages. "Last year's proposal that won." She leaned toward him. "Several studies in the past five years on sexual attraction and mating rituals. We might ask the librarian to pull all university studies on the subject in the past three years."

Surprisingly, she also had an outline of what questions they might use for their survey.

"Please feel free to edit or add. I did it while I was watching *CSI*." She giggled. "I can solve the crimes and work at the same time."

Benjamin didn't dare ask her which *CSI* she was watching. Probably *Alien Crimes on Mars*.

He studied each paper she handed him. Before he'd realized

it she'd drawn him into the project. Three hours later they were both on their computers polishing the questionnaire. Ten questions on what attracts one person to another.

When they stopped at noon, he had to acknowledge that Miss Clark had a brain under all that red hair. She might drop down some wild rabbit-trail now and then, but her ideas, hypotheses, and theories on a subject he'd thought would be boring were actually very interesting.

The theory that people were attracted by smell surprised him. He would never have thought of smell until she explained many studies found attraction to someone's smell was a strong factor.

As they walked downstairs to the coffee shop that served sandwiches, curiosity got the best of him. "Why haven't you gotten your doctorate?" He leaned down a bit as he asked and discovered she smelled of chocolate.

"I started the program once at UT and a few years later at A&M, but life got in the way. It had always been my goal, but there were so many other paths to follow. At forty-three I feel like it's too late."

He didn't ask more. When they entered the coffee shop area, he relaxed. After months of doing little more than nodding at each other, they were actually talking.

Lucky for him, he wasn't the least bit attracted to her, even if she did smell like chocolate. She wasn't his type. Correction, he didn't really have a type. Women, in general, confused him. The games they played irritated him. Why couldn't they just come out and say what they wanted?

Benjamin ordered at the counter and they sat by the window so they could watch the rain. Some called Clifton College a suitcase school because most students went home on Friday.

On weekdays there was always a line of students to pick up coffee before class, but on Saturday, they were the only two customers. The coffee shop and the library usually kept shortened hours over spring break.

"I'm glad it's raining." He broke their first silence all morning. "That way I don't feel bad about not working with my dad."

"Your dad still farms?"

"He does, but every year I take a bit more of the load. When I first came back, I was just free labor now and then, but the past few years I feel myself taking over more. It's not that he's slowing down. It's more like he's losing interest."

"What about your mother?"

"She lives in Europe. They met in school right on this campus. She was studying to be an artist. Him a farmer. Dad doesn't talk about her leaving, but I was just old enough to remember seeing him standing in the middle of the road watching her go. I've never seen him look as broken as he did that day. I don't think he's said her name since. Seems to me they had nothing in common, but Mom still broke his heart."

"Attraction fades sometimes," Jenny said. "Or maybe she couldn't live in such a quiet place. Maybe she needed more color, more noise, more excitement."

"Right. But something must have pulled them together in the beginning."

"Maybe your dad was a hunk?"

"I doubt it. He is tall and lanky like me. His sentences are usually three words or less, and I've never heard him talk about anything but the weather, farming, or what he eats." Ben leaned back, beginning to feel comfortable around Jenny. "You know, in the years I've been teaching, he's never asked me one question about what I do."

He noticed Jenny had a way of listening, really listening.

Like she cared about what he was saying. He'd count that as a point of attraction on a survey.

As she ate a chip in little mouse bites, she added, "Maybe he was a great lover, or she liked the way he felt. Touch can be powerful. I've heard people say they never forget the feel of someone's heart beating against theirs."

Ben had never thought about it, and he wasn't sure he wanted to think of his parents in that way.

When he pulled out a small notebook to make notes, she asked, "Can we take a break, Benjamin? My brain needs a few minutes off." She lowered her fingers atop his hand that held the pencil. "I'm enjoying just talking to you. It's nice to have a conversation with someone my age."

Touch, he thought as he stared at her hand over his, one of the ways couples show interest. "We're not the same age. I'm forty-two."

"Then think of me as the older woman." She winked at him.

"Of course." He pulled his hand away slowly, having no idea what she was getting at.

They ate in silence for a while, then she smiled. "This research reminds me of the first time I fell in love. I was fifteen and he was a senior in high school, a star basketball player."

Benjamin just kept eating. He wasn't sure he wanted to hear this, but it was hard not to listen when they were the only two in the place. The kid who'd served them had disappeared in the back.

"I went to every basketball game and never watched anyone but him. Turned out he didn't even know I was there."

He took a deep breath and decided to make an effort. After all, they were working together on a project. "At least you shared a love for basketball."

She shook her head. "Not really." Then she leaned forward and whispered, "I put my panties in his locker with my number written on them, but he never called."

"Oh." Benjamin would have said more, but he was choking on his ham sandwich.

To his horror, she stood and started beating him on the back. This time her touch was definitely not a sign of affection.

When he turned to tell her to stop, his face bumped into her rather large left breast. His only escape was to go back to coughing. She ran for water, and he tried to calm down.

Maybe she hadn't noticed their intimate contact.

But he had noticed. Soft, yet nicely firm and at least twice the size he remembered it being. Yes, he remembered . . .

Without warning, the past he'd pushed to the back of his mind came back, avalanching down every nerve, every sense.

He remembered her. The memory he'd tried to forget about a girl people called "Red" almost twenty years ago. They'd met in January and traveled with a group of mutual friends the week before spring semester started. Most were first-year grad students looking to relax and have fun before they started back into endless circles of study, research, and lectures.

One cold January week to relax before the work began.

He'd pushed it so far back in his mind that he seldom thought about those foolhardy days. There were more important goals, things he had to do, but for one moment in time, he'd let them slide.

When he'd met Virginia Clark this past September, he'd thought she looked familiar. Only she had a different last name than the girl she reminded him of. Different first name as well. Benjamin passed the feeling off by commenting that they might have met at the university years ago or maybe simply been in a class together. It made sense; they were both science majors.

She'd agreed.

Now, in the silent coffee shop, he knew it had been far more than a class they'd shared. He might have been a bit drunk, but he'd seen her, all of her. He'd held her closer than he'd ever held anyone.

When she returned from the coffee shop counter and handed him the water, he thanked her and turned away. Pushing away the memories, Ben stood and said he had to leave.

They parted with a "See you Monday" goodbye.

An hour later he was working on a tractor in his dad's barn. Slowly, he let the memories drift back.

His father had been angry that January that Ben hadn't stopped with one degree. He wanted his son home. They'd argued over the Christmas holiday, and Benjamin returned to the university early. For once in his life Benjamin wasn't sure of himself. The workload had been far more than he'd anticipated the first semester at UT. He'd decided to move off campus with new roommates for his second semester.

But the week before classes started, there were parties, and Benjamin jumped in. Red had been his first lover, though neither talked of it.

When he'd come home for spring break two months later, he'd worked at the farm and somehow found his footing once more. His dad had talked to him about how proud he was of his only child. When Benjamin went back to school after that spring break, he went back with purpose. He pushed away the wild time he'd had, as if it never happened.

A year later another chemistry student, Marti Ranehart,

walked into his life. She was like him, shy, studious. Their dates were to the library and to lectures. He'd thought they were just friends until one night she asked if he'd sleep over. The encounter was awkward for them both; almost like making love was a homework assignment they had to get through.

Throughout the semester, she'd ask him now and then to sleep over, and he thought they were improving a bit each time. Their lovemaking reminded him of two people dancing together while each listening to different music.

He thought they had moved into a relationship, maybe one that would eventually lead to marriage. But it turned out she just wanted to sleep with him every Wednesday. Sex relaxed her, she claimed. He remembered they'd had sex every night during finals, and then she'd politely said goodbye. She was going to Mexico for the summer to study and he was going back to the farm. She didn't come back to school in the fall, and in truth, Ben barely missed her. In his memory he called her Marti Wednesday.

He found out online that she'd stayed on at the university in Mexico, but he didn't try to contact her. What had started had never taken root. Now, analyzing their relationship, he couldn't remember one thing that had truly attracted him to her.

Strange, he'd slept with Red one long weekend, and the memory of her filled his mind far more than the semester he'd been with Marti.

Benjamin stopped working on the tractor engine, closed his eyes, and tried to remember what Red had looked like. Chatty, funny, loving, bouncy, and short.

Marti had been tall, long brown hair, thin. He couldn't remember the color of her eyes or how it felt to make love to her. It had almost felt more like a lab experiment than passion. But with Red it had been natural, and the hours with her were waiting in the shadows of his mind, ready to be pulled out and relived now and then.

When they'd had sex, Marti hadn't liked him to touch her breasts. They'd been friends, both absorbed in their studies. Dating was more of a convenience now and then. Go out for a pizza. Meet friends for drinks. Sleep together. Sex was just what they did, but the desire never happened for Benjamin, and he had a feeling it was the same with Marti. Maybe she found passion with some guy in Mexico.

Thinking back, he realized he hadn't touched a woman's breasts in years. There had been other dates through college, but his studies came first. Once he'd accepted the teaching position, he'd thought it improper to date his students, and no one else seemed to be around.

So he settled in Clifton near his home and rarely thought of the past or the future. The wild, loving relationship he'd had with the girl called Red could not happen again. It made sense to him that Jenny had obviously forgotten it all. For her it had probably been just one of many weekends.

He couldn't remember how they'd ended up in bed that first night, but if he closed his eyes and traveled back in time, he could almost feel his hand moving down her body. He remembered exactly how she had felt, how she'd tasted. He also remembered he hadn't just had sex with Jenny. He'd made love to her.

In a world of men claiming to be oversexed, Ben figured he must be on the other end of the curve. Undersexed. Oh, he thought about it now and then, but logic always won out. An affair or a weekend fling wouldn't be worth upsetting his ordered life.

Plus, if he were honest with himself, if he couldn't love

like he had with the redheaded girl, he'd rather not settle for what he'd had with Marti. The act without passion.

And now, before Monday, he had to push a memory back into the shadows of his mind and never mention it to Professor Clark. They were different people now.

Benjamin decided the next month would be the longest of his life.

Chapter 5

Ketch

Afternoon

The phone on the windowsill woke Ketch with a jolt. "Crystal," he whispered. No one ever called on weekends but her. Maybe she'd changed her mind. Maybe?

Not likely.

Step back into reality, Kincaid, he told himself.

Dragging his hand through his hair, he groaned when he passed over the bandage, then glanced at the stranger sitting at the head of his bed.

For a moment he looked at the girl as if part of his dream had decided to come alive. In the cloudy daylight she looked more like a vision than a real person.

Faraway lightning flashed across the huge windows and reflected as she opened her green eyes. Rainy-day green, he thought. Beautiful eyes looked at him, and he knew she'd been watching over him.

Then he remembered her name. Tuesday Raine, the waitress from the bar. She had walked him home and she'd apparently stayed.

The phone rang again. He ignored it.

"Anyone ever tell you that your name is a weather forecast?"

She rolled those jade eyes and didn't bother to answer. For no reason at all, he smiled.

In the shadowed light, she was prettier than he remembered. No makeup on now. Her hair pulling loose from the ponytail. Her clothes wrinkled and spotted with blood. Her sad stare seemed bottomless.

The phone rang for the third time.

He grabbed it and sat up. "Morning, Professor," Ketch said as he noticed the caller ID.

"Good afternoon. I hoped you'd be home. Not much roofing happening during thunderstorms."

"Thanks for calling in the weather report, Professor." Ketch sat up and fought down the urge to swear. He liked his chemistry teacher, but he didn't feel much like talking. "Can I help you with something?"

"I'm calling to ask if you're interested in helping with research for a project I'm working on. Pays twenty an hour and it will look good on a job application after you graduate. I'm working with Miss Clark in biology, so this could mean two letters of recommendation in your file."

Ketch lost interest in the conversation as he watched the girl stand, stretch, and walk to the bathroom. She'd spent the night, probably to make sure he didn't fall out of bed. He seemed to have developed a habit of toppling over.

He pulled himself back to the phone conversation. "This research have anything to do with construction?" Ketch had helped the professor with two projects on his little farm. The guy might be a solid teacher, but he was worthless with power tools.

"No, but it pays good. Probably take about ten hours a week from now to graduation."

Ketch took a deep breath. He'd make twice that in

construction, but this would be something different, and most of the Randall projects were waiting on lumber. The brothers wouldn't mind if he took a few days off.

"I'll take it." He'd been carrying a full load of classes, working thirty hours a week, but right now giving up all free time seemed like a good idea. "Sleep is overrated anyway."

Professor Monroe laughed as if he thought Ketch was kidding. "Great. We'll talk more Monday, about ten."

The phone went dead, but Ketch didn't move. He just stared at the closed bathroom door and wondered what he was doing with the barmaid in his room. He wasn't sure what had happened. He didn't remember a fight, but his body felt beat up. His boots and jeans were off, but his underwear was still on. She'd been sitting up when he woke and looked to be fully dressed.

Ketch had a blurry memory of falling. Once, maybe twice. No memory of having sex. If that had happened, it had been so long since he'd hooked up, no amount of alcohol could have erased that memory.

He did recall seeing Tuesday at the bar last night. He'd danced with a blonde once while he was counting down bottles of beer. He thought he remembered leaning on someone as he walked home. It had to have been the girl in the bathroom. The blood on her shirt was probably his. But she was small. She couldn't have held him if he passed out.

She opened the door, her hair was combed and her face damp. Without looking at him, she circled the room, picking up her shoes.

"I don't do one-night stands," he said as his foggy brain tried to put pieces of last night together.

"Neither do I, mister."

He'd heard rumors and doubted her story, but then he didn't have a story to remember. He took a stab at what had happened. "You brought me home last night, right?"

Looking down at all the Band-Aids on his leg, he added, "And doctored me."

"Right, mister." She sat on the corner of the bed and tied her tennis shoes. Her voice sounded cold, and she was acting like she wanted to get out before he yelled at her.

The "mister" was starting to bother him. Like she thought him old or maybe she didn't know his name.

"My name's Ketch Kincaid." His head was pounding now.

"I know. I heard your friend call you that." Still not interested in talking.

"I'm in my last semester of college and I work for the construction company below us. I don't usually drink. I was just in a really bad mood. I got dumped." Too much information, he decided.

"I don't really care." She stood to leave. "Look, Ketch Kincaid, nothing happened between us last night. Not that anyone will believe it. Say whatever you want. I'm beyond being hurt by rumors."

It seemed to be storming in his brain as well as beyond the windows. She was mad for some reason, and he wanted to throw up. "If nothing happened, how come you spent the night?"

She leaned so close her nose almost touched his. "Because you told me you didn't want to be alone and I know how that feels. I felt sorry for you."

For a moment he just stared. Ashamed of his weakness and fascinated that she'd listened. He couldn't deny hating to be alone. He could say that he was drunk or kidding, but they both knew the truth. He had said the words real enough to make her care.

"Thanks for staying," he finally said, his tone low and honest.

Surprise flashed in her eyes. "You're welcome."

He stood, took one glance at his bloody jeans and grabbed

a pair of sweats from a shelf. "I'll walk you out, or drive you home. I seem to remember walking here last night." He tossed her a clean T-shirt. "I owe you one."

She took the shirt that had been army issued years ago. As if she didn't notice he was in the room, she stripped off her bloody shirt and pulled on his. It was so big it hung halfway to her knees.

Ketch closed his eyes, trying to get the picture of her small breasts covered in only blue lace out of his head. She was so small. Almost more girl than woman.

"No need to see me out. I know the way back to the bar." She lifted a small backpack. "You don't have a car, so we'd have to walk anyway. No sense both of us getting wet."

Tuesday almost smiled as she watched him dress. "In case you forgot, you told me you left your pickup at the library. Claimed your truck was smarter than you last night."

"Right." He wasn't just an idiot; he'd been a drunken idiot.

She looked so young in her jeans and his T-shirt that she'd knotted just above her waist. "How did you manage to get me up the stairs, Tuesday?"

"It wasn't easy. You leaned over the railing a few times and kept mentioning how you didn't want to think about someone named Crystal." She shrugged. "I'm guessing she is your ex."

"Correct." Anger washed over his mind, riding a headache. "My fiancée sent me a letter. Damn, that was cold." He scratched his hair, then yelped in pain. "I don't want to talk about it."

"I know. You told me several times last night in your sleep." She turned. "So long, Ketch. Have a good life."

"Wait. I can borrow one of the work trucks downstairs. I'd really like to drive you home. No one will be working today, so the trucks are just sitting there. We could stop for coffee. Or maybe lunch."

She studied him for a long moment. "All right. I don't care if you want to thank me or you still don't want to be alone. But I am starving. All you have in your fridge is water." She frowned at him. "This is not a date or anything, but if I stand around here much longer you've got to feed me."

"Totally. What would you like to eat?"

"Food. I've already eaten the six crackers you had."

Chapter 6

Amelia

Amelia Remington buttoned her gray raincoat as she rushed out of her office and through the silent canyons of books in the college library. The weak stormy-day sunshine lit her path toward the glass front door.

She'd only meant to pick up yesterday's notes from the library board meeting, but she'd stayed to check the mail that had been dumped on her desk and open several boxes that arrived.

At thirty-six she'd learned to hate loose ends or clutter on her desk, but today she'd remained too long. Now it was late afternoon and raining hard.

The schedule for next month's student workers hadn't been posted yet, so that would have to be her first job Monday. It might be spring break, but she'd insisted the library remain open for those who wanted to study. Clifton College was small, but its library was grand and linked in to the top research libraries in the country.

"Note to self." Amelia's soft voice echoed down the eight-feet-high stacks. "Re-shelf the rare-book room Monday. Begin the list of books to order before fall. Order three new study desks."

Rain pelted the glass doors as if demanding she stay inside. Watching the storm dropped her spirits.

Her usual Saturday night of relaxing would be cut short. Routine was important. A balanced life was essential. "Everything in its place," she whispered, remembering when she'd been a child and all was always in its place or there was hell to pay.

But today, the rain had shattered her plans. Every Saturday afternoon she drove over to Honey Creek to shop the market's organic-foods section. Then she'd put on her one pair of jeans, make herself a salad, and work on next week's calendar while watching the news.

Today, since she'd worked late, she might go a bit wild and buy a ready-made salad and a whole-grain muffin, then eat at the roadside park between Honey Creek and Clifton Bend. If it was too cold at the covered picnic table, she could eat in her little car. After all, spring was her favorite season in the valley and the damp air would smell wonderful if the rain slowed.

Twenty minutes of being outside, watching the stars come out, might be the perfect ending to her day if it would just stop raining. Her mother had always complained that she was high-strung, but Amelia never exactly understood what her mother had meant or how to fix the problem.

She wondered what it would feel like to have one moment in her life when she didn't follow a routine.

Her first memory was learning her numbers by her father's watch. "Time is important," he used to say. "Control your time and you control your world."

She wasn't sure she believed him, but she'd had the saying made into a plaque that hung beneath her office clock.

Amelia braced herself for a run to her car. She couldn't

wait any longer. She had groceries to buy and Rambo to attend to.

Once outside, she locked up. With her arms full, she stepped off the curb on her way to the faculty parking lot. Without warning, rain suddenly rode the wind, splashing against her face, washing away her plans and spotting her glasses.

The roar of a motorcycle dueled with thunder. Glancing up, she glimpsed the last bit of sunshine fighting through storm clouds to the west. *I'd better hurry*, she thought. Rambo hated thunder. He'd be panicked, alone in the house.

One blink later, something slammed into her arm, whirling her around as if she were nothing more than a human turnstile in the middle of the road.

Two seconds ticked by before she hit the pavement so hard her head bounced off it.

Three seconds until the bike scraped the ground in front of her like a huge metal bird diving to earth. Steel slid across the rough asphalt, rattling and screeching as if in pain.

Then, one breath later, almost silently, a man's body landed twisted and boneless like a rag doll five feet from her.

Stillness blanketed them, as if all time had frozen.

She closed her eyes and stopped counting. Her world began to fade, leaving only a black canvas.

As if from miles away, someone screamed and she heard the squeal of car brakes.

A high-pitched cry for help drifted through the muddy water Amelia's mind seemed to be floating in, but she paid no attention. Neither did the man lying a few feet away. His hand was stretched toward her as if he were reaching for her.

She moved slightly, reaching over the rough ground until the tips of her fingers rested over his bloody hand.

With the few brain cells that were still working, it occurred to her that they'd almost met amid the sounds of cars braking, people shouting, and an ambulance's scream growing louder.

She bit back the pain as she held his hand. She might not know his name, but she shared his pain.

"Miss Remington, can you open your eyes?"

A worried woman's voice was pulling her from a deep sleep. This person was demanding, but Amelia didn't respond.

An impatient male tone came next. "Miss Remington, can you hear me? I'm Dr. Hudson. You've been in an accident. Can you hear me?"

Amelia tried to ignore the question and go back to floating. Only now, more voices were mumbling in the mud in her mind. Too many voices to count. Too many to disregard.

She opened one eye slightly to see what was happening and pain crawled over her entire body. First it tiptoed along her limbs, then sank into her skin, flowing toward her core until she couldn't breathe without hurting.

"Miss Remington!" A middle-aged woman in green scrubs moved closer. "Welcome back. We've all been waiting hours for you to join us."

The room came into focus. White with blue trim. A strong smell of antiseptics. A huge window with rain dripping in tiny streams. Only blackness beyond.

The world seemed to be crying just beyond her room.

"Where am I?" she whispered, but no one answered.

She had lost part of her day. She'd lost time. For a moment, she slipped back to being a little thin girl who was late getting home. Her father interrogated her as he jerked her arm so hard her entire body reacted like a whip.

"What time is it?" she asked aloud as she realized she

hadn't made it to the market or had supper. It might even be too late to do next week's schedule or watch the news.

"I lost time," she wanted to scream, but the memory of a hard slap from thirty years ago came back. Her father yelled, "If you lose time, you lose your life."

But no slap came now. Only a calm voice. "It's almost midnight, miss. You were in an accident." The nurse put her hand on Amelia's shoulder. "Dr. Hudson says you're lucky to be alive."

Amelia knew she'd have to keep her eyes open to find a clock, but she wanted to go back to the muddy place where there was silence and no pain. This room was too bright. Strangers surrounded her. She wasn't in control.

The doctor's voice came again, softer now. "Miss, you're going to be all right. You've got a bad sprain to your right wrist, but it's not broken. Your left leg is fractured. You have a cut on your head, nothing serious, and a dislocated shoulder along with scrapes and bruises."

"You're going to be fine, miss." The nurse patted her on the arm. "Don't you worry."

Amelia swallowed and whispered, "What happened exactly?" Details were the backbone of her life.

The nurse huffed. Her name tag said BETHIE WEST, RN. "Harrison Norton flew around the corner and ran over you like he was late to his own funeral. When he was in his teens, he was wilder than any preacher's kid should be. Then he rode the rodeo circuit for several years like the devil dared him, and now he's back in town running over our librarian. Clifton College should sue him for being born to be nothing but trouble."

Amelia tried to make the pieces fit together. She'd only been in Clifton Bend for a year and had no idea who Harrison Norton was.

The nurse barked a laugh. "I've a good mind to call the

pastor and tell him what his offspring did," she added as she began checking Amelia's IV. "But if the preacher couldn't control him at eighteen, he'll have no influence now. It's been twenty years since high school. I swear if being a bad boy was a sport, Harrison would have made the Olympics."

Amelia felt an impulse to smile, then moaned as her mind finally began to clear. Her bottom lip was busted. The doctor had left that out in his assessment of damages. "I don't know the man." Amelia tried not to move her lips. "But I doubt Harrison Norton cares what his daddy does or says."

Nurse West nodded. "Pastor Norton is as near to being a saint as any mortal can be, and his only son seems to be determined to fly into hell at full throttle. I hear Harrison visits a couple times a year and there is always talk. Some think he turned into one of them Hells Angels; others figure he's doing drugs. He's got a ponytail and that right there tells you something about the man."

The wreck came back to Amelia in flash cards. The noise. The pain. The man flying over her, then lying mangled and still.

She had to ask, "Is he all right?"

The nurse shrugged. "I guess. He's hobbling around out in the lobby cussing like a drunk sailor. One of the nurse's aides grabbed him and wrapped his hand. She said she was tired of mopping up blood."

Amelia smiled, then groaned again. "You see a great many drunk sailors, do you, Bethie?"

Before the nurse could answer, Amelia gave in to sleep.

When she finally came back to consciousness, she opened her eyes and noticed someone had turned down the lights a bit, and the room was empty except for a few machines. The rain tapped lightly against her window, almost playing a melody. Pain seemed to be running in her blood, but the feeling wasn't new. No matter how many years passed, she'd never forget the pain of her childhood.

She'd been about four or five when it started. She'd be asleep in a room which she had made sure was clean, with all her toys in place. The sound of the door hitting the wall always woke her, then a big, beefy hand would grab her. Sometimes there were slaps sending her head first one way, then the other. Sometimes she'd be swung over her father's knee and spanked as he yelled at her for something she'd done or something her mother had reported Amelia hadn't done.

But what she hated most was the whiskey smell of his breath as he shook her while he yelled a few inches from her face.

When he got tired and short of breath, he'd toss her back in bed and walk out. If she cried too loud, he'd return for another round. On those nights, she'd crawl under her bed after he left, too afraid to make a sound.

Come morning, her mother would see the bruises and say simply that Amelia better "get with the program" or "straighten up and be good." Somehow, no matter how many times he beat her, Amelia still couldn't be the perfect child her mother wanted. If she was a minute late getting home. If she didn't act fast enough when her mother gave an order. If she changed the channel on the TV and forgot to change it back.

Her mother never touched her. She didn't have to. All she had to do was inform Amelia's father.

Her childhood came back as she lay hurting all over now in the silent hospital, but she didn't make a sound. She'd learned early what happens when you cry.

In the shadows, a tall, lean form slipped into the room.

For a moment, she thought it might be the angel of death coming to claim her, but logic told her people rarely die from a broken leg. Her father and mother had no interest in knowing where she was. No one would come to hurt her again. She was safe.

As the stranger moved closer, she heard the clink of metal on boots, almost as if he wore spurs.

"You all right, lady?" he asked in a gravelly voice that seemed meant to sing country songs.

She tried to see details as he came closer. Black leather jacket. A dark bruise across his strong jawline. Hair dirty, dark, and too long. His left hand bandaged. The smell of whiskey flavored his breath as he leaned closer.

Amelia tensed at the familiar smell.

She should be afraid of this man who'd wandered into her room, but then she saw the sorrow in his gray eyes. Old eyes, she thought. Ancient eyes in a man who hadn't lived half a lifetime.

He looked as if he were truly worried about her, not himself. He might be slim and near six feet, but he wasn't young. Twenty years out of high school the nurse had said. Twenty years of hard living, she'd guess.

"Are you hurt, Mr. Norton?" she asked. The man had to be Harrison Norton, the preacher's wild son.

"No. I'm fine. I just had to check on you. You look like you were run over by the devil himself." He smiled and the pain she'd seen in his eyes eased. "You know my name. I'm the one who was riding the Harley that plowed into you."

"Are you the devil himself?" She fought not to smile.

"Some say I am, but I swear I never wanted to hurt you, pretty lady."

Amelia almost laughed at his joke. No one had ever called her "pretty." She was born plain and never wasted time mourning beauty.

To her surprise, he touched her hand lying atop the covers and held it gently. "I didn't see you. You were no more than a blink in the rainy sunset."

"I was running, worried about being late and not wanting to get my hair wet. It tends to curl out of control when it gets wet. I look a mess." She was rattling. She never rattled. Maybe the doc forgot to mention brain damage?

Amelia lightly moved her fingers along his hand, feeling calluses and the bandage. "You are hurt, Harrison," she whispered again.

"It's nothing and call me Hank. No one but my father calls me Harrison." He smiled. "Looks like you got the worst of our first encounter, Millie."

She couldn't look away. No one had ever called her Millie, but she didn't correct him. She was far too interested in the lines of character in his face. She saw intelligence, worry, and caring. He reminded her of a young Hemingway double, come to life.

His free hand reached up and brushed a lock of her curly, mousy-brown hair behind her ear so he could see her face.

"I'm so sorry," he whispered. "Chestnut," he added with a one-sided smile. "You have chestnut-colored hair, Millie, with a few strands of red and a touch of sunshine blended in."

His words didn't seem to fit the man. "You know about hair colors, Harrison?" She never would have taken him for a hair stylist.

"Sure, but mostly on horses' manes. I had a chestnut horse once. Beautiful animal."

"Will you do me a favor, Harrison? I have no one to ask."

"Name it."

"Would you go over to my house and let my dog out? He'll do his business and come right back in."

"Sure."

"Thirty-fourth and Elm. One block north of the campus.

The house with sunflowers. Tell Rambo I'll be home as soon as I can. He'll understand."

Harrison Norton nodded, but he had the look of a man talking to a nut case. "Rambo. Does he bite?"

"Yes, but just tell him to stop."

"Great," Hank whispered as he looked down at his already bandaged hand.

Dr. Hudson turned up the lights as he walked in with the county sheriff behind him and ended their conversation.

Hank straightened but didn't pull his hand from hers.

Dr. Hudson was a foot shorter than most men and the sheriff was a foot taller. They made an odd pair. Both frowned at Hank.

She closed her eyes to the bright light and curled her hand around two of Harrison's fingers as if she were a child and needed to hold on tight.

Sheriff LeRoy Hayes pulled out a pad and pen as he leaned a hip against the bed's frame. "Miss Remington, do you feel up to answering a few questions?"

The sheriff might be all-official, but he looked tired. A long Saturday night, she guessed.

"I'm a bit tied up at the moment," she answered glancing down at both her bandaged arm and her leg in a brace.

Three feet away, the old doctor stood guard as if planning to order everyone out at any second. With his short stature and out-of-control mustache, he reminded her of a Smurf. She fought the urge to see if he wore shoes, but she guessed it would hurt too much to lean over and look.

LeRoy glared at Harrison Norton, and Amelia thought she heard the lawman growl. "You want to press charges against this man, Miss Remington? I could take him in right now. Hit-and-run, probably a DWI to start with. It's been a few years, but it wouldn't be the first time Norton has crossed the law."

Harrison's hand tightened slightly over hers. "I wasn't drinking, Sheriff, but I have been in the hours I've been waiting. I'd rather have a few drinks for pain than what they serve in here."

Amelia cleared her throat. "Sheriff, Mr. Norton sustained some injuries as well in our accident. To my knowledge he did not leave the scene of the accident. When I passed out, he was lying five feet from me."

Dr. Hudson cleared his throat. "He refused medical care."

"So, if it's all right with you, Doc, I'll take him in for questioning? He can't just roll into my county and start causing trouble." LeRoy turned to Harrison. "Damn it, Norton, did you have to run over the college's only certified librarian? Took the school two years to find someone who'd take the job."

"You can't arrest him, Sheriff." Amelia forced her tone to be professional as always. "I'm the one who caused the accident. I stepped off the curb without looking. I was not in a pedestrian walkway. I was in a hurry and rushing through rain. Take me in if you must. I caused the wreck. I hurt him."

Dr. Hudson and the sheriff squared off like two mismatched boxers beginning round one.

"You're not taking Miss Remington out of my hospital, Sheriff. She needs care now and will require round-the-clock help when she gets home." The doctor's tone left no room for discussion. "Her left leg is broken in two places and may need surgery to heal correctly. She can put no weight on it. Her shoulder has hairline fractures, and her left arm must remain stable against her side. The head wound is also problematic."

LeRoy didn't look like he cared.

The old doctor continued, "I have no room here to keep

her for more than twenty-four hours and I'm short at least one nurse on every shift. Because of the head injury, she needs to be watched, not just checked on. To top it all, now I have to deal with you, Sheriff, coming in to arrest her. I suggest, if you want to help, you contact her next of kin to take over her care."

"Someone is to blame for this accident." LeRoy backed a step closer to the door as if he feared the doc might have rabies.

The big lawman might be past his prime, but he looked ready to run away from this mess. No one would care if he arrested Harrison Norton, but the whole town would be in his office yelling if he jailed the librarian.

Amelia leaned her head sideways, gazing at the sheriff from another angle. "Maybe you should be in charge of me, Sheriff? I can't go home alone, and everyone knows both nursing homes are full. I have no kin. In jail I'll have round-the-clock care. The doctor thinks someone needs to be responsible for me. It is obvious my brains are scrambled. I can't walk or use one arm. Maybe I'll go with you."

Hank grinned, clearly loving how she fired back at LeRoy.

Amelia hadn't allowed anyone to boss her around in years. "I've changed my mind. Take me in, Sheriff. Have the hospital send all the supplies to your office. I'll need a wheelchair, a walker, and probably a potty chair. And, of course, three meals a day and sponge baths."

LeRoy looked like he thought she was serious. "We only have one holding cell, miss."

She noticed Hank was now choking down a laugh as she continued, "One cell is fine. If you want to arrest someone for the accident, take me away."

Amelia did her best to make her point from a hospital bed, but the reality of her predicament hit her hard. She was alone. She knew half the faculty and a few students, but not one had ever been in her house. No one would offer to care for her, and she wasn't sure how long she'd be able to pay for in-home nursing, even if she could find some- one to hire in this tiny town.

She tried to straighten just a bit and gripped the stranger's hand to hold her steady. "Thank all of you for your concerns, but I can take care of myself. If you don't plan to arrest me, I'll be going home come morning."

The old doc shook his head. "You'll need help, miss. I can't discharge you without someone to see to your care."

Amelia saw no other way. She had no relatives, no friends. "I'll manage." She'd been on her own since she'd graduated from high school. Her parents said they'd done all they could for her. She'd moved to a one-room apartment a day later and worked six months to make enough to take a few night classes. Her folks went to Hawaii on the money from her college fund. A year later when she stopped by their house, they'd moved.

"I can't release you, Miss Remington. One fall could cause another break. You can't stay alone."

Harrison Norton's low voice ended the discussion. "I'll be responsible for her."

"How you going to do that, Norton?" the sheriff barked. "You'd have to stay sober. You wouldn't even know what to do."

"I'll figure it out." Hank wasn't looking at the men, only Amelia. His voice lowered. "I'll get you home, Millie, if that is where you want to go."

LeRoy seemed to realize this might end the discussion of her staying in his holding cell. "You'll have to make her place handicap accessible. Make meals. Stay around if she needs anything." The sheriff glared at him. "And don't think I won't be checking on you."

Harrison's eyes never left Amelia's face. "I'll watch over you, pretty lady."

Every logical thought told her to find another way, but his hand held hers tightly and his gray eyes bore a promise.

"It'll take a week, maybe more, to fix my bike. Will that be enough time, Doc?"

"If all goes well. She will not be healed, but she will have figured out how to get around."

The sheriff shook his head at her. "You are not seriously letting this man in your house?"

"I am." Amelia almost laughed. She had nothing to steal, and he'd already taken his best shot at killing her. "He's my best friend."

The nurse, who'd been standing just inside the door, moved to the bedside. "He's wild," Bethie whispered, "but he comes from good people."

Amelia closed her eyes and silently whispered, "I don't." Not one of her kin would come if she called.

Chapter 7

Tuesday's World

Tuesday watched the big guy called Ketch fight not to limp as he headed down the stairs of his warehouse apartment. He wasn't like most men she met. There was a politeness about him. A kindness in the way he moved, as if he didn't want to frighten her with his size. The mouse and the elephant, she thought.

It had been her experience that big men often pushed their weight around. Not just in bar fights but in the way they handled women as well.

At five feet, four inches tall, she felt small next to Ketch Kincaid. There was a shyness about him, almost like he was new to having a woman close.

Another surprising thing about him. The man acted like he didn't even notice she was a woman. When she'd changed T-shirts, he'd turned away as if not interested in looking at her body.

They passed through a metal door that opened into a warehouse bay. Supplies were stacked everywhere in order. Four trucks were lined up at the front, all loaded and ready to roll out. Two fire-engine-red pickups were parked by another huge bay door. They were filled with orange cones and yellow barrels for water.

"The Randall brothers handle most of the construction in the valley," Ketch said as he headed toward one of the pickups. "Dan Randall was my first drill sergeant seven years ago. He told all the guys when we finished our tours and needed a job to come here. He claimed this valley was the best place on earth. Since Clifton also has a college and I knew I had a job waiting, I headed to Texas."

"What about your family?" she asked as they began unloading cones from one of the pickup beds.

"No family. I was left on a dock wrapped in a worn square of a sailcloth when I was a week old. Someone had written on the box I was in, *His name is Ketch Kincaid. Tell him his parents loved him, but we weren't born with roots.*"

"Seriously?"

"That's what I've been told." Ketch laughed. "I imagine my parents being kids taking off to sail the seven seas."

"Do you have a love for sailing?"

"No, I get seasick in a pool. That was probably why I was left behind."

To her surprise, he opened the company pickup door and offered to help her in.

Tuesday grabbed the handle and climbed up without assistance and heard him say, "Good job, kid."

She watched him cross to the driver's side. He couldn't be out of his twenties, but there was something about him that made her think of him as much older. He seemed far more mature than men she usually met at the bar, but that wasn't saying much. "How old do you think I am?" she said as she settled in the huge pickup.

"Eighteen." he glanced in her direction as he pulled the keys from the sun visor. "Maybe nineteen."

"I'm twenty-two, old man."

He smiled as if knowing she was teasing him. "I'm twenty-six, so you can stop calling me mister or old man."

"And you can stop calling me kid." As he backed out she added, "You think we could be friends?"

"Why?"

The rain seemed to cocoon them as they pulled away. "There's something about you, Ketch, that makes me think you might be a good friend to have." She laughed. "I don't know why. You're a heavy drinker, a friend of brain-dead Wynn, and you have a tendency to topple over."

"Sure. I could use a friend who'll patch me up and watch over me." He winked at her. "Why not. If you grow a few inches up and out, you'll be just right."

When he glanced down at her breasts, she caught what he meant by "out." She hit him hard on his shoulder and noticed he hadn't even flinched.

"Look at it this way, old man. You saved me in the bar's parking lot, I doctored you, and we slept together. I guess that bonds us for life."

"Damn straight. Where would you like to eat, friend?"

Looking down at her clothes, Tuesday knew going into a restaurant was out. "How about we drive through someplace and eat after you drive me home?"

"Sounds great." He turned into the bar's parking lot.

She jumped out before he could tell her to wait and tossed her old bike in the truck bed.

When she climbed back in, shoving her wet hair out of her face, Ketch smiled. "You look like a drowned rat, kid."

"I know, mister, but at least I didn't have to dig you out of the mud. The way you topple over, you'd never be able to stand in water."

They both laughed, knowing that the nicknames would stick.

"I know a barbecue stand a block away, but with this rain I have no idea where we'll eat."

She sat silently, facing straight ahead. Last night she hadn't thought much about helping him get home, or patching him up, or even staying with him watching him sleep. But now, in the daylight with him sober, she felt strange. He was a stranger who had broken through her defenses. He was right. They were friends now, and the strangest thing was he appeared fine with it.

"Barbecue OK?"

"Sure. I don't eat out much. I like to cook." She glanced at him, wondering when he'd turn into a jerk. In her experience all men did. "Get the food, then just drive me home. We can sit on my porch and watch the rain while we eat."

"You got it." He smiled at her for a moment, then turned into the drive-through lane.

In ten minutes they had their bags and drinks and she was giving him directions to her place. "It's only a few miles out of town, but no one ever comes there. Not even a mailman. I have to pick up my mail in town. I don't think my home has a proper address. It's just been Primrose Hill for as long as folks can remember."

When he turned onto a muddy trail that couldn't even be called a road, he asked, "Cars ever make it to your place?"

Tuesday laughed. "Nope. I consider this road my security system."

"You mind if the next time I have to dump some dirt from a construction site I drop it off here?"

"Nope."

She stared through the rain as her great-grandmother's house came into view. "You're on Primrose Hill now. My great-grandparents came from England after the First World

War. He planted fruit trees and she planted flowers all over the hill. When I was a kid, I moved in to help my Grannie Eva out, or that's what my mom said when she dumped me off. My great-granddad was long dead. Grannie died two years after I came to live here and left me the house."

"What about your grandmother and your folks?"

"My grandmother died soon after my mother was born. No man in the picture that anyone ever mentioned, but there must have been at some point since my mom came along. So Grannie raised my mom. Mom hated small towns, so she left as soon as she could drive. A few years after she left, she had me. Again, no guy stayed around. A dozen years later when she finally decided to get married, I was in the way, so she dumped me with Grannie Eva. The old girl raised three generations of daughters before she died."

Ketch pulled his truck close to a rundown porch and seemed to be studying the old house in the rain. "Fascinating design. I can even see a bit of England in the lines."

She tried to see the house through his eyes. The steps up to the sagging porch were broken and wooden shingles looked like they'd slide off the roof any second. Several windows were boarded closed upstairs. Parts of the home were beautiful but most looked like they needed care.

But she loved the rounded rocks that formed the foundation and natural beams that seemed to guard the big old house whose roof brushed hundred-year-old trees.

"Looks like the electricity is out again," she said when he didn't move.

Finally Ketch said in almost a whisper, "This place is magic. The craftsmanship, the balance, the beauty, the soul of the place."

She'd never thought of the house like that. "Grannie Eva said her husband's brother, Tony, built it for them. It took him years because he loved my grandmother's cooking.

Over the decades, Tony would return between jobs to add on and keep up the place. He built the four big rooms downstairs first, like it was the whole house, then they built the rest of the house around the base. Tony claimed it was never finished. One summer he added an attic floor just for the fun of it."

"Where will we eat?"

"The porch, of course. Since my grannie died, I live in the four original rooms she called the base. It's enough for me. I use the porch as my little dining room."

"When we finish, will you give me a tour?"

"Sure."

They grabbed their food and ran for the house. Just enough sun filtered through the clouds and low-hanging branches to make it seem like twilight on the corner of the porch.

Ketch laughed as he shook off water and for the first time she saw a young man beneath the drunk, wounded, sad stranger of last night.

An old three-legged table sat in a corner sheltered from the rain. She motioned for him to take the one chair. He draped his jacket over her shoulders before he divided up their food while she sat on the railing, patiently waiting.

Her knee brushed his shoulder and the quiet shelter made her feel like they were alone in the world.

They ate and talked about the weather and the food. Then they both silently enjoyed the stillness and beauty of this strange little farm called Primrose Hill.

She looked at him, knowing they'd probably reached the limit of their conversation skills, but they were comfortable.

He wasn't facing her but staring out into the rain. Finally, his words came low. "I want to talk to you, Tuesday. I just don't know how to start. I like the idea of having a friend.

I haven't managed to find one at the college. I know lots of people, but not one who'd watch over me when I sleep."

"Me either. I thought I had a few, but they vanished when someone started a rumor about me."

"Was it true?"

"Yeah, some of it was." She was glad he didn't ask what the rumor had been.

He was silent for a while as he stared at the rain dripping off newborn tree branches. "It's beautiful out here."

"I know. This place, this land is part of me. Maybe someday I'll have the money to fix it up. I'll live here the rest of my life, just like my great-grandmother did."

Ketch stood beside her and tested the porch pillars before leaning against one. "You going to pave the road?"

"Nope. Never."

He nodded as if he understood, and a comfortable silence stretched between them.

She decided to give conversation a shot. "Maybe we need to start this friendship off with a few rules. I'm not going to ask you any questions. You tell me what you want me to know. I'll do the same."

"Fair enough. I don't have much to tell. I joined the army after one year of college. I'm not from anywhere really. No relatives. No ties."

"I started school at Clifton College four years ago. I wanted to be a nurse."

She left out how she'd hated school and it felt good that he couldn't ask questions. "I was shy. That strange girl who lived on Primrose Hill who never talked."

He nodded. "You do have some nursing skills. You patched me up."

"I'm glad I was there." They smiled at each other. "Sometimes I dream of trying school again."

Ketch realized it was his turn. "Once I joined the army,

all I thought about was being my best. I was looking for adventure. I figured if I traveled enough I'd find home, but I never did. Four years later I got out and started college again. In a few months I'll be graduating with a chemistry degree, but I think I like building houses more. The Randall brothers have taught me more than I ever learned in school. I like working with my hands."

A comfortable silence drifted between them once more. There was a freedom in not having to answer questions. She felt half the things people asked her about didn't have an answer. Now she could tell him just what she wanted him to know.

"I like baking on cold days and I love rain," she said softly. "Sometimes, if it's warm enough, I dance in the rain."

"I can see you doing that, kid."

She grinned. "If you were younger and more steady on your feet, I'd suggest you give it a try, mister."

"I used to like rain until I camped out for four nights in a deluge. I swore my toes were webbing together. If I'd stayed out one more day, I would have turned into a duck."

She laughed. "A six-foot-five duck would be noticed."

"I figured that, so I'd probably wear a hat."

She giggled and met his eyes. "Rule Two: If we're going to be friends, we promise never to lie."

"Just the truth. You've got a deal. And since we're being honest, I can't dance."

"I noticed that last night. You looked like a tree, and the blonde was dancing around you like a fairy." She hesitated and added, "I should tell you that you're my only friend."

"You're my only one too. Between work and school I don't have time." He smiled. "I don't think of Wynn as my friend, but he's probably as close as I've come."

"You get to set the next rule."

He shrugged as if he wanted nothing, then he finally

added, "Rule Three: You have to hug me every time we see each other. It can be when we meet or we part, but it's got to be a real hug." When she didn't question, he added, "I haven't had enough hugs in my life."

She stood, wishing she could ask him why, but there was Rule One: no questions. Without a word she walked to his side and leaned on the railing. When he turned toward her, she put her arms around his neck and hugged him.

He wrapped one arm around her waist and hugged her back.

When she pulled away and began to clean up lunch, he added one more fact. "Tuesday, I'll never be the first one to pull away or the first to start hugging."

She didn't know what to say. She felt like he'd just given her a gift. Her choice. She could pick the time.

As the evening shadows grew around them, she brought out a lantern. "We'll have to save the tour for another time."

He raised his hand, caught a low beam above his head, and patted the wood as if silently saying goodbye to the house.

They walked back to the truck when the rain slowed, and this time he lifted her bike down. "Could we allow one question, kid?"

"Depends."

"You going to be all right here?"

"I am. Will you be all right without me, old man?"

"I'll do my best." He nodded. "But, if you ever need me, just call or drop by."

She turned, hopping over puddles as she moved to the house. "You too, mister."

As he slid his way back to the county road, she stood in the porch shadows and watched him.

Ketch Kincaid was a strange man. A friend. Someone she could almost believe was real.

Sunday

Chapter 8

Harrison

Midnight

Hank Norton walked the three blocks from the hospital to his motel. The town never seemed to change, even though businesses on Main faded and others grew like weeds amid the rubble. Rustic old storefronts became antique shops and fishing gear huts that had seen their glory days in the '50s gave way to coffee shops and eyebrow spas that drew the college crowd. It reminded him of two worlds that had blended together, not in harmony, but in ragged hunks of sidewalk.

Every muscle in his body felt bruised from the wreck, but Hank's thoughts were on the lady he'd hit. He'd left the librarian sleeping in the hospital. She'd looked so fragile. So alone. She might be an important lady at the college, but she'd needed someone to help her tonight. He was a loner, not a caretaker, but he'd have to do this for her. It was apparent that he'd been her only offer, and he guessed she'd be too proud to ask for help.

He wondered if he should tell her that the one pet he had as a kid, a puppy, ran off, and the cactus in his apartment died a year ago. Not much of a reference. He'd tried being a big brother to a kid in Houston whose dad had died, but they'd had nothing in common. The kid read biographies and played video games. When Hank took Simon to an Astros game, the kid was bored. About the third inning the kid turned backward in his seat and played games on Hank's phone.

Hank smiled as he walked through the sleeping campus. If Simon hadn't liked the action of a major league game, he'd hate this little town.

But then, Clifton Bend was growing. The place would have had only a two-room clinic off the one doctor's office if the college hadn't started a program of continuing education for healthcare workers years ago. They trained everyone from EKG technicians to phlebotomists and won a grant to build the ten-bed hospital.

Hank's dad had told him every detail a few years ago when he'd circled by to visit. Since Pastor Norton had moved to the retirement home, his favorite topic, next to the sins of his son, was healthcare.

Hank unlocked his motel room, the last door on a long line of rooms for rent. Ten rooms, about the same size as the hospital. But the old motel was only stocked with the basics.

Out of habit he looked back for his bike. The old Harley was gone, hauled away after the wreck. He'd left home on it twenty years ago. He'd trailered it with his horse during his rodeo days, and now he pulled it out of storage every time he came back to Clifton Bend.

It had taken him five years to break his promise and come back to Clifton Bend. After that time, he made a point to call every few months to check on his dad and drop by now and then. He'd stay one night, maybe two, never three. He always came on his bike, to remind his father he'd never change.

But this time, Hank might not be able to fix the old bike. Maybe, like it or not, it was time say goodbye. Freedom was a drug he craved, but lately he wanted more in his life.

"Evening, Hank." A low voice came from the shadows at the end of the parking lot.

Since he couldn't think of anyone looking for him lately, Hank forced himself to relax. The light from the ice machine blinked across a man's boots and tan dress slacks.

Hank smiled. "Evening, Colby. Or should I say, Ranger McBride. Haven't seen you since you were promoted from trooper to Texas Ranger."

The tall, young ranger stepped into the light and held up two beers. "Welcome home, Captain Norton. I heard you might have taken your last ride on the old hog today. If so, it wouldn't be right not to toast the passing."

They laughed as Hank took a beer. "How'd you know I was in town anyway? And drop the Captain. You'll tarnish my bad reputation."

"I probably wouldn't have known you were in town. I don't usually keep up with you, but you ran over the librarian. In a valley this size that's a federal offense."

Hank took a long drink. "Yeah, I feel bad about that. The sheriff wanted to lock me up."

The ranger leaned against the railing. "You know, you might think of filling LeRoy in on who you really are these days. I was surprised to learn the folks around here think you're wild, a rodeo bum, a drifter."

"Don't enlighten them, Ranger. You make a few mistakes in a small town and folks never forget. I'll always be that wild kid who hit eighty on Main in Honey Creek and set off fireworks in the middle of Clifton College's graduation. They say I took the virginity of half the cheer squad, but I only parked out at the lake with one and she was teaching me things."

"That's all you did? One night with a nympho cheerleader marked you for life as wild? Doesn't seem enough to build up to legend."

"I was the preacher's only son." Hank laughed without much humor. "If I stepped one foot off the straight and narrow, I was next week's sermon. After a while I didn't give a damn. I started looking for trouble. My father could have written a book on my hell-raising."

The ranger nodded. "I have a hard time seeing you that way, but if you want to keep your rep, I'll keep your secret. If you need anything, just call. I owe you a bucketful of favors. Last summer in downtown Austin, when you walked what the paper called 'the silent walk' straight toward a ticking bomb, I aged a year in ten minutes just watching you."

"Just doing my job like you do. Keep what I do for a living quiet."

"Will do." When the ranger turned toward his pickup, Harrison added, "Thanks for the beer. Just the medicine I needed."

Colby McBride waved, tossed his half-full beer in a trash can and climbed into his pickup.

"Wait, Ranger. There is something you can help me do. Could you drive me a block north of the campus? I got to do a favor."

"Sure, climb in. What you got to do this time of night, or should I say morning?"

"Break into the librarian's house and feed a dog named Rambo." Hank got in. "And, Colby, you're my partner in crime."

Five minutes later Hank was prying the door open of what he hoped was the librarian's house. She didn't have enough light in the front for security, and the back door was flimsy. In the moonlight huge sunflower heads bobbed in the wind as if watching his every move.

"How big do you think a dog named Rambo is?" Colby asked, as he held the flashlight on the lock.

"I don't hear a bark, so he's not much of a guard dog."

"The big ones just have a low growl before they bite."

Hank laughed. "Great. You go in first."

"Not me. This wasn't my idea. I'm just here to arrest you if an alarm goes off or drive the getaway car if it doesn't."

"She doesn't have an alarm." Hank popped the lock.

"How do you know?" Colby asked.

"Because no one in Clifton has an alarm."

"You got a point. Half of them probably don't even bother to lock their cars at night."

Hank opened the door three inches and a tiny ball of fluff ran out and attacked his shoelace.

Colby shined the flashlight on Rambo, but he was laughing too hard to hold it steady. "Watch out, Captain, he might be deadly."

Hank scooped up the two-pound ball of hair and held it in the light. "This is a dog? You've got to be kidding. It looks like a hairball some cat coughed up."

He put the pup in a fenced-in area the size of a playpen, and both men waited until Rambo did his business.

"I got to tell you, Hank, your wild days are a bit off-kilter."

Hank hurt too bad to laugh. He picked the dog up, patted its head, and gently tossed him back inside. "That dog is guarding the house about as completely as this tiny push button is locking the house. She needs a bolt and an alarm."

Colby shrugged. "She's got Rambo."

The ranger laughed as they walked away.

Five minutes later, Hank stepped under the blast of hot water and closed his eyes. He remembered how, after an aide had wrapped his hand in the hospital waiting room, he'd asked about Millie and learned she'd listed no one to call. No kin. No friend.

Ripping the bandage off his hand, he thought about how she'd gripped his fingers when he'd stood by her bed. The nurse had been trying to tell her what to do, but the lady didn't want anyone to make decisions for her or handle her future. Independence must run to her core, but for a moment she needed someone. Someone had to help her and, for some crazy reason, she'd turned to a stranger, him.

He knew her name, address, blood type. She was thirty-six, two years younger than him. Probably twice as educated. Stubborn as a boulder. Thin as a rail. And one other fact. She needed a friend.

Hank had offered, but had no doubt that the moment she could manage alone, she'd tell him to get lost, in a nice way, of course.

He had a feeling independence was what Amelia Remington valued most.

As he was drying off after his shower, he remembered the way she'd frowned when he'd called her Millie. Just for the hell of it, he thought he might call her that now and then. He liked seeing that touch of fire in her eyes.

Another bet he'd make with himself. She'd probably never call him Hank. To the little librarian, he'd be Harrison.

After he bandaged the spot still dripping blood, he stretched out on the bed and decided he'd do this one thing for her. He'd get her home and make sure she was safe. He wouldn't try to tell her what to do. He'd just offer assistance for a few days. He could build a ramp if needed, or move things around so she could reach them from a wheelchair. He'd make sure she had what she required. Then he'd leave.

Hank shook his head. He was good at leaving. He never

stayed in a relationship long enough to be missed when he closed the door on his way out.

He fell asleep remembering the feel of her hand. He wasn't attracted to her. The lady was plain, too thin, and had bookworm written all over her. They had little in common.

Except the wreck and maybe a strong need to be alone.

When he closed his eyes, the accident came back. The fact that she'd fallen without a sound haunted his dreams more than if she'd screamed.

A little after nine the next morning, Hank walked into the hospital in what he called his street clothes. Dark slacks, white button-down shirt, and a smoky-gray sweater wrapped over his back like a cape. His dark brown hair was pulled back.

Little of the biker was left. If he'd shaved his short beard, he'd almost look like a preacher's son.

He always packed the same outfit when he came to Clifton Bend to see his dad. It eliminated at least one lecture, and his dad never noticed he'd worn the same clothes for a dozen visits. If he'd had any sense, he would have driven his Audi up from Houston, but he couldn't quite conform that much.

He loved roaring into the valley, circling Honey Creek on a bike, just as he'd ridden out at eighteen. It had been twenty years ago, but he wanted to let his dad know he was still wild. The preacher would never win.

As he walked past the nurses' desk, heading toward Miss Remington's room, Hank noticed a woman in a navy suit waiting just outside the librarian's door.

"You Miss Amelia's friend?" she asked as if she'd already figured out the answer.

Hank frowned. He didn't know Amelia Remington well enough to be a friend, but since he was taking her home, it would make more sense to say yes. "I am. Is everything all right with Millie?"

"Of course. I have her discharge papers ready. The nurse is making the final check now. The doctor ordered our ambulance to take her home. He thought it might be easier than getting her into a car."

Hank nodded, feeling like the village idiot. He hadn't even thought of how to get her home. He'd walked from the hotel to the hospital. He doubted Clifton Bend even had a taxi.

He guessed her car was still at the college, parked somewhere in the faculty parking lot, but he had no idea where the keys were.

If he was the only friend she had, Millie didn't have much.

"Any problem if I ride along?" He could walk, but he wanted to be with her.

"Of course not." The woman made a note. "We'll make sure she has crutches and a wheelchair. The doctor reminded me to tell you that she's to put no weight on her left leg until she comes back in three days." The lady in the suit finally smiled. "You may have to carry the librarian around, unless she's in the wheelchair." The clerk studied him up and down. "You look like you can handle that job."

"Understood." Hank didn't smile. The last thing he wanted was someone starting rumors. He'd had enough of that the year before he'd left town.

He also didn't like the look the checkout clerk gave him. A lopsided smile, a lift of her eyebrow, a glance down his body. That "come get me" look cowboys on the circuit often get. If it had been ten years ago and they'd met in a bar, he might have taken her home, but not now. He was older, wiser, and had a few other things to think about than mindless sex with a woman who'd probably cry while claiming she loved him, at the same time she was trying to remember his name.

A friend told him once that he used women, but Hank didn't see it that way. He never made the first move. He never said a word that hinted of love or a future. If anything, women used him. They wanted their one wild night with a cowboy at the rodeo or their encounter with a biker who was riding across the country. They wanted the fantasy lover, not the reality.

When he'd left the rodeo to work on oil rigs, he'd abandoned that life as easily as he'd left his life in Clifton Bend. The bar games and the women who giggled constantly no longer interested him. Two years later he'd studied enough to hire on at an oil company as an explosives engineer. Two years after that he was in the EOD, the Explosive Ordnance Disposal branch of the Houston police. Moments of excitement hidden inside hours of waiting. Just like riding bulls. A clock in his brain that ticked out seconds still seemed to be ticking.

Moving inside Amelia Remington's room, Hank thought he could go over to his dad's house and borrow the preacher's old Lincoln, once he got her settled. If the boat of a car would start. He might even go get his dad and take him for a ride one morning before he left town. They could drive by the old house, the church, and maybe his mom's grave. One place his father had probably never been.

But right now, he had to get Millie home and settled.

He had money and plenty of vacation days, but maybe it would be easier to hire an aide to sit with her. Hank wasn't skilled at this kind of thing. She would probably be better off with professional help.

He stood just inside the librarian's doorway and watched as the nurse slowly applied cream to Millie's arm, then moved behind her to untie her gown. As the cotton slipped away he saw her back. From her shoulder to the small of her back there were black bruises and places where missing skin was raw. The line of her body as she sat so straight reminded him of a painting. Graceful.

Hank couldn't move as the nurse worked. Bandaging first her arm, then her neck. The woman he'd hit made no sound. Her chestnut-colored hair lay over a place where they'd shaved her head to put stitches in.

This quiet view of her hurt him deep inside. He'd been the cause of her pain. He had to help her.

He'd done this to the lady, and yet she'd taken the blame last night. She'd told the sheriff she'd stepped out without looking. She was stronger than he was, even when he'd been riding bulls and working the oil fields.

Hank would take care of her. Not because she needed him, but because he needed to. Penance, maybe, for all the wrongs he had done.

Slowly he slipped into the room and watched everything the nurse did. The way she secured the sling. How she checked the brace on her leg. How she touched Millie lightly to balance her for even the smallest movement.

As the nurse worked, she talked to him as if giving a demonstration.

He moved closer, learning as he watched. Her hospital gown came loose and slipped, barely covering her breasts. He didn't miss the bruises along her collarbone.

The nurse spoke softly to Millie, but her gaze met Hank's eyes. "There will be more bruising, dear. Deep bruises coming up. It looks like your left side took most of the impact. Make sure you take all the meds for a few days and talk to the doc before you go off painkillers. Keep all wounds clean and dry. Don't push yourself. Let your friend help you."

"I don't want painkillers," the librarian said. "Only over-the-counter."

He couldn't see Millie's face, but she sounded determined.

"All right," the nurse answered. "But you're going to hurt all over."

"I can take the pain," she answered as she pulled up her gown with her right hand.

Hank moved forward and tied the gown behind her neck. "I'm here to help," he said almost against her ear, as he lightly placed his hand on her right shoulder. "You'll have to tell me how."

She turned and looked at him, showing no surprise that he came back. Her eyes were clearer this morning, but the left side of her face was bruised. "I'm glad you came. Promise not to boss me, Mr. Norton. I'll take the help when I must, but I want to manage if I can."

"I promise." He grinned. The lady had strength in her that surprised him.

He thought of all the promises he'd broken over the years, but he wouldn't break this one. "I'll stay with you for as long as you need me."

"Thank you." Her hand touched his fingers still resting on her shoulder. "I'll heal fast."

"Until then, I'm near." For a moment he thought he saw the little girl in the woman. A blink of fear in her eyes a moment before she straightened.

Damn, the lady was in a bad place if he was the one she turned to.

The nurse finished her checklist. "That's a good friend you've got, Miss Remington."

She smiled. "Best one I've ever had."

Hank winked at the librarian and he could have sworn she was blushing beneath the bruises.

Chapter 9

Ketch

The church bells were ringing as Ketch drove toward Tuesday's place. For once he had a day off, and it wasn't because of rain. No work to finish up and no papers due, thanks to spring break. He'd loaded down his truck with tools and enough lumber to keep him busy. He wanted to pay Tuesday back. The least he could do was fix her porch.

The day might be sunny, but the last half-mile to her place was still muddy. She'd been right about the unpaved road being protection. Her great-grandparents' place wasn't easy to find or get close to. He drove over prairie grass to keep from making the ruts deeper.

Ketch unloaded and went to work. A half hour later, Tuesday leaned out the front door, wearing nothing but his army T-shirt, knotted at her waist, and pink panties. "What do you think you're doing?"

"Fixing your porch before it falls down on you."

"Oh," she said and closed the door.

Ten minutes later, she appeared still dressed in his T-shirt, but the panties were covered by shorts. Her hair was combed and her smile came easy. "Morning, Ketch."

Then, without a word, she walked out to him and gave him a quick hug. "Go away. I don't need any help."

He shook his head. "Not till you feed me. You said yesterday you liked to cook. Well, cook or feed me leftovers. I'm here to earn a meal." He turned back to the saw he'd set up on the solid wing of the porch. "This project is going to take a while."

"What do you want?"

"Food. Real food that doesn't come in a frozen box or a take-out bag. Prove it. Cook me something. I grew up on cafeteria lunches and army grub. I'm not hard to please."

She turned around and headed back in as he added in a whisper, "Your legs are longer than I thought they'd be, kid."

Two hours passed before she returned with a tablecloth and real napkins.

He'd taken his shirt off and had sawdust all over his chest. When she walked past him, he raised an eyebrow. If he didn't know better, he'd think she was checking him out.

She stopped at the door and turned back. "It's Sunday. When company comes on Sunday, I set the table proper."

"That mean I have to put my shirt back on?"

"If you plan to eat, you do."

The minute he smelled the food, he dusted off and dressed. It took her three trips to bring out the meal. Chicken-fried steak, mashed potatoes, fresh carrots, peas, and biscuits.

He just stared as she poured tea.

"You made all this in two hours?"

"No," she said. "The pie is still in the oven."

Ketch pulled out her chair and for a moment felt like he was on a date. He could never remember a woman cooking a Sunday meal just for him.

Laughing, she watched him taste everything as he put a serving on his china plate, then took another spoonful.

When they began eating, his plate was piled high and hers looked like a kid's meal.

While he ate, she picked at her food and told him about coming to live with her Grannie Eva when she was half grown. Tuesday swore she was Chicago tough when she arrived, raised by a mother who never had time for her. She was afraid of the country and angry at the world. Grannie Eva had treated her as if she were a great gift and, to her surprise, nothing she said shocked the old lady.

"She was shorter than me but four feet nine inches of pure love. I couldn't hate her even if I tried."

Tuesday talked about how everyone at school made fun of her accent and the way she dressed, but she loved coming home to this house. Her grannie had traveled the world as a kid, then the war came and, at fifteen, she'd married just to get away. Her husband, Frank, was older, a friend of Eva's father. He treated Eva like extra baggage and that's all she ever was to him.

Tuesday smiled as she remembered. "We might not have owned a TV, but we always seemed busy with just living. Grannie could cook all kinds of food.

"I don't think she ever worked, other than to help Frank sell a few sculptures. She said she had a small trust fund. After Grannie passed, my mother's lawyer took what was left in the bank when he visited after the funeral. He told me my mother needed the trust money, but he said the deed to the house had been made out to me. He also told me that my mother thought I'd never go anywhere, so she wouldn't fight me for this worthless spot. She claimed she would rather die than live in Nowhere, Texas, again. Except for the lawyer, I haven't heard a word from my mother since."

Tuesday leaned back in her chair, and Ketch mentally filled in the story. "It must be hard keeping this place up."

"I'm managing." She looked over at the work he'd done. "Well, I've tried. Thanks for fixing the steps."

He saw steel hardening in her veins and knew it was time to change the subject. "Why were you named Tuesday?"

Tuesday shrugged. "I was born on Tuesday. Why were you named Ketch?"

"My folks loved to sail, I guess. A ketch is a kind of sailboat."

She smiled for the first time. "I guess you're a leftover kid too. You know, a couple has a great time, and nine months later you pop out. Maybe they love you for a while, but you're just left over after the party's forgotten."

"That how you feel?"

"That's how I've always felt."

He leaned closer and brushed her hair back from her face so he could study her. A whole world of sadness lived behind her green eyes. "I don't want to ever have a leftover kid," he whispered as if he was making an oath. "If I ever have a kid, he'll never doubt for one day that I love him."

"Me too," she answered as she slowly straightened away.

A silence settled between them as they finished eating. She didn't show much interest when he pulled a four-foot pipe forward.

As he leaned back in his chair and grabbed the rusty pipe, he said, "I found the strangest thing under the porch."

He held out the pipe like it was a treasure. "At first I just thought it was trash left behind, but then I noticed a tube inside the pipe. I recognized it as an architect's tube, like we use on commercial buildings to store blueprints."

They moved to a table he'd rigged with a few boards and a sawhorse. As she helped him unroll the paper, Tuesday got excited. "It's my house."

Ketch studied the plans. "This is no ordinary house plan. This one was done in great detail. Look here how the window is turned sideways, not straight. That man named Tony must have designed the entire house and then built it in stages. That's the only way this place could have fit together so seamlessly."

Tuesday moved in front of him, her back fitting nicely against his chest. "That's the dining room. That window catches the morning light in spring. And this window that I thought was always put in the wrong place catches the winter sunrise."

The hole in the porch was forgotten as they examined their find. Ketch could read the plans and Tuesday remembered the odd turns in the house. They were both Christmas-morning excited.

"The guy who built this house was an artist, and every detail was built with love."

Lifting the plans, they hurried inside to explore. "By the time I moved in with Grannie, we only lived on the first floor. I've walked the rooms on the other two floors, but I didn't know them."

"We'll start with these four rooms." Ketch thought out loud. "The base first." He moved around, touching every wall, then read the blueprints as if they were explaining every step of the construction.

When Ketch found a slot in the wall of Eva's pantry, he laughed with excitement. He pushed his fingers in and lifted a lever up. A wall panel swung open. Tuesday squealed, and they both rushed in to see a secret room. Four feet by three feet, with two steps that led up to nowhere.

"This makes no sense," Tuesday whispered as if a ghost might hear. "It's too small to be used for anything."

"Every detail on the plans was worked out," Ketch whispered back. "This space has to have a purpose." Ketch saw this as a puzzle, but Tuesday's eyes told him she saw it as frightening.

He stretched his arms, as if trying to push the walls.

The ceiling above them was ten feet high, with what looked like a slated covering that let a bit of light in from above. When the panel door suddenly closed, they found themselves standing in a coffin-sized room.

Tuesday stood on the second step that went to nowhere. Nose to nose with Ketch, she announced, "We're trapped. Pull the door back up."

"I can't. There is not enough room for me to bend down. You give it a try."

She tried as her body moved over his. She could lean down a few inches, but his big frame took up too much room. When her soft parts pushed against him, his solid frame didn't give.

When he smiled, she hit his shoulder. "Stop enjoying this! We're going to die. We're trapped."

Ketch tried to look frightened. "Yeah, we'll die in here. No way out." He moved closer to her ear. "The upside is I've been wanting to get this close to you all day."

"Why?" She put her hands on his shoulder, almost close enough to choke him. Some of her fear vanished. Now she was looking at him as if he'd gone mad.

"I was thinking about asking for my T-shirt back."

"What? Are you crazy? We're trapped. There is probably not enough air in here for two people. We'll starve to death before anyone finds us, and you are worried about your T-shirt, which I am not giving back, by the way."

"You'll starve long before me. I ate all my lunch."

She was back to panic. "There has to be a button or a lever, some way to get out. She bumped against him as she turned, searching every inch of the walls. "Lift me up."

His hands circled her waist and lifted her up as she patted the wood above them. When her breast bumped his eye, he groaned and she hit him hard on the head.

He couldn't help but laugh. The panel that had closed behind him would shatter with one kick, but he'd hate to damage the house. Plus, he was having too much fun. For a man who never got close to anyone, he was loving being close to Tuesday.

"Even if I stand on your shoulders, I can't reach the slats above."

"We should try anyway," he suggested. "I'm starting to feel like a tree you're climbing." One of her shoes dropped and he cupped his hand beneath her foot to hold her up. Her bare waist brushed against his lips.

"You taste great," he whispered.

She patted him on the head. "You are a very noisy tree." The other shoe dropped. "Can you lift me higher without kissing your way down my body? Keep in mind that if you don't behave and we live, I will kill you later."

He lifted her higher. "I'll be a perfect gentlemen, but it's not going to be easy." He listened to her patting the wood above them as her body brushed against him. She was slender but soft. He breathed her in, inch by inch.

"Lower me," she finally said. "It's hopeless."

As he lowered her to the step, his arms closed around her. "It's all right. I can get us out, but I hate to shatter the wood."

"I thought of that. There has to be another way."

Ketch leaned his hand behind her to kiss her. He'd waited long enough. She was inches away from him and the nearness was driving him mad.

Just before his mouth reached hers, the wall behind her gave.

Tuesday squealed and twisted against him to turn into a tiny open stairway. Then, like a spider, she climbed up.

He was right behind her, climbing toward the pale light.

A moment later they crawled onto the dusty floor of an attic, both laughing.

Long windows slanted into the roof, showing the land below. The trees she'd said her great-grandfather had planted from the stream all the way up the hill. Grannie Eva's huge vegetable garden, now still sleeping in winter, lay east of the house. And the first blooms of flowers planted everywhere beside paths weaving among the trees.

From this lookout point, Ketch realized he could see pretty much every foot of her land.

He sat beside her on a quilted cushion almost wide enough to be a bed, his elbow on his knee as he studied the land. From this angle he couldn't see another structure, not even the road. All the world seemed made up of only nature. "The architect who built this place was a genius. The whole house is built to catch the light and show off the beauty of nature. This little space was a private lookout."

He leaned back against the quilt to look up at the cloudy sky.

Tuesday lay down using his chest as a pillow. "I remember Grannie Eva saying she'd traded one of her paintings for lumber." Tuesday laughed. "When I would cry, Grannie would climb the two flights of stairs to this attic and we'd watch clouds. Wonder why she never showed me the hidden steps."

Ketch said his thoughts. "Maybe it was a secret passage for lovers?"

"But there were only three people in the house when it was built."

Ketch grinned. "And only two knew about this passage."

She shook her head. "Not my grannie. She'd never . . ."

He leaned close. "She wasn't always a grandmother. Once she was a girl married to an older man and maybe, just maybe, in love with his brother."

"Impossible." Tuesday giggled.

"No ordinary builder designed this house. You mind if I take the plans and study them? This Tony, who worked for meals, could have made a name for himself."

"Sure. You found the plans. You can have them, but you're not getting this T-shirt back. You gave it to me and I'm never taking it off."

She patted him on the chest. "Stop laughing. You're making my pillow wiggle. After our near-death experience, I just want to lie here for a while and watch the clouds go by."

And that is exactly what she did as he smiled, thinking of all there was to explore in this place.

As Tuesday drifted off to sleep, he thought of the letter from Crystal. If it hadn't been for the letter, he wouldn't have gone to the bar. If he hadn't gone to the bar, he wouldn't have met Tuesday. He didn't care about the rumors circling her. He didn't believe them.

Maybe nothing more would ever happen between them, but she'd taught him a lesson. No matter what came of their friendship, he'd learned to always look around the next corner.

Ketch closed his eyes, still seeing the puffy clouds in his mind. For the first time in his life, he felt at home. Maybe it was a person, maybe it was the house, or just maybe it was a career.

He didn't belong in chemistry; he belonged in architecture. This house was making it plain what he loved.

Chapter 10

Hank

When the ambulance brought the librarian home, Hank took one look at the winding path up to Amelia Remington's front door and lifted her from the stretcher. "You mind if I carry you, Millie?"

"It seems the most practical way." Her voice was soft, tired now.

One of the EMTs took her keys and ran ahead to open the door.

Hank carefully walked up the path with her right side resting against his chest. He didn't want to bump her braces or her left arm. She was lighter than he'd thought she'd be and he could feel her heart racing. In a strange way she was his, or maybe more accurately, he was hers.

There was an easy feeling between them, almost familiar, almost comfortable, almost loving.

He'd accidentally run over a fragile bird and the thought of what he'd done hurt deep inside of him. For once in his life he planned to correct the damage he'd caused.

One of the EMTs followed them into a tidy little house with the walls lined in books. The ambulance driver brought in equipment. Harrison stood in the center of the room, holding her as she told the two men where to put everything.

Her voice grew a bit stronger now, but he could almost feel her strength melting in his arms.

He turned his face toward hers, almost touching her ear. "I need to put you down, pretty lady. That all right with you? Bed or couch?"

"Bed," the EMT answered for Millie. "The nurse gave her something to help her make the trip. She'll sleep for a while."

Hank didn't move. "Your call, Millie."

"Take me to bed, dear knight." She smiled a tight little smile, as if she were teasing him. "Rambo is probably hiding under there. He's afraid of crowds."

Hank followed instructions, thinking there were other ways he could have taken that order "take me to bed" if she'd been pretty much any other woman. But the librarian wasn't his type, and he'd bet she had no idea how to flirt. Plus, if he made a pass, Rambo would attack his shoelaces again.

When he picked up a woman, usually at a bar, she'd be curvy, definitely big chested, and probably blonde; not tall, thin, and bookish. In fact, he could never remember talking about books with any of his midnight dates.

Within a few minutes, Amelia Remington was in bed with her leg atop pillows and her left arm banked with a soft throw. Hank dug around under the bed until the pup bit his finger, then he pulled Rambo out, took him outside for a few minutes, and finally put him beside Millie.

The little hairy rat seemed to sense her pain. Rambo curled up next to her hand and began to lick her fingers.

As the men left, Harrison leaned down close to her as he carefully brushed her hair from her face. "Will you be all right for an hour? I need to go get a car, pick up some groceries, get your prescriptions, and check out of my motel."

She looked exhausted. "Where will you sleep?"

"On your couch. I'm on guard duty in this tiny castle of yours."

Millie didn't argue. She was already asleep.

He covered her with a quilt designed with sunflowers. Without much thought, he leaned down and kissed her cheek. "Sleep, little bird. I'll watch over you." On his way out he picked up her keys.

Two hours later, when he made it back with his dad's Lincoln loaded down with groceries, Hank was having an anxiety attack.

What if she woke and was in pain? Or sick? He wasn't much of a knight. He hadn't even thought to leave water by her bed.

When he found her exactly as he'd left her, he took a deep breath. "Thanks for watching over her, Rambo," he whispered. As silently as possible, Harrison unloaded food, checking on her every few minutes. All he'd seen in her fridge was yogurt, eggs, and lettuce. He bought a bit of everything that he could cook and enough beer to last a week.

On his last trip in from the car, a neighbor stepped out on her porch. Seeing her bulldog expression, he braced for an attack. "Is Miss Remington all right, and who are you? I've never seen a man walk into her place. I think I may need to call the sheriff."

Hank wanted to tell her to mind her own business, but that wasn't likely in Clifton. Sheriff LeRoy wouldn't be happy if he had to drive over from Honey Creek to "not" arrest him again.

"I'm an old friend of Miss Remington. She's had an

accident, and I am watching over her until one of her family arrives."

"Oh." The neighbor, still in her bathrobe, didn't look happy. "What happened to her?"

"An idiot ran over her in front of the library."

Hank took a chance, since the nosy neighbor obviously wasn't heading to church and didn't look old enough to have heard old rumors. "I'm Pastor Norton's son. I just happened to be in town visiting my dad."

"Oh," she said again. "I've heard the name." She seemed to relax, but she didn't offer to help. "He's retired, isn't he?"

"Yes, ma'am. Left the calling five years ago, but still teaches Bible studies at both of the nursing homes, if you're interested. I'll ring you if I need any help with Miss Remington. Thanks for your concern."

The neighbor took a step back. "I work nights and sleep days. Not much for nursing, but if you need something from Walmart, I could pick it up for you."

"Thanks, you're very kind," he lied as he closed the front door.

He had a can of soup warming and a sandwich made when Amelia woke.

She looked surprised to see him but not frightened.

"You hungry?" he asked. She didn't look all that proper with her hair wild. It was long, and he'd bet she usually wore it in a knot on the back of her neck. That was how all librarians wore their hair, right? He had to fight not to kid her about letting her hair down.

She shook her head no, then saw the plate with the sandwich beside her bed. "I could eat a little."

He awkwardly lifted her to a seated position and put every unused pillow he could find behind her. When he stood back, tears filled her eyes but she didn't complain.

He brought her a cup of soup he'd been rewarming while she slept, and she asked if he'd eat with her.

He set a tray beside the bed so he could face her as they ate. She handled the soup fine, but he ended up helping her with the sandwich.

"What do I call you?" he asked. "Miss Remington?"

"Call me Amelia and I'll call you Harrison."

"I think I'll call you Millie, pretty lady. I've always liked that name, and it fits you."

She looked up at him. "I guess Millie is fine since you seem stuck on it, but why do you call me pretty lady? Unless you are blind, you must see that doesn't fit me."

He studied her for a minute. "You're wrong, Millie. You are pretty. Don't tell me no one has ever told you how beautiful you are. There's a grace about you."

"You're not going to compare me to a horse again?"

"No, but I do love that chestnut-colored hair of yours."

He could see it in her eyes. No man had ever noticed her. He'd seen a hundred women who thought they were beautiful and were not, but he'd never seen one who was lovely and fragile but didn't know her worth.

Finally, she spoke. "I'm smart. That's enough for this lifetime. I've never been pretty."

Hank knew if he said anything more, he'd be arguing with her. He couldn't change her mind now, maybe ever. So he switched the conversation to how he fixed his father's car.

She leaned back and closed her eyes as he watched her. Once more, the line of her neck, the classic strength of her face reminded him of a painting. He couldn't resist brushing his fingers lightly over her hair to push it away from the porcelain perfection of her.

"Pretty" wasn't the right word for her. "Graceful" was.

An hour later she woke and said she had to go to the bathroom. He had no doubt he turned redder than she did.

Without a word, he lifted her gently and carried her to the bathroom. He set her down with her hospital gown draping her in front. Then he closed the door and prayed she could handle the rest.

When he heard her say his name, he opened the door and waited.

She grabbed his arm and pulled herself to stand on her good leg.

He moved his free arm down her back, over her hips and lifted her. The sight of her bare back and hips reminded him once more of her slim perfection.

It crossed his mind that the hit he took to his head might have made him see women differently.

Without looking at him, she thanked him, then added as he put her back on the bed, "My gown doesn't cover my backside. Would you mind getting me my robe?"

He placed the pillows around her. Tears were flowing again, but she didn't complain. "Don't worry about it, Millie. I've seen a thousand butts. When I was working cattle, the back side of them was pretty much all I saw every day."

She let out a little squeal that he wasn't sure was a cry or a laugh.

"Sorry. That didn't come out right. Your bottom isn't anything like a cow's." If he didn't shut up, he'd be the one blushing before long. "Yours is real nice, I mean. Not that I looked."

The next sound was definitely a laugh. "Under the circumstances, how about we simply be honest with one another? No flattering to make me feel better."

"All right. I'll stay honest, since I'm a knight. Only the truth. You are a pretty lady, and you have a pretty backside."

Millie met his gaze. "And you, Sir Knight, are blind."

Hank winked. "Nicest thing I've ever been called." Suddenly, despite the accident and the fact they were strangers, she made him feel young, not almost forty. He hadn't felt young for a long time. In his twenties he'd lived hard and fast on the rodeo circuit. When he turned twenty-eight and was still riding bulls, he was considered old in the game. He'd known it was time to get out, so, thanks to a friend, he'd switched his occupation to the oil fields. Then he'd studied nights and weekends to become a specialist, an expert at something, even if it was considered one of the most dangerous occupations around.

From fighting oil fires and handling explosives, he moved to the police force and prepared for one of the most challenging teams. The bomb squad.

He had a feeling all Millie's adventures had been in books, and somehow her life had slipped between the pages. Or maybe the accident had rattled her brain as well as his. It didn't matter. He'd play along with the knight gig. He felt like he'd been playing one part or another all his life.

"Would you like me to move the TV in here? Or get you a book? Or tell jokes? No, forget that. All I know are dirty ones."

He'd won another smile. "Can we just talk for a few minutes?"

"I'd like that." Without asking, he began to comb her hair while she sat straight and still. "How did you end up at Clifton College?" he asked after a moment.

She took a deep breath and seemed to relax. "My parents lived in a trailer and moved around when I was a kid. Strange, but wherever we moved, the school and the libraries seemed my home, my safe places. When my teachers said I should go to college, my parents said I'd had enough learning. So I moved out, got a job, and started night classes. When I checked on them, they'd moved on. I think they were accidental parents who never settled into the role."

"Did you find them?"

"I didn't look."

The pieces of her life seemed to explain Millie. An only child. A mother and father who didn't care about her. She'd finished college alone and shy, with the library as her hiding place.

Her words were orderly, organized, without emotions. "It took me six years to finish my degree, then I drifted from library to library looking for a home. I thought maybe this small place might be where I'd finally settle. I always thought that people who had a hometown were lucky."

But she hadn't settled here, he thought. The small house with all her things packed inside was more a storage place than a home. No relations. No friends to call. She didn't fit in, no matter how perfect the library. Hank would bet she was still looking for *home*.

He sensed she was a person who wasn't comfortable in her own skin. It seemed to him that she was a stranger to herself. He'd heard an old legend about a tribe of people who were all that way. They moved over the land like smoke, sentenced to live life over and over without ever finding their place. The elders said they were rootless because Mother Earth would not accept them.

As he braided her hair in one long rope, Hank told her about his rodeo days. Even showed her a few scars. Leaving out the drinking, the fights, and a few not-so-legal pranks he'd done, he managed to make riding the circuit seem fun. "Now I'm settled in Houston, but I drive up to see my dad a few times a year."

"The pastor?" she asked.

"Right. Believe me, he was much more a preacher than he ever was a father. My mom died when I was fourteen. He told me not to go to the cemetery because she wasn't there. I knew that, but he wouldn't let me mourn. He caught me crying about a week after she died and lectured me for hours, then preached about how weak I was the next Sunday."

Hank couldn't believe he'd just told her something he'd never told anyone. In this town, Pastor Norton was a saint to everyone but his son.

She moved her hand over his, just as she'd done at the hospital. "That must have been hard," she whispered.

Rambo belly-crawled to his hand and licked his wrist. The pup seemed to agree with her.

He sat on the edge of her bed and leaned back against the wall. Maybe she just wanted someone close or maybe he didn't want to leave. Like two teenagers, they just held hands as the room grew darker. They talked like old friends who had nothing to hide, and he loved the growing intimacy between them.

When she placed her cheek against his shoulder and settled so near, he didn't move. Hell, he felt closer to this stranger than he'd felt to most women he'd slept with.

She seemed to be waiting for him to say more, and for once, that was all he needed.

He told her that when his mother died, he was lost. "Dad took on preaching like a quest and never mentioned her. Since I couldn't cry for my mother, I went wild. My way of balancing out the world, I guess."

To his surprise, she laughed, then added that she'd never done one wild thing in her life.

Hank kissed her hand and continued, "It was like my father died, too, when I was fourteen. There were times he'd stare at me as if wondering who I was. The only time he noticed me was when I was in trouble. Finally, I just left. I sent him an announcement when I graduated from college. I don't know if he even opened the envelope. When I made the papers for just doing my job, I gave him the article from the *Houston Chronicle*. He thanked me and put the page down without even looking at the headline.

"It wasn't like I was lost. I had a cell phone, but he never called."

When her eyelids begin to droop, he tucked her in and kissed her on the cheek again. "How about when you get well I teach you to ride the wind, Millie? That could be your one wild thing."

"I'd like that," she added, already more asleep than awake.

Hank meant to leave, but she was still holding his hand. Her trust in him was the one thing in the world that mattered to him.

He leaned back against the pillow that braced her shoulder and closed his eyes.

He wasn't going to leave her alone. He had a feeling they'd both been alone too long.

Chapter 11

Ketch

Ketch left Tuesday Raine asleep in the attic room and retraced their steps back to the tiny passageway. On the opposite wall, halfway down, he noticed a lever that easily opened the hidden panel door into the kitchen. Anyone could take the stairs to the attic from the main stairway, so why did the builder include a secret passage?

"And are there more?" he asked himself aloud. Nothing about this house was standard construction.

He left the passage open so Tuesday could find her way down and went back to work. The hammering and whine of the saw didn't wake her. When she finally wandered down wearing his T-shirt and her shorts, she stretched and yawned.

Ketch had packed up his tools. "Finished," he said.

She admired his work. "Thanks. What do I owe you?"

"Another dinner sometime?"

"Anytime."

Neither said a word. He knew their friendship was too fragile to tease about. He simply walked to his truck with the house plans tucked under one arm.

"See you, kid," he finally managed as he climbed into his truck.

She waved. "See you, old man," she answered.

Ketch grinned. At twenty-six he was her old man and at twenty-two she was a kid. Between them, they had a lifetime of living.

Later that night, in his apartment, he studied the plans and thought there was one thing he should have done before he'd left.

He should have kissed Tuesday. She'd looked so adorable in his old army T-shirt. He loved how she'd slept on his chest like they were wild pups.

Trying to get his mind off of the way Tuesday's body felt bumping against him in the tiny passage, Ketch googled Tony Raine. If the brothers had kept the same name, he might find out if Tony Raine ever worked on any other house.

No luck.

Ketch tried Anthony Raine.

His laptop lit up. An artist turned architect, he had worked on county courthouses all over the state. Every county in Texas, all 254, had a county courthouse in the center of town. Picture after picture of stately buildings appeared.

Uncle Tony hadn't been simply a construction worker. He'd been a true artist. One article said he was buried in Texas State Cemetery in downtown Austin. According to the article, he died with no living kin.

The last line noted that Anthony Raine never owned a home but left his mark on Texas.

Ketch leaned back and stared at the screen. Tuesday's great-great-uncle's home was Primrose.

Chapter 12

Benjamin

Dr. Benjamin Monroe planned to make it in to work on time every morning though it was spring break and the college was officially closed. If he kept to his work schedule, he'd still have time to get his lesson plans for the rest of the semester mapped out. Somewhere during the week he had to make time to complete at least a first draft of the survey with Professor Clark.

Now the hallways were empty and he relaxed as he stared out the long row of windows on the third floor at his peaceful town. A college town, he thought, with school colors flying, shops for the young, and sidewalk chalk announcing every sorority fundraiser or party. Campuses were tiny worlds inside the real world, and only those enrolled were natives. The campus seemed to be paused, waiting for the students to come back.

Memories of his first year in grad school had filled his mind all weekend. The few days when he was twenty-one and searching for his North Star. He'd almost dropped out after a semester working toward his master's. The only time in his life that no order reigned. The only time he'd truly doubted himself. The only time he'd fully made love without boundaries.

Those cold January nights he'd been an adventurer running wild, lost without direction. One woman had affected his direction more than anyone ever had. He'd only known the girl they called Red a few days, but she'd changed him forever.

She'd done more than just make him a man. She'd made him believe in himself.

The redhead beauty had told him how smart he was. And how kind. She'd held his hand and, like a fortune-teller, said she saw his future. He could be anything he wanted, and she'd made him promise he'd never stop until he'd climbed the mountain of his potential.

She'd laughed when he'd told her he was shy. This woman he hardly knew explained that he was an inside thinker and if he didn't let his feelings out, he'd explode one day.

After growing up ten miles from Clifton Bend, then attending his first two years of college here, this place would always be home. His mountain seemed to be only hills surrounding a wide valley, and his inside thinking would have to stay hidden.

Those few days with Red, he'd felt like he'd stepped on the moon.

Everything before her was confusing and hard to grasp. He not only had to deal with the huge campus but also wild, quirky Austin. Suddenly, a million people were circling around him shouting new ideas and beliefs.

All he'd done that fall semester was study. He'd wake up every morning with too many things on his to-do list and fall asleep cussing himself that he didn't get it all done.

When he went home for Christmas break, he wasn't sure he could make himself go back to college. He was out of his depth.

The farmer had welcomed his son home but said nothing. They worked together from before dawn until after dark. The winter sun warmed him and for the first time in months he slept solid each night. Father and son finished one project after another.

Ben felt himself growing stronger, not just physically but mentally. He made a stand. He not only went back, he went back early, if for no other reason than to prove to his father that, though he loved the land, he wasn't a farmer. Or a quitter.

For the first time, Ben had felt angry at the world. He had wanted more than just studying. He'd wanted freedom and he needed to know his own strength. Moving off campus was one step. Drinking became the second. The first week back was always a party going on round the clock somewhere, and he managed to find the location. A new year. A new semester. A new world.

His friends were new, too, and another kind of education began.

Most of January had been a blur. He did remember what an idiot he'd been, trying to find life. If he hadn't wised up, he would have lost his scholarship. He would have lost the future he wanted. The future he now had.

But that cold January in Austin, there was one weekend that stood out. Three days, two nights with a girl at a waterfront house on Lake Travis. The place was packed that weekend, but he remembered only one person. They'd spoken of things he'd never talked about with a girl and made love without saying a word.

She'd told him they were two souls, lovers in another lifetime, who were just meant to cross once. He didn't really understand what she meant, but he'd wanted to believe her.

Then she'd slipped from his bed and his life without saying goodbye. People at the lake house knew her nickname was Red, but nothing more.

He skipped classes for a week looking for her and drank her memory away at night.

She'd said she was in her last few months of school and then she planned to travel for a while. She was almost two years older than he and much more experienced in everything. The things she'd taught him still warmed his blood when he thought of them.

As the years passed, Benjamin did what he always did. He pushed the fuzzy memory of her back where all the sad ones from his childhood lived. An only child on a farm with no one to play with. A kid too shy to make friends. A student who felt alone most of the time, even with people around.

The one time he'd really connected with someone hadn't stuck. The lake weekend was just a fluke, nothing more.

Then, years later, with one brush of his cheek against her breast, a twenty-year-old feeling came back. The one weekend when he'd totally connected with someone.

Every memory rolled over him like a tidal wave now.

The biology professor, the woman he'd avoided since she'd started in the fall, the noisy, bothersome teacher had once been his lover for a blink in time. His only true lover.

Fate hated him. When you're young, you think love is easy to find, but as you grow older, you realize how rare it is.

"Dr. Monroe?" came a low voice from the back of the room.

Ben turned to face Ketch Kincaid, a young man who would make his name in biochemistry one day. "I'm ready, Kincaid." Ben pulled back to reality. "We're meeting Miss Clark in the conference room. With few people on campus, we can spread out on the big table and work there."

Benjamin noticed a cut ran along Ketch's hairline. "You all right?"

"Yeah. I accidentally ran into the road." The ex-soldier

grinned. "After three years I decided to try Clifton's night life Saturday night. Big mistake."

Ben shook his head. "I tried that once in Austin."

They moved to the meeting room, and Ketch politely said hello to Professor Clark and two of her students she'd recruited to help for extra credit.

While they planned the schedule, Ben stared at the biology teacher. It had to be her. The girl called Red. Most of the gang called him Farmer that winter. It seemed a time when everyone had nicknames. She'd been thin twenty years ago. Her hair had been darker and much longer. But her smile was the same. She'd seemed more girl than woman then.

He wondered if she remembered him. He'd had a beard then, like everyone had. His hair was longer. Gray peppered his once dark hair now.

Jenny looked directly at him and said, "Let's get to work, Doctor. We've got one week to do the research and get the study ready."

No smile. No wink. She didn't remember their weekend at the lake house. He was sure of it. She didn't remember him. For all he knew she was at the lake house every weekend. After a few years of grad school, minus holidays and bad weather, that meant she could have had a hundred weekend lovers.

He remembered their silent lovemaking when they'd communicated only by touch. Like passing through Heaven blindfolded.

Ben fought down a deep anger equally divided between her and him. Why hadn't they tried harder to find one another?

While Ketch and Miss Clark talked, Ben did what he

always did. What his father had taught him to do. Push all feelings aside and work.

When he eventually joined the planning, Jenny commented, "Glad you're finally with us, Dr. Monroe. You're so quiet most of the time, I can't tell if you're thinking or sleeping with your eyes open."

He didn't even try to smile.

Within less than an hour they'd finished the planning session. The two underclassmen recruits would help with the survey and enter data. Ketch would run the programs.

Ketch had to check in at his construction job but said since it was spring break, other part-time students could take over most of the work. He promised to drop by in the morning to pick up the survey.

Benjamin and Jenny agreed to pick three community classes to answer questions. One hundred people should be plenty. One of the undergrads would collect data by mail from parents of students, and another planned to hit the local senior citizens' center.

As if they'd heard a bell, all three helpers disappeared at once.

Jenny fussed over her papers while Ben watched. They were alone, but they might as well be miles apart. He'd never be able to mention the lake house weekend, and she obviously had no memory of it. Miss Clark wasn't the type to remain silent on any subject.

Ben moved closer, noticing that she smelled of strawberries today. The need to touch her hair made him ball his hand.

He considered the possibility that he was cracking up. Since when had he started smelling women? He wasn't sure, but he had a feeling they probably locked men up for doing

that kind of thing. If it got out, the locals would start point-
ing at him and saying things like, "There goes the sniffer."

Jenny looked up as she shoved one last paper into her
case. "Was there something else, Benjamin? I really need
to hurry."

Ben had to think of something. Telling her he was just
standing around smelling her didn't seem like a good idea.
"I thought . . . I thought if you're not busy . . . we could have
a late lunch." He silently cussed, then added, "I've a few
questions about the survey."

"Sure." She didn't sound very excited. "Your office?"

"Sounds practical. I'll pick up lunch. Same as Saturday.
Tuna sandwich, cheddar chips, and Diet Coke."

She looked up at him and grinned. "I'm surprised you
remembered, Benjamin."

"I remember," he managed as his hands fisted at his
sides, keeping him from admitting that he remembered the
way she felt. Soft and warm. He remembered the way her
breast felt in his hand. The way she wiggled in her sleep.
The way her wet body sparkled in the shower.

Suddenly, he needed fresh air.

Before he reached the door, he thought he heard her say,
"If strange had a market value, that man would be rich."

An hour later, Jenny rushed down the hall toward Dr.
Monroe's office. She'd forgotten about the late lunch and
spent too much time cleaning her lab.

When she hit the door of his office, she rattled the glass
in his window.

He stood and frowned at her, making her want to turn
around and rush back out, but then she saw lunch arranged

on his desk. He'd even gotten her a napkin to use as a placemat.

"I'm sorry I'm late. This was kind of you, Benjamin." Maybe, for once, the professor was trying to be friendly.

"Not kind, just expedient." Ben nodded once.

He just stood there waiting for her to take her seat. When she did, he folded into his chair. The desk made an ocean between them. For a few minutes they didn't talk. They simply unwrapped their meals.

Jenny knew she'd have to be the one to break the silence. "When I was in Italy, I had the most delightful sandwiches. It's been twenty years, but I still miss the taste."

"Were you studying there?"

"No, I was about half finished with my doctorate when I decided to follow a dream. A friend encouraged me. So, I dropped out of school and traveled for a year. I wouldn't have changed one moment of it, even though it meant not finishing my degree."

"Did you go to Paris?"

"I did, but I only stayed a few days. It seemed filled with tourists. I wanted to stay in small fishing villages and work the vineyard to the north. I wanted to know the people."

"So you never went back to school?"

"No. By the time I came home I decided I wanted to teach, but the need to wander is still in me. Every few years I move to another college, somewhere I've never been. New York, Atlanta, North Dakota. I even taught one year in Alaska."

"Why here?"

She took a drink and noticed he hadn't taken a bite. "I always want something different. The nice thing is, students are pretty much the same anywhere. Someone long ago told me this was a nice town."

"How do you like it so far?"

"I love it here. It feels a bit like home. I'll stay the two years, maybe longer this time."

Benjamin picked up an apple, but didn't eat. The man looked deep in thought. "I had a friend who also told me to follow my dream. It changed the direction I was headed at the time."

She couldn't decide if she was more surprised that he had a dream or that he had a friend. Dr. Monroe was always so formal. "What is the craziest thing you ever did, Benjamin?"

He took a bite of his apple, but she waited him out.

After he swallowed she swore he stuttered, coughed, cleared his throat, and finally said, "I went swimming in the horse tank when it was snowing."

"You're a wild man, Professor."

He grinned. "I was buck naked."

She laughed so hard tears came to her eyes. She could not imagine the proper Dr. Monroe doing such a thing. "Where was this horse tank? Not in town, I hope."

"It's on my dad's place, about ten miles from here."

She dried her eyes on her napkin. "You'll have to prove you did such a wild thing, Benjamin. I find this story hard to believe."

"How could I do that? Have my dad testify? I'm afraid he wouldn't want to get involved."

She smiled. The professor was actually talking about himself. "Doesn't care?"

"No, he's just busy. He raises mostly cash crops on his farm, and runs a few cattle. I've been experimenting with grapes on a small spot of land on his place. Got a few acres that I'm turning into a real vineyard."

"I'd love to see it. I spent a month working at a winery once. Though, I'm no expert."

"The crop is small. You'd be disappointed."

"Try me. I should go out to see the grapes. Who knows, I might be some help, and more importantly, I could question your dad about the horse tank."

He was staring at her again but she waited him out. Finally, he said, "All right. You're invited the next time I drive out. But you'll have to see my grand vegetable garden as well. Knowing Dad, if you step onto our land, you'll have to stay for supper. Then we'll go look at the horse tank."

For the first time since she'd been in Clifton Bend, Benjamin Monroe seemed interested in talking to her. There is a lesson she never seemed to remember: Most folks are interesting if you take the time to know them. Maybe she should make an effort to make a friend.

She wasn't attracted to him, she thought, but the stiff, cold, silent man was starting to grow on her.

That reminded her why she was in his office. "We'll see your farm later in the week, Professor. Right now, we need to get down to your questions about the project we're working on."

Jenny wasn't surprised when he picked up a notebook. The man had written his questions down. For a moment, she'd thought he was human. Now he was back to being a robot. He probably hadn't swum in the horse tank. His father more than likely had tossed him in to see if he'd rust.

Answering his questions as concisely as possible, she secretly smiled. She might not be attracted to Ben, but the curiosity in her decided to push a bit harder to find the core of him.

He could experiment with plants. She planned to experiment with him.

Chapter 13

Harrison

Tuesday
The Librarian's Checkup

"Millie, you are not going to try to put that shirt on by yourself. It'll hurt like hell." Hank paced the small bedroom lined with books. If her house ever caught fire, this place would burn for days.

She looked at him with her proper librarian stare. "I'm not going into my appointment wearing a hospital gown. I've had this thing on for three days. I can move the sleeve of the shirt an inch at a time, so turn around, Harrison. I'm not letting you see me nude."

Hank fought down a dozen swear words. They'd been together three full days and nights. He'd helped her eat, carried her around, even helped her take a sponge bath under a tent he'd rigged. When was she going to figure out they were not strangers?

"You are a stubborn woman, Millie. Modesty has its limits. The dog agrees with me." When she looked away from him and toward the pup, Hank nodded his head.

Rambo did the same.

Millie huffed as if they were ganging up on her. "Don't push me, Harrison."

She was fighting back tears. They both knew the arm would hurt if she lifted it away from her side. But she wouldn't let him assist her. He couldn't help, but he wondered what she thought might happen if he did see her thin frame or her small breasts.

He had no modesty. One night he woke her to give her pills. All he'd had on was underwear. From the panicked look she gave him you'd have thought he was buck naked. Since then he slept in his jeans. Heaven forbid she saw his hairy legs.

Harrison fisted his hands. "I'd wear a blindfold, but I doubt I'd be much help." He tried another angle. "I've seen a hundred women totally bare in my thirty-eight years of living. Believe me, honey, I won't see anything I haven't seen before. You're taking this shyness too far. We're two grown-ups. Hell, we're both moving into middle age."

She'd refused to wear anything but the hospital gown because it was open in the back when she needed it to be. But now she wanted to look proper.

They'd been together since she'd left the hospital. They'd talked. Told secrets. Admitted fears and laughed. They'd eaten every meal together and devoured ice cream sandwiches as their guilty delight. Showing a little skin didn't seem a big deal to him.

"I don't suppose you'd go naked if I did. Then we'd be even."

She almost smiled. "Not a chance, cowboy."

Hank walked to the bedroom door, turned, and walked back. If they'd been living together, he would have stormed out and gone for a drink, but that wasn't possible. Damn, damn, double damn. It's hard to argue with her all crippled up. Every time her face tightened with pain or she moved and let out a cry reminded him all this was his fault.

He knew her. How she liked her steak cooked. How she hated ketchup. How she loved reading. He'd carried her around the whole house and even outside to check on her dumb sunflowers. He'd seen her backside several times, even though she tried to keep the gown closed.

He'd even slept next to her that first night. But they were now going outside their cocoon, and she did not want to be seen in her stained gown.

She looked so upset and it suddenly hit him that she'd never been bare before a man. The very proper librarian was a virgin. How on earth was that possible? She'd told him she was thirty-six. To his way of thinking she should be wiser.

Dealing with a virgin was way out of his league. How could a woman make it halfway through life and not have let a man see her bare? She'd never felt another's body, skin-on-skin against her. He'd bet she'd never been held all night while she slept or pulled so close she couldn't tell if she heard his heart beating or hers.

Hank had to tread softly.

"I got an idea." He walked out of the room and returned with an apron. "Now be still. Trust me on this, pretty lady."

He tied the apron around her neck and untied the gown. "Pull the gown off. You'll still be covered with the apron."

She made sure the sheet covered her to her waist, then tugged the gown away.

It worked.

"Now, lean forward." He untied the sling and carefully moved one sleeve up her left arm, then looped the shirt behind her and she slipped her unharmed arm in the other sleeve. The shirt was open a few inches as he untied the apron and buttoned her blouse. The cotton top was big and white and clean. It also showed the outline of her breasts, but he wasn't about to mention that.

She smiled. "Thank you, Harrison."

"You are welcome. There's nothing I can't figure out if you give me time. That shirt is long enough to be a short dress. I'll put a blanket over your legs and you'll look all proper."

She raised one arm and circled his neck as he lifted her. When he lowered her into the wheelchair, she kissed his cheek.

He didn't move away. "Your aim's off, Millie. Try again."

To his surprise, she did. One chaste kiss against his lips.

Hank nodded once and straightened. He was back in middle school with the vanilla kiss. If his hunch was right, she knew little of what goes on between a man and a woman. They'd have to go back to "first date" level to start anything happening between them. Not likely, he decided. She wasn't his type and she probably wasn't interested. Millie lived her life in books.

Though he had to admit, her breasts were nicely rounded, even if they were small. The minute the thought came into his brain, he wished he could knock it out.

After tucking her blanket in on both sides, he pushed her slowly out the back door, where he'd rigged up a ramp that rolled her right to his dad's old Lincoln.

He wasn't surprised the neighbor was watching. She never offered any help or brought over a meal. She must just be the town watcher.

Hank waved.

The woman didn't wave back.

Another day, another time, he would have waved with one finger, but not today. Hank even caught himself driving like an old man, slowing down at green lights, letting other drivers cut into his lane. If he didn't straighten up, he'd be leaving his blinker on and flashing his brights for no reason at all.

"Will your dad miss his car?" Millie fought to keep her voice calm, but he knew she was hurting.

"No. He hasn't driven for three years. I suggested selling this old clunker, but it's a symbol of his freedom, I guess. He won't sell the house either."

"Do you stay there when you come to visit?"

"No. I stay at a motel. Feels more like home." He winked at her as if silently saying that she already knew that about him. "We're friends, Millie. Right?"

"I don't think I've ever talked to a member of the opposite sex as many hours as I've talked to you, so I guess that makes us friends."

"I agree." He'd probably shock her if she knew there were women he'd picked up and not said a word to them until after they'd had a midnight ride.

He caught that tight little smile shine for a moment and guessed she was happy about something.

As they pulled up at the doctor's office, she asked, "Will you stay with me?"

"You bet, babe. I'm your knight and a knight never leaves his lady," he answered.

She laughed. "No one in my entire life has ever called me 'babe.'"

"You mind?"

"No. I don't mind." The very proper librarian winked, then looked away. It was as if she couldn't let out too much joy. Everything in her world was measured, from the way she cut her meat in tiny pieces to how she drank only a half a cup of coffee each morning.

Hank found himself wondering if she'd measure out love as well.

Watching her was like studying an alien. He guessed she

felt the same way about him. Last night when he'd told her he'd gotten his degree by taking online classes after he'd worked in the oil field all day and studied half the night, she'd been fascinated.

When he lifted her from the car to the wheelchair, a nurse came out of the office to help. She pushed the chair as he gathered up her things. From the time they stepped inside the doctor's examining room, he felt invisible, and in truth, he liked it that way. Hank wasn't sure Amelia Remington even remembered he was in the room when the doctor started asking questions. She sat up so straight, hiding her pain, answering every question as if she were testifying.

Hank stood in the corner, leaning on a counter and staring at her back. She had a very nice back, he decided. If he were a sculptor, he'd like to reproduce the lines.

When the nurse helped Millie out of the white blouse, he thought of leaving, but the pretty lady had asked him to stay.

The bruising on the left side of her back seemed a bit lighter and the doctor was nodding and saying everything was beginning to heal. When she cried out as the doctor lifted her arm, Hank had to stop himself from going to her.

He noticed the nurse made sure only the damaged flesh showed. They treated Millie as if she were made of glass. The dozen times he'd been treated in an emergency room, he remembered he'd felt more like a piece of beef on a grill.

As the nurse helped her with her blouse, the doctor turned to Hank. "Has her family arrived yet?"

"Not yet." Hank didn't add that no one had been called.

"You still able to stay until they arrive?"

"Sure. We're friends."

The doctor shook his head, then turned to the librarian. "You all right with this, Miss Remington?"

"Yes. May I go home now?"

The doctor nodded, then glared at Hank. "You take good care of this lady, Norton."

"I plan to."

As Millie raised her unharmed arm, Hank slid beside her and lifted her. He didn't bother with the wheelchair; he just carried her to the car with a nurse rolling the empty chair behind them. Another aide rushed out carrying paperwork and all the things Millie had brought. Her purse. A sweater in case it was cold. A small umbrella in case it rained. A book to read if she had to wait. Oh, don't forget the snacks in case they got hungry waiting.

Hank swore families traveling west in wagon trains brought less.

He got her settled, then headed around to the driver's side of the Lincoln. He was able to make out what the nurse was murmuring to her colleague. "He's taking care of her, but what a strange pair. I heard he's been in jail, even after he grew up as a preacher's son."

The aide stared at him. "Maybe someone should call the sheriff. I saw that scar on his throat. Knife fight probably."

"The admissions clerk already did; Old LeRoy told her to mind her own business."

In the car, even with pain in her eyes, Millie had a tiny smile on her lips. Apparently, she had also caught the conversation. "Are you going to do bad things to me, Harrison? You being so scandalous and wild and all."

"Only if you ask me to," Hank answered.

For the first time he heard Millie laugh. "Maybe I'm the one who might be wild and scandalous."

"I already thought of that. The quiet ones always are." He stretched his hand out and she laced her fingers in his.

* * *

He got Millie settled in her bedroom, with Rambo standing guard. She was asleep before he left her room. Half an hour later he was ushering Ranger McBride into Millie's living room.

"What's up?" Hank asked.

"Maybe I just came by to check on you?" Colby McBride grinned as he took off his Stetson and took a chair too small for his frame.

"I doubt that. How can I help?" Hank took the chair across from the ranger. "If you've got your hat in your hand, you come for a favor and you already know the answer will be yes."

"You guessed right. I could use some advice about a local problem before I call the FBI in." Colby looked frustrated. "LeRoy and his deputies have found several pipe bombs in mailboxes on rural routes. The homemade jobs were placed there the last three nights, we think. They were not properly wrapped, so they didn't go off. The first ones were too poorly made to be more than just supplies, but whoever is doing it seems to be getting better. Farmers circling Clifton Bend are finding them and calling in. It's keeping LeRoy busy just going out to pick them up. He won't let his deputies but I'm not sure LeRoy has enough training or equipment."

Hank had seen this before in his work. "You want me to tell you if we're dealing with a kid just trying to stir up trouble or someone honing his craft."

"Right." Colby let out a breath. "This isn't my territory really, but this valley is my home. Yours too. I'm just helping the sheriff out and you'd be helping me out."

"I'll help but off the books. Set it up for just me and you to go in to look at the bombs. No one else."

"Will do. I'll pick you up at six."

"No. I'll meet you. Text me where. I don't want Millie to worry." Both men stood. "And, Colby, I should tell you that the odds are good that this guy probably will not stop until he blows something or someone up. The thrill of making any bomb isn't the thrill of frightening people. It's the excitement of knowing he's caused bedlam."

"That's what I'm afraid of. I told LeRoy to call this in, but he thinks he can handle it."

Hank pulled a card from his wallet. "Email me the files. Anything you've got. I'll break into Millie's laptop and study them before we meet."

"You know her password?"

"Yeah, I got it on the first try."

Colby nodded and walked away. Hank sat down at Millie's computer and typed in her password. RAMBO.

His first email was to headquarters asking for all he needed if he had to suit up. If they got the request today, he'd be able to pick it up in Clifton Bend in two days.

He continued working while Millie slept the rest of the morning away. Then he left Rambo in charge and drove over to the barbershop for a haircut. When he glanced in the shop mirror, he almost didn't recognize himself. Surprisingly, he looked like the man he was. A captain in the Houston police force. *The commander of an elite division who handled explosive problems*. Bombs, toxic waste, ammo, and the list went on.

Hank tipped the barber a twenty and smiled. The one thing he didn't look like was a preacher's son.

One stop at a shop that sold workout clothes and he was headed back to Millie.

She was still asleep in her white blouse with white flowers embroidered on the collar. Without thinking much about it, he stripped his dirty, wrinkled clothes off and pulled on a new pair of jeans and a black T-shirt. He'd also bought sweat pants to sleep in and a comfortable pair of shoes.

When he turned to check on her, she was watching him.

"What do you think of my new clothes? It was all I could find that wasn't in school colors."

"You look very presentable. Thanks for going with me this morning." She noticed a late lunch waiting on her nightstand and picked up a chip.

"So, you owe me a favor, right?"

"Right, but I don't want to play dominoes again. You can take them back to your dad's place."

"How about a date?" His tone was low, almost a challenge. "I have to go visit a friend, but about seven I'll be back and we can have dinner and watch a movie."

"I can't go out."

"A date right here. I'll come in here and pick you up. Carry you to the couch. We'll have popcorn for dinner. Turn the lights down and watch a movie."

"All right. You've got a date. And now I think I'll eat a little lunch and then take another nap."

After she was settled, Hank moved to the computer set up in the kitchen to study all the info Colby sent over. Rambo thought he should sit in Hank's lap and watch the screen.

After twenty minutes, the dog was still watching.

"When you figure this out, pup, let me know." Hank nodded at the dog and Rambo nodded back.

Just as he was about to shut down the computer, an email came through.

Captain, having trouble with your almost nephew, Simon. His mom left for a few weeks with work and Ray says the kid is not talking or listening until he sees you.

Hank emailed back: *Why? He doesn't even like me. Why would he want to see me?*

Headquarters: *That should give you a hint of what he thinks of us if he's demanding to see you. His after-school babysitter quit and his grandmother, when she finally picked up her home phone, told me she was out of town.*

Hank: *Tell him I'll talk to him tomorrow before school. Facetime. 7:15 A.M.*

Headquarters: *Will do.*

Hank shut the computer down before more bad news came in. When Simon's father had died two years ago, he'd been part of Hank's team. Three other men besides Hank, all single, swore they'd watch over Simon and his mother. At first all the kid did was read and play games. Then after a few months he stopped listening to anyone. It wasn't like he was acting out; it was more like Simon didn't notice anyone in the room. He wouldn't eat when they asked him to, or go to bed, or pay any attention. The kid gave his four guardian-angel-uncles hell when his mother had to go back to work.

Hank swore when he got back, he'd try harder to reach the boy.

Chapter 14

Ketch

Ketch Kincaid finished his job for the Randall brothers by four. For once it felt good to be pulling the construction trucks into the bay early. Thunder warned of rain in the lower valley. He could have pushed the crew a bit more but they were at a good place to stop. He needed to head for the night classes that would be taking Dr. Monroe's survey.

As he double-timed the stairs to his room to clean up, Ketch couldn't stop smiling. Surprisingly, he was interested in what the professor's testing would find. He felt like he was starting over in this game men and women play. Maybe he'd find out what attracted him to the kind of woman who didn't believe in forever.

For six years he'd thought he'd found his life partner in Crystal. They'd had everything in common. The army, both wanting a big family, an education. They seemed to speak the same language, or at least he thought they had. He and Crystal had talked about what to name their kids, where to live, what kind of house they wanted, where they'd go on vacations.

They matched. The sex was primal and great. Both were

in top shape and planned to stay that way. They even liked the same movies. They finished each other's sentences.

But she'd broken it off. About the time they were going to become two sides of one coin, Crystal ended it with a letter. Not even a kiss goodbye, just a letter.

How could he have read the signals so wrong?

As he showered and dressed in his standard jeans and pullover shirt, he realized that he knew nothing about the chemistry of mating. He would help with the survey even if they weren't paying him. At twenty-six he didn't have much time to be wrong again.

An hour later he was in the first community class for seniors in high school who were trying to get into college. Questionnaires were on the desk in front of him. Most of the crowd seemed interested.

Slowly he explained the rules and the importance of being honest. He even made a joke about not cheating off anyone.

One kid made a comment that if any girl wanted to mate with him, she only had to follow one rule. Show up at his dorm door next semester. He believed in love at first sight and he'd welcome all types at all hours of the day or night.

Another added, "Why do we have to learn to talk to the opposite sex or take them out? The point is to insure the continuation of the species."

Ketch smiled, waited for the room to settle, and repeated the rules. Then he looked at the instructor. The man nodded once, and the survey began.

An hour later he was in another class. This time senior citizens. Several students appeared to be sleeping. Those taking notes seemed to take the questions much more seriously than the high school students had.

By eight he was watching his third group, a couples' cooking class in the community center. To relieve his boredom,

Ketch looked over the room trying to figure out if anyone attracted him. All his adult life he'd always looked for the tall girls. He liked a woman to come at least to his shoulder. Five-nine or taller.

By now he should know what turned him on. Tall. Street smart.

The students seemed to fade like wallpaper as he thought of Tuesday. She wasn't tall enough or old enough, but there was something that pulled him to her. He could almost feel her head lying on his chest. The time in the attic had seemed removed from everything else in the world. Time passed as silently as the clouds above and for once Ketch had felt at peace.

Suddenly, there she was at the back of the room, standing in the doorway as if he'd conjured her up. Worn blue jeans and a shirt two sizes too big. She might be twenty-two but she still looked like a kid.

As he collected the completed surveys, he kept checking to make sure she was there. He hadn't seen her since Sunday, and in an odd way, he missed her even though a week ago he hadn't even known her.

After thanking the chef, Ketch headed for the door. "Any chance you'll feed me?" he said to Tuesday. "I'm starving."

She laughed. "I can't afford to feed you. How about you buy a pizza and give me a slice?"

Sexual attraction was standing right in front of him. He didn't need any survey.

When they arrived at the café, he ordered a meat lover's pizza with extra cheese while she found a table. As they waited, they talked of everything and nothing. Her garden. His work. How the students had reacted to the study on attraction.

She said she was attracted to men who made her feel safe.

Then she laughed and said she liked men who smelled of sawdust.

"The bad news is I'm not a good judge of men," she admitted. "Correction, I think they are men, but they're still little boys. Most of the boys I've gone out with get mad if they don't get what they want. A few took it out on me. Because I wasn't interested in them, something was obviously wrong with me."

Ketch studied her. "You know I'd never hurt you, don't you? We're friends."

She didn't answer back, but something in her eyes told him she didn't entirely believe him.

When the pizza arrived, she claimed no one in the history of the world had ever ordered so many meat toppings on a pizza.

He looked confused. "Next thing you're going to tell me is you don't like beer."

"I don't. Veggie pizza and tea, that's me."

He ordered her a small veggie and tea and let his pizza get cold while they talked. They were learning one another. She liked country music; he loved rap. He liked suspense movies with lots of action and she liked Disney. They had nothing in common. She hated guns and he owned half a dozen. She'd never been in a church and he'd changed religions every time he changed foster homes.

As he took his last bite, Ketch asked, "Anything else you can think of that we'll probably argue over one day?"

"Well, I hate to mention it, but you're too tall for me. I like men that I don't have to jump to kiss."

Ketch laughed. "I get your point. When I walk beside you, I'm talking to the top of your head."

Smiling, she fired back. "And I'm talking to the underside of your chin."

"We were meant to be friends, Tuesday, nothing more.

But I promise, if you ever want to give me that kiss, I'll be happy to lift you up. After all, we're friends."

"That's not a bad thing to be. I've had few friends in my life." She offered him her last slice of the veggie pizza. "When I was in grade school, kids were afraid to come to Grannie's old house. I used to think I lived on another planet."

"Me too. I moved around so often I never learned my zip code. When I joined the army, I felt like I had a home for the first time, even if it was just a locker and a bunk."

Unfortunately, Wynn Wills and his brother walked in with a couple of losers. All looked drunk, and the brother was so stoned his eyes didn't seem to be working together. Ketch had no idea if Wills was still hungover from last weekend or getting a head start on next weekend. The guy needed a keeper, and his brother wasn't smart enough to be a pet.

He hoped WW and the drunks wouldn't notice them, but no such luck.

"Helloooo," Wynn shouted. "Evening, Ketch." One drunk looked toward Tuesday as if trying to draw her into focus.

"Ketch, old man, what are you doing eating with the barmaid?" Wynn slid into the extra chair as if he'd been invited. "She's Saturday night fun, not midweek pizza."

"Tuesday is my friend. We're having a pizza after class." Ketch hoped Wynn was sober enough to see a warning in his eyes, but Ketch's hand molded into a fist just in case.

The drunk disappointed him. Wynn leaned over the table and winked at Ketch. "I get it, man. Bed buddies. Hope she doesn't play dead . . ."

Wynn didn't have time to say more. Ketch's big hand slammed into the back of Wynn's head and the drunk rocked in his chair, spilling beer.

WW slowly raised his head, eyes wide. "What happened?"

Ketch slapped Wynn on the back a little too hard. "You're welcome to the last of the pizza, WW, but we are just leaving. See you in class."

Ketch took Tuesday's hand and walked out while Wynn just sat there, trying to figure out how he spilled his beer.

As soon as they hit fresh air, Tuesday burst out laughing. "I can't believe you did that."

"I didn't want to hurt him, just shut him up." He laughed. "Beating up WW would be like slapping a frog. Not much fun."

She waited for Ketch to lift her up into the truck. "I don't care about what people say about me. Most of it isn't true."

He put his hands beneath her arms and lifted her up so they were face-to-face. "I do. I care, and while you're at eye level, kid, there is something I've been wanting to do for a while."

His lips touched hers lightly, testing to see if his advance would be welcome. When she opened her mouth slightly, he wrapped his arms around her and prayed he didn't squeeze too hard.

When she finally pulled away, he let go. "I guess that kiss took us beyond the friend category. I can take it back if you want me to."

"It wasn't a bad kiss," she said. "I think I'll keep it. Now, put me in the truck and drive me home. I'm not a toy you get to keep just because you picked me up."

Chapter 15

Harrison

Tuesday

Hank waited until almost dark before he decided it was time. He woke Millie with a gentle brush of her chestnut hair and a whisper. "Wake up. You've got a date tonight."

She opened her blue eyes that spoke of so much more than she'd ever express in words. He'd seen the pain she'd never complain of. The relief when he'd said he would take her home. He hadn't missed the stubborn look that told him there was no use arguing.

But in the twilight tonight he saw fear as he swooped down to pick her up. For a blink Hank could have sworn he saw the panic of a child. As if the monster she feared had appeared and she had no way to run.

"Millie, it's all right. You're safe. I'm here with you." He set her back on the bed. "We don't have to do this. If you'd like to go back to sleep, that's fine. I just thought it would be fun."

"No, let's watch a movie. You just startled me, that's all." The truth lay unsaid between them.

He lifted her again and set her on the little couch, then covered her legs with a throw. "I'll get the popcorn."

Before he left, he flipped on the news with the volume down low. The windows were open and a cool breeze drifted on the night. All was calm in her little house now. All but her. The librarian held herself stiff.

As the popcorn cooked in the microwave, he thought of how she'd reacted. He'd seen mistreated horses react the same way. And whatever had happened to her, he'd bet it happened at night. Maybe she'd been startled awake. Someone had hurt her, not just frightened her.

The memory of the wreck came to mind. She hadn't cried out when hurt. Not when she was hit. Not when she was lying in the road, staring at him. Not when the nurses and doctors poked on her. Through it all she hadn't made a sound.

The pieces began to slide together in his mind. Someone had hurt her, probably repeatedly, and she hadn't been allowed to react.

He was sure it had been a man, which would explain her not dating, too.

Hank hoped he was wrong, but sometimes it seemed all the people in the world were broken somehow. Everyone held a story they would never voice.

When he returned with the popcorn, he sat down next to her and handed her the control. "I set you up on cable. I'll show you how it works after the movie?"

"All right." She was almost touching him. "What are we watching?"

"Harry Potter. I've never seen it, have you?"

"No, but I read the books."

He pulled the bowl of popcorn atop his leg and carefully

placed one arm behind her. Rambo jumped up on the other side and put his chin on her broken leg.

If Hank had to go all the way back to a first date experience, he would.

As they watched the movie, their bodies seemed to settle in closer to one another. He held her hand and kissed her fingers once, which made her smile.

After the movie was over, he told her that in a little while, he needed to go out for an hour, but that he'd be back after that, and sleeping on the couch if she needed him.

As he left the room, he was thinking: *If she were any other woman, I'd . . .*

He considered slamming his head against the wall. She wasn't any other woman. He was helping her, nothing more.

Chapter 16

Benjamin

Wednesday

Pushing himself into peril, Ben tapped on Professor Clark's office door. It was after five, but he could hear her bouncing around talking to herself.

"How may I help you, Ben?" she asked in a none-too-friendly tone as she opened their connecting door. She had her cell in one hand and a pencil in the other. A warrior working.

Ben almost backed away. But he knew if he chickened out this time he'd never work up the courage again. "My father called and said he was heating up the grill. You want to drive out to the farm for ribs?"

She looked over at the paperwork on her desk.

Ben braced himself for rejection. He couldn't remember the last time he'd asked anyone to dinner. And this wasn't anything, really. He just wanted to get to know her, see how she'd changed. Maybe even talk about that weekend twenty years ago. Problem was, how could he talk to her about their shared weekend when she obviously didn't remember him?

"I could show you the start of my vineyards. All three rows." He didn't want to build the outing up too much.

She finally looked at him. "I'd love to. Can I bring dessert?"

"No. Dad invited a few of the neighbors. Sarah, from the farm to the north, will bring cobbler, and if Donna and Rex come, we'll have homemade ice cream to go with it."

Jenny leaned her head sideways. "People make ice cream?"

Ben nodded slowly. "City girl," he whispered, remembering he'd called her that twenty years ago when she didn't know how to bait a hook and she'd called him "farmer."

She was too busy organizing her desk to have heard him. When she saw that he was still standing in her doorway, she said, "I'll be ready in a minute, Dr. Monroe. Just let me get my purse." She bumped the door between their offices closed with her hip.

Ten minutes later, Jenny was climbing into his Jeep, looking like she thought it might be a killer ride at the county fair.

"Do you drive in from the farm every day?"

Ben took a breath. An easy question. "No, I live in an apartment over the drugstore. It's close, and most days I ride my bike to work. I help my father farm on weekends and do research during the winter in a greenhouse we built out of a little barn. Chemicals used on crops have always fascinated me."

"Oh." She seemed to be waiting for him to say something interesting.

He'd already looked her up in the faculty directory so there was no need to ask where she lived, but he decided it would be polite to talk.

She answered simply, "I live near the river in one of the little cabins that used to be fishing shacks before the town grew out that way years ago. It's quiet but way too few streetlights. I'm a city girl. I like to see in the night."

"Oh," he echoed her.

They drove out of town toward the farm-to-market road. She wiggled in her seat, played with one curl of her hair, and watched the houses become fewer and farther between. "This isn't a date, is it?" she asked.

"Do you want it to be?"

"No. Definitely not. I haven't had a date in years. When we finish dinner, you will bring me back to my car? Right?"

"Of course. I'll have to pass by the campus to get home, so it's right on my way."

He slowed, and they drove along a field that looked like a dying vineyard. She asked questions and he tried to answer them. It didn't take long for Benjamin to realize she knew a great deal more about growing grapes than he did. Finally, they had something in common to talk about.

Benjamin was surprised when she wanted to get out and walk the rows. He had his passions, just like everyone else, but his were tied to the earth, and few of his colleagues wanted to hear details. Town folks didn't understand the importance of weather or rain, and most farmers weren't interested in growing grapes.

As they walked into the farmhouse where he'd grown up, they were both talking as if trying to get a few points about grapes in before they had to postpone the conversation.

At the door, he paused, smiling down at her. She stopped in midsentence and grinned. "I like it when you smile, Doctor."

There was no time for him to respond, but he did let his hand brush her back as he ushered her into the house.

Ben introduced Jenny to his father and two couples almost as old. The neighbors. To his surprise, the biology teacher joined the old folks' gang. By the time they sat down to dinner, he was the outsider.

She might not know much about farming, but she asked questions and listened to the answers. As the sun set, everyone gathered around an old picnic table beside the pecan trees. As Benjamin poured the wine he'd brought for his addition to dinner, everyone else watched the sun set.

Jenny's way of pulling folks out of their shells fascinated him. He learned things he'd never known about people who'd lived next to him for years.

When Ben helped carry the dishes inside, his dad leaned close to him and whispered, "Any chance you like that girl, son?"

"I do, but that's all, Dad. Just like."

"Well, work on it. I'm not always going to be around to watch over you. She's a keeper."

Ben wondered if his dad was seeing the same woman he saw. She was chubby, laughed too loud, her hair probably glowed in the dark, and apparently she never met a stranger.

A few minutes later, when he handed her a plate with a helping of cobbler topped with ice cream, she said, "Thank you, dear. I just couldn't make up my mind. I have to have both."

Both Donna and Sarah puffed up a bit with pride. Donna said she'd give Jenny her secret recipe for homemade ice cream and Sarah let her know that the cobbler recipe was in the 4-H cookbook.

His dad must have heard Jenny call his son "dear," because the old guy wiggled his eyebrows at Ben. An hour later as he said goodbye to them, Dad leaned over and whispered something to Jenny.

She nodded, then kissed the old guy's wrinkled cheek.

Ben considered the possibility that his father had taken

up hard drinking. He'd never seen Dad do much more than scowl at a woman.

As they walked to his Jeep, she slipped her hand around his arm. "It's so dark out here, I need to hold on to you, Ben. City girls sometimes have problems walking on dirt." She sighed as she looked up at the stars. "I can see why you'd love the farm."

In the car, Jenny told him that his father had showed her the wall of pictures of Ben growing up while Ben was clearing the table. "You were a cute kid, Benjamin. Every birthday, every Christmas, every graduation from grade school to college. It was like watching you grow up."

"Dad marked time with me at every age like he was keeping a log . . . So what did my dad ask you as we left?"

"He asked if I was in my gestation years."

Ben almost missed the curve. He gripped the wheel, slowed, then pulled off into a grove of low-hanging cotton-wood trees.

Turning toward her, he forced words. "I . . . I'm so sorry. I hope you're not sorry you came. My dad talks to so few people; he's forgotten how to have a conversation."

"Nonsense. He's a sweetheart. I've already been invited to Rex and Donna's place next week. She said they're planning a clambake. She grew up in Galveston, you know."

"No, I didn't know. I also didn't know that this dinner seems to be a weekly thing."

She patted his leg. "You're not in the gang, Ben. We're playing games next week. Sarah said I can bring you as my date if I want to."

After a long silence, she cupped the side of his face and kissed his lips. "Stop worrying. You're too young to be senile."

He didn't move. "Why did you do that?"

Her face was only a few inches from his, so she whispered,

"Since you pulled off to park, I thought I'd give it a try. You want to touch my breasts?"

"No." He straightened. "And we are not parking. I just pulled over to talk."

She laughed. "So you don't want to touch my breasts?"

"Where is this coming from, Professor Clark? Have I ever made an improper advance toward you or treated you as anything but a colleague?" He pushed aside the memory of bumping against her breast when he was coughing and the touch of her back when he directed her into his dad's house.

"No, sir. You've been a perfect gentleman," she snapped. "Let's blame it on your father giving me ideas. Since we are parked out on a country road with no one around, I figured a kiss and a touch might get the ball rolling. To tell the truth, it's been a while, so if you're not interested, I'd understand. You do seem about as cuddly as a scrub brush right now."

He sat perfectly still as he put the pieces together. "But you don't even know me. Once you get to know me, you might not like me, and then we'd be in a mess."

"Ben, we're both in our forties. We don't have that much time."

He sat frozen. The evening had turned into something that he'd never meant it to be.

After a while she patted his knee again. "It's all right. Just a misunderstanding. We'll laugh about it tomorrow, then forget it ever happened."

"I lied. I do want to touch your breasts . . . but it seems such an adolescent thing to do. I'm forty-two, far too old to be parking on a country road."

"Drive me home, Dr. Monroe, and we'll discuss this problem."

He gave her a hesitant kiss, and then another, as if relearning an old skill.

As the kiss warmed, he moved his hand along her back, then to her waist, then up until he finally cupped her breast.

She placed her hand over his heart as if she knew what he wanted. What he needed. "About time you found me, Farmer," she whispered.

Chapter 17

Benjamin

Thursday

Dr. Benjamin Monroe always woke before dawn. He'd decided years ago it was in his blood. No matter how much education he had, he was still a farmer.

For a moment he thought he was still dreaming. The shadowy room was unfamiliar. The ceiling seemed too small for him to stand. Books and boxes and quilts were everywhere. Half a dozen fishing rods stood in one corner. His clothes were scattered on the floor.

He was waking up while some crazy dream was still rolling through his head. In the dream the window had been left open, but he didn't feel cold. He wasn't wearing his pajamas. He was naked!

Soft hair brushed against his chin and the whole night slammed back into his confused brain.

He'd followed Jenny into a dark room. No, she'd held his hand and pulled him into the room. They hadn't said a word, but he remembered leaning down and kissing her like he'd never kissed anyone. It felt right. Familiar. A hunger grew to be closer to her.

They'd made love. If possible, it was sweeter than it had been twenty years ago. He had taken his time, wanting to remember every touch, every smell, every heartbeat. Ben wasn't adventurous or even spontaneous, but for once he'd decided to try. Even when the loving was finished, he couldn't let go of her. She'd made him feel fully alive.

She'd fallen asleep in his arms with his hand moving over her soft flesh, exploring every inch. Now and then she'd make a little sound of pleasure and Ben would smile and repeat his last touch.

He rubbed his cheek against the top of her head now. He wasn't sure how it all happened. From the time she'd kissed him in his Jeep, his brain seemed to have stopped working.

The first light of dawn colored the night with morning. He didn't move. He just watched the window and let this newborn memory float in his mind. Every detail. Every feeling. Every movement. He wanted to catalog each touch so he'd never forget. He didn't need to study chemistry; he was drawn to her like a moth to light.

For once in his life he hadn't been shy or hesitant. He'd been a lover. No. He'd been *her* lover.

Logic told him that he shouldn't have followed her inside her cabin. This should never have happened. Not without love or words of commitment. But logic was no longer ruling his actions, evidently. And his brain, which he'd always considered to be above average, had turned to mush.

Right now, in the stillness between night and day, he could feel her hand on his heart and her breast against his side. Heaven seemed nestled in the stillness.

He was losing his mind and he didn't care.

Benjamin closed his eyes, trying to think as she wiggled beside him, touching him from shoulder to knee. Then she rose slightly and kissed him. Not a good-morning kiss but a lingering, passionate kiss. Her warm breast brushed over his bare chest as she continued nibbling at him as if just discovering something she craved.

He was lost again. His last sane thought was that he was hers. Whatever she silently asked him for, he would give her. The feel of her was addictive.

She knew it, too, because she laughed just before she ran her fingers into his hair and pulled him to her.

An hour later when he woke again, she was gone, and for a moment the loss of her felt like a blow.

Then he saw the light on in the bathroom. Dawn was now shining brightly. He relaxed back amid a mountain of pillows. Reality and memories blended in his thoughts.

She walked out of the bathroom wrapped in a towel and smiled down at him. "I'm not touching you, Benjamin, or we'll never get out of here, and we both have work to do." As she issued her order, he noticed she let the towel slip to expose one of her breasts.

Scrubbing his face, he asked, "Mind if I use your shower?"

"No, I don't mind, as long as I can watch."

"You may not watch." He grabbed a pillow and covered himself as he rushed around her. "Don't even think about it."

Jenny laughed. "Of course, Benjamin."

Now she calls me Benjamin, he thought. Who would have guessed that all he had to do was sleep with her for Jenny to get his name right.

Ten minutes later when he'd showered and shaved with a funny razor he'd found in the soap dish, he stood stone still as he faced himself in the mirror over a tiny sink.

What would he say to her? Should he tell her it was just as good mating with her last night as it had been twenty years ago? Maybe he should establish a few ground rules for the next time. If there was a next time. What if there was? What if there wasn't?

He stared at the man in the mirror and decided they were both insane.

Benjamin took his time combing his hair, and brushed his teeth with a travel toothbrush that had been left on the counter.

When he came out of the bathroom, his clothes were on the bed. The trousers were black and a bit wrinkled, but it looked like she'd ironed the shirt.

As he dressed, Ben looked around the room. Every corner was packed with junk, but there seemed an order about the clutter. One small bookshelf held half a dozen bamboo rain sticks along with a djembe drum and castanets. A table in another corner displayed jars of all sizes that held buttons. Under the window were a dozen boxes stacked like a pyramid.

When he wandered into the tiny kitchen, one place setting of ten different patterns of china hung on the wall.

Jenny didn't look up from her paper as she handed him a glass of orange juice.

He saw two paper plates with two pieces of toast on each. Jelly and butter were between them. They stood on either side of a three-foot counter and ate.

"Thank you," he finally managed. "You didn't have to feed me."

For the first time she met his gaze. "I don't do anything but what I want to do. I wanted to feed you and I wanted to sleep with you, Ben."

Ben didn't lower his eyes. "I wanted the same." The night was over. Now might be a good time to get everything straight between them. "This . . . what we did . . . doesn't go with us to the college, agreed?"

She picked up her briefcase. "Agreed. You can continue to speak to me as little as possible, if you like."

He opened the door and held it for her. "Purely professional."

"Purely professional."

As she passed him, she patted him on his bottom.

Chapter 18

Ketch

Friday

The phone rattled a shill cry in the stormy night. For a moment Ketch was back in the army, reaching for his weapon.

It took him a second before he realized where he was. No army. No fear. No shells exploding. Only faraway thunder and lightning.

He was in his apartment over the construction offices. Safe. Home. Three years out of the army.

He picked up the phone. "Kincaid here."

The sky was dark with clouds. He hadn't overslept. He wasn't late for work or school. The only other person who might call him besides his boss or Dr. Monroe was Tuesday and his boss or the professor wouldn't call this early. "What do you need, kid?" he said, a smile already spreading across his face.

"Kid! You've never called me that." The familiar voice came strong and fast, not soft like Tuesday's low tone.

"Crystal?" He sat up and tried to scrub sleep from his head.

"Did you forget me already, Ketch? We only broke up a few weeks ago."

"I got the letter one week ago. The wound is still raw." He didn't feel like arguing. She'd probably written the letter two weeks ago. What did it matter?

"About that." She giggled as she always did when she was nervous. "I've changed my mind. I went out with a few guys here at the fort since we broke up and I realized what I had with you. The guys here are jerks. The letter was a mistake. Can we just forget that I wrote it? At the time, I thought I'd be on leave with someone else, but now that's over. I'm coming to see you as soon as I can book a flight."

When he didn't say a word, she added, "Or, if you can get away from that little school, I'll meet you anywhere on the West Coast. You are on spring break this week, aren't you?"

When he still didn't answer, her voice hardened. "Oh c'mon, Ketch. We've been together for years. You know how I get restless now and then. What's one hiccup? You know me. You probably knew I'd change my mind. Right?"

Ketch disconnected the call. He did know her. Crystal wasn't going to give him a chance to say a word until she'd presented her case. If she'd been in front of him, she would already be teasing him with her body, making him forget about what they were arguing about.

But she didn't know him. He'd stopped listening.

He sat waiting. She called back four times. He sat watching the day begin, loving the dawn spreading over a rain-soaked valley. The newborn sunlight sparkled like diamonds over spring's bright colors.

Finally, the phone was silent. He dressed, erased four messages, and dialed Tuesday.

When she picked up, he said, "You awake, kid?"

"No . . ."

"You hungry? I know a café in Honey Creek that makes the best buttermilk pancakes in the world."

"I'll be ready by the time you get here," she said with a squeal.

Ketch laughed. He could almost see Tuesday running around trying to find her clothes, her shoes, her funny little band that held her hair up. As he pulled on jeans and a pullover, he noticed Crystal's letter on the dresser. With one toss it landed in the trash.

They talked as he drove toward Honey Creek, making plans for the day. She said she'd go with him to the library to meet with the college librarian. Dr. Monroe wanted Ketch to dig up as much research as possible on the chemistry of mating, and Miss Remington wanted to help, even though she had a broken leg.

He winked at Tuesday. "For research purposes, what attracts you to me, kid?" Right now, with her bare feet on the dash, she looked about sixteen.

"Who says I'm attracted to you, Ketch? You were just a stray dog too drunk to walk. What else could I do with you except bring you home?"

"I think it was me who took you home."

"Just one stranger helping another." She winked at him. "You slept in my bed the night we met, even if all we did was sleep. You cooked for me. I'm thinking you wouldn't have fed me if you wanted me to leave. Tell me there must have been something that drew you to me."

"Your size frightens me, but you're kind, Ketch. And funny."

"You left out handsome."

She knelt beside him in his truck and started fixing his hair and digging the collar of his shirt from beneath his pullover. "Let me work on you a minute before I make up my mind."

He circled her waist and pulled her between him and the steering wheel.

In a blink, the playful mood was gone and he saw anger in her green eyes.

She scrambled away and hugged the passenger door, and he tried to figure out how to say he was sorry.

Ketch pulled off at an abandoned roadside park. He cut the engine and swiveled to face her. A dozen questions were on his mind, but he remembered that first morning when she'd made the rule of no questions.

"If you want to talk about something, kid, I'm here."

"No. It's just dangerous driving like that. I'm fine." She opened the door and stepped out of his truck.

Ketch did the same, but he didn't move toward her. He put his hands in his pockets and rounded his shoulders as if to make himself smaller and not as threatening.

She picked a few bluebonnets growing around the broken bones of a picnic table. In a small voice she said, "I'm little compared to you, but I'm not a child."

He kept his voice just as low. "I'm big, but that doesn't make me a bully. You got to know, I would never hurt you."

He watched her, thinking how beautiful she was. She couldn't have had it easy. Growing up with a single mother moving her around, and then her only parent sending Tuesday to live with an old woman. She'd told him she'd been just a kid when Eva had died and she'd had to take care of everything. No one cared, or maybe knew, she was out on Primrose Hill alone. She'd had to ride her bike to school. It crossed his mind that she was still riding a bike at twenty-two.

"You know how to drive?" He finally broke the silence.

"Nope. Don't need to. I don't have a car."

He smiled. "I could teach you."

"When?"

"How about right now?" He relaxed as he saw her smile.

Five minutes later they were on a back road. He was laughing and Tuesday was screaming about loving driving and yelling for help at the same time. He claimed she drove like a snake wiggles along, and hit every hole in the dirt road. The third time his head hit the roof of the truck, Ketch figured he'd better finish the lesson before he got brain damage.

When they finally made it to the Honey Creek Café, they were starving. They each ordered the special. Ketch added a side of sweet potato fries and pie.

She drove the dirt roads back with less screaming and a lot more laughing.

When she pulled up to her house, she cut the engine and danced out, whirling. "I love driving. Thanks."

"No problem. I'll help you find a car, or a little pickup if you like. I could probably find something for a thousand that would run."

"I could dip into Grannie Eva's nest money. She moved stocks and cash over in my name so my mother wouldn't accidentally take everything. I guess it would help to have something other than just a bike."

Ketch held out his hand. "Deal." He'd find her something even if he had to come up with half the money.

She hesitated, then slowly walked up to him. She didn't take the handshake he offered. "Lift me up, Ketch. I want to hug you."

He carefully placed his hands on her waist and lifted her to his eye level.

Tuesday put her arms around his neck and hugged him, just like she said she would.

Ketch fought the urge to pull her closer just as he fought the urge to love her.

Friends. That's what they needed to be. It hit him that he'd rather be a friend to Tuesday than a lover to Crystal. Tuesday was far easier on his heart.

Chapter 19

Benjamin

Benjamin walked through his last day of spring break. Empty hallways. Spotless lecture rooms. An organized lab.

In a little over a week the governor of Texas would be dropping by to deliver a grant to Clinton's library. The award and grant were given to small colleges with strong education programs.

If he and Jenny could win the Westwin Research Award, that would be another feather in the college's cap.

He grinned, thinking of Jenny. The break hadn't been as silent as he'd thought it might be this year. He closed his hand, wishing he could keep the feel of Jenny's skin on the tips of his fingers. He loved touching her. They'd been professional yesterday, both busy, but when he went home to his place he'd slept around the clock without dreaming. After all, he was now living his dream.

Benjamin sat down in his office chair and prepared his lectures for Monday. When he'd entered his forties, he'd decided keeping an exact routine would eliminate a lot of wasted energy. He got up at the same time, ran his classes and labs on time, and ate his meals by his watch. Now that Jenny was in his life, he'd make adjustments.

He smiled to himself. She *was* in his life once more.

When Ketch caught him at his desk eating his lunch a few minutes later, Benjamin simply paused to check a few points on the project so Ketch would be ready to run the survey results.

"Dr. Monroe, you're not going to believe what some people are attracted to. I'm getting an education just reading the answers people wrote down."

Benjamin nodded as he checked the findings.

Ketch continued, "You'd think it would be beauty or brains, but it's not. They talk about how their partner smells, or how she feels naked beside him, or how he whispers against her throat. One guy even said he gets turned on every time his mate hiccups."

Ketch shook his head. "Name a body part and someone is attracted to it. Except elbows. Seems no one is attracted to them."

When Ben finished a final check of the survey and looked at Ketch, the big ex-army ranger leaned back in his chair.

Ben had known Ketch for a few years, and for once the guy looked happy, really happy.

"Anything else you need?" Ben asked.

"One question that has nothing to do with the survey." Ketch hesitated. "I figured you could answer since you grew up around here, Professor. I was at an old house this week, working on a broken-down porch. It looked like it was built seventy or eighty years ago, but it's different than any building around here. There's something old-world about it. Like it was crafted by a master."

"The house on Primrose Hill," Ben said simply.

Ketch looked surprised. "You know about it?"

"Sure. My dad's farm borders one side of the place. At one time I heard the story surrounding it, but I've forgotten the details. In high school, kids used to whisper that Primrose Hill is haunted."

Ketch leaned forward. "Mind telling me what you remember?"

Ben hesitated, then began. "My dad said it was built by a foreigner, Frank Raine's brother, if I remember right. Raine and his wife lived out there, but the brother came around now and then to work on the house. Tony was his name, and he built it between other jobs. Frank, the older brother, had an injury from the war and could barely stand without a cane. My dad helped the younger brother haul lumber a few times back in the sixties.

"Dad said Frank was maybe twenty years older than his little wife. His brother was closer to her age. Dad said she was usually the one who helped Tony and him unload."

"What were they like?" Ketch seemed fascinated with the old story.

"They never had much to do with the folks around here. Artist types, you know. When Frank died, some said he hung around to haunt the place, but I think it was just his younger brother dropping by now and then to check on his sister-in-law."

Ketch raised an eyebrow. "So you don't believe in ghosts, Professor?"

"I think people make up things, especially if the story around the place is sad. Eva had her only child several months after her husband died. Some said the birthing almost killed her."

"Tell me more." Ketch's request seemed to whisper off the walls.

Ben shrugged with little interest, but he continued. "There's no record of when artists started settling here, but by the roaring twenties this little settlement was full of them. Some say the first art-loving couples found this place after the First World War, then more foreigners, mostly friends of the artists already here, settled in after the Second World War.

"They must have had it bad during the war. I heard someone say Frank Raine had been an established sculptor in England and lost everything, but they had enough money to buy Primrose Hill and make a new life. After a while, I heard his art was selling in New York.

"Eva buried her husband and raised her only child, Gabriella. Some say the kid was wild and crazy. Ran off with some guy while she was still in high school. Years later, Gabriella came home to deliver a baby and then disappeared again, leaving the baby with Eva. Gabriella's daughter, Anna, lived with Eva until she was grown. Folks said Anna was wilder than her mother. And, like her mother, Anna dumped her kid, Tuesday, on Eva, who was in her eighties by then."

Ben stopped.

Ketch leaned forward. "Tell me the rest."

Though Ben didn't like talking about people, he guessed this was more of the town's history than gossip. "Eva died when Tuesday was about fourteen. Four generations of women have lived at Primrose Hill. Tuesday Raine is the last."

"What about Frank's brother, Tony? Did he ever live there?"

"I heard he'd come in the winters to stay a while. The house grew every time he dropped by."

Ketch stood and paced. "If Tuesday was only fourteen when the old lady died, didn't the county take over her care?"

Ben shook his head. "I don't think that many people knew about it at first. Tuesday stayed in school and claimed an aunt was living with her. Only she didn't have an aunt. By the time folks figured out no one was there to watch over the girl, she was seventeen. So, I guess they just let her stay."

Ketch's voice rose in anger. "Are you telling me Tuesday lived out there alone?"

"I guess everyone thought someone else was taking care of her. I've heard a few rumors about her, but for a kid who raised herself, I'm thinking she did all right."

Ketch picked up his books. "Thanks for telling me the history, Dr. Monroe. I thought I had it hard in the foster system, but not like her."

Before Ketch reached the door, Ben said, "You've been out there. You know how unique it is."

"Yeah. When I fixed her porch I kind of felt like I was adding Snoopy on the cliffs of Mount Rushmore. You're right, the house is a work of art."

Ben smiled. "As far as I know, you and Sheriff LeRoy are the only two who have ever made it down that road. Too many ghosts and potholes for most people. Most folks in town have probably forgotten it's there. Legends and midnight stories are only mentioned around firepits when camping out."

Ketch looked back. "I don't believe in ghosts, Professor, but I can testify to the holes in the road. I plan to fill them one at a time."

Ketch waved. "See you Monday."

Ben sat back in his chair and returned to thinking of his night with Jenny. He'd needed the sleep last night, but he would have given it up to be with her.

Her office had been silent all day, but he tapped on their connecting door anyway, just in case she'd dropped by.

When he packed up to leave, he found a note taped to his office door. The envelope was addressed to Dr. Benjamin Monroe. In a hurried hand Jenny had written, *Have to think. Don't call. See you Monday. VC.*

She hadn't even taken the time to write her name. His Jenny had left again. Only this time she'd left a note and said Monday. This time she'd be back. Ben walked down the two flights of stairs thinking that the note was a good sign. The "have to think" might be a bad sign, however. And the signing of her initials might just be the professional part. After all, he'd set that rule.

Ben nodded once to his reflection in the windows. He'd go to the farm, help his dad this weekend, and give Jenny her time. That would make sense.

His mind was made up, but his hand opened and closed slowly as he walked to his Jeep. He couldn't feel her skin. The memory of touch had left his fingers.

He drove by the cabin. Her car wasn't there. The place was dark. He had no idea where she was.

Just like the last time.

Then he patted the note in his pocket. Monday, she'd said. He'd wait.

Saturday

Chapter 20

Ketch

Ketch walked across the empty campus, feeling a stillness drifting over the old buildings and wide sidewalks. The grounds reminded him of an old warrior resting before the next fight. Now and then he'd stand and fight to change lives with the battle cry, "Grow. Learn. Evolve."

Most schools would be gearing up for the weekend, but as far as Ketch could tell, there weren't a dozen people back from spring break yet. Clifton College didn't have much of a party life, or a single frat house, so no students were in any hurry to come back early after break.

That was one of the things that attracted Ketch. After four years in the army, he'd been looking for someplace quiet.

Thoughts of Tuesday Raine drifted in his mind as he headed toward the library. She'd wanted to help him on the research, but she'd been called in to help her boss do inventory. Ketch felt like he'd found a treasure in her. A unique soul, but he'd have to handle their friendship with caution.

The library closed at five on Saturdays and he needed to ask the librarian a few research questions. Miss Remington had access to studies on attraction from universities all over the world.

When he first saw the librarian, Ketch thought she looked fine. But as he stepped farther into her office, he saw bruises on the side of her face, and instead of her office chair, she sat in a wheelchair.

But, to his surprise, she smiled at him.

A man in his forties sat a few feet away from her, reading a book he didn't look that interested in. He was friendly enough, but it was obvious he was there to watch over Miss Remington. Within ten minutes, Ketch explained the study the professors were doing, and she promised to get him material that might be helpful as soon as possible.

As she worked on her computer, Ketch became the runner who collected the few resource books and articles that were in the Clifton Library.

An hour passed before the man stood and whispered something in the librarian's ear.

She nodded to him. When she turned to Ketch, he could see the exhaustion in her eyes. The man must have gently reminded her that it was time to leave.

"Thank you," Ketch said before she needed to tell him she had to go. He guessed the librarian must be a workaholic who lived in her office. She wasn't young or old, early forties, he guessed. Amelia Remington was probably called *ma'am* before she'd been out of college. He'd always seen her hair curled in a knot, but now only a ribbon at the base of her neck bound it. Her wavy brown hair hung halfway down her back.

She handed him a list of studies on his topic that she'd ordered. "The articles will be scanned and emailed by Monday, and I'll ask that the books on interlibrary loan are sent as fast as possible. There may be a small charge."

"Put it on Dr. Monroe's bill," Ketch said.

The man she'd called Hank stood and very carefully picked her up before he faced Ketch. "Would you mind taking the chair outside and down the steps? It'll be faster."

"Sure." Ketch dropped his books in the wheelchair and rolled it out behind the couple. The guy looked a few years older than the librarian, but it's hard to tell with people over forty. He was fit, and even holding the lady, he walked like a man in balance. Like at one time he'd been a fighter or athlete.

Ketch thought about being a bit older than Tuesday too. He wondered how she really saw him, not as just four years older, but really an "old man." He'd seen the world and been in combat by the time he was twenty. He'd have his degree before he turned twenty-seven, so he didn't figure he was much behind those who skipped the army.

Funny thing about going into the service: You think you're going to be behind when you get back home, but when you come back, you notice no one is moving that fast.

So, if he measured age in experience, he probably was an old man to a twenty-two-year-old who'd never gone anywhere. Smiling, he thought of how much fun it would be to show her the world.

Hank lowered Miss Remington into a boat of a Lincoln. Then he shook Ketch's hand. "Good luck with the study. Sounds interesting."

"Thanks," Ketch managed to say as they put the wheelchair in the back. "Nice car," he lied.

Hank laughed. "Yeah. You want to buy it?"

"No, thanks. I couldn't give up my truck."

"I know how you feel. I've never been able to give up my Harley. Nice meeting you, Ketch Kincaid."

He had the feeling the stranger had just filed information about him in his brain.

Something made him say, "If you or the librarian ever need me, just call." He looked at her curled up in the seat, her head resting against the window. "She is going to be all right?"

"Yes." Hank turned back to the car and smiled. "I'll get her home. She's kitten strong right now, but she'll heal."

As Ketch drove home, he wondered how Tuesday had survived adolescence alone.

She'd survived alone, just like he had.

In Tuesday's case, the old house protected her. She had fruit trees and a garden.

He realized he was probably attracted to her because she needed him. It had been the same way with Crystal that first year they'd met. She'd told him a dozen times that she would have washed out if he hadn't always been by her side. He'd coached her, pushed her, and sometimes carried her through that first year in the army. And then he'd fallen so hard in love with her that he didn't believe she didn't feel the same way.

One line in her letter echoed in his mind. *I'll always love you, but it's time I choose my own path.*

Now he'd help Tuesday as a friend. Only this time he wouldn't ask for anything, even friendship. Then he'd move on down his own road, alone. He wasn't sure he could take another heartbreak.

Without much thought he climbed into his truck, then drove home to get his tools. With a free afternoon, Ketch planned to head out to Tuesday's place. He'd help her get the house in shape. If flirting came as a side dish, he'd keep it light.

When he returned to her front door, she came out on the newly repaired porch.

"Why are you here?"

"I'm your handyman for the day. What do you need fixing?"

Tuesday stared at him for a few minutes, then answered, "Pick a room."

Two hours later he'd put doors back on their hinges, hung pictures, sealed windows, and fixed two sinks. When he walked in the kitchen, she had a late lunch waiting.

"You're going to feed me?"

She pulled out a chair and he folded in, feeling a bit like a bear come to tea. "Have you ever considered that what holds us together is food? We seem to be eating all the time."

"I tend to do that about three times a day. It's a habit that's hard to break."

Tuesday hadn't just made a sandwich; she'd made a meal. Meatloaf on the spicy side, baked potatoes, a fresh salad, and a chocolate pie.

After he tasted everything, he asked, "You always eat like this?"

"Once a day, I do. Most of my pantry comes from the garden or the orchard. I trade out at the local grocery, fruit for meat. Last time I checked, he's a few hundred in the hole to me. I cook one meal a day and eat leftovers for the other meals."

"How long have you been doing that?"

"What? Trading or eating?"

"Trading out fruits."

She shrugged. "Always, I guess. When I was half grown, I remember watching my grannie do it with half the stores in town. I work at the bar for any money I need. Plus, I mentioned my Eva left me what she called 'nest money' at the bank, already under my name. I used some for tuition, but college wasn't for me."

He talked about how he'd saved money all the years he was in the army. "I thought I'd buy Crystal and me a house after we finished school."

She patted his arm and he thought about how tiny her hand was next to his.

As he downed the last of his iced tea, she whispered, "I've got something to show you."

She led him through the rooms of the house. Each window was angled toward a view.

"Whoever built this was a genius."

"You've said that before. My great-uncle built it. My great-grandfather was too old and crippled up to be much help.

"Tony, her husband's younger brother, built the upstairs just for Eva."

Ketch could see the brother's vision. Everything downstairs had wide doors and railings to hold on to. Wide, low windows. Built-in seating, so a frail man could find somewhere to sit within a few feet anywhere downstairs. But as they climbed the stairs, the rooms were smaller. Everything had been made for a woman's touch. A little daybed to nap on in front of a bay window. Tiny drawers built into the wall beside mirrors so no dresser took up space in her little rooms.

The second floor reminded him of a dollhouse created with fine details. For Eva. "Let me guess, your Grannie was small like you."

"I was as tall as her by the time I was twelve. I thought I was grown up then. In our last few years together I grew taller and she seemed to shrink."

As they explored the rooms, he said his thoughts. "Tony,

old Frank's brother, must have loved Eva. Even the pulls on the shutters up here are hand carved."

"I think maybe he did," Tuesday whispered. "My mother told me once that Eva and Tony might have been lovers. They never married, not even after Frank died, but Tony never stopped coming to visit and worked on the house until he died in his sixties. Then she lived almost thirty years in the house he built her on Primrose Hill."

Ketch noticed a closed door at the end of the hall. "What's there?"

"Eva's studio. I wasn't allowed in there, but when she passed I went there to cry. It's just a long office that runs the length of the back of the house. There are lots of file cabinets and ink drawings of flowers, all black on white paper. There's even room for easels by each window. All face the clear east light."

Ketch's big hand turned the carved knob. As he pushed the door open, it creaked, almost as if warning them not to come in. The room was in twilight and the air so still he felt like he was stepping into a forgotten graveyard. The sketches that lined every wall had a haunting quality. Beautiful. Lonely. Almost as if her garden drawings had died on the paper and only left their shadow in ink.

Tuesday opened the shuttered windows and light seemed to fight its way in through floating dust.

"They are wonderful." Ketch studied a wall of sketches layered atop one another.

"The files are full of more. They make me want to cry. It's like looking into Eva's heart. Her life was so dark."

"No. Tuesday, I don't see it that way. She spent her time drawing something so beautiful with only a pen. She didn't need a hundred colors to create. She saw the beauty of nature in lines."

Tuesday smiled. "Thanks for that."

She took his hands and placed them on her waist. "Up," she whispered.

He raised her to eye level as she circled her arms around his neck and kissed him.

This one gentle kiss, Ketch thought, was worth a week with Crystal.

Chapter 21

Hank

Hank stood in the doorway of Millie's bedroom and watched her move slowly from the bed to her crutches. Every bone in his body wanted to help her, but she wouldn't have it. Since Thursday she'd insisted on doing as much as she could by herself. To his surprise, every day she did a bit more.

He'd watched over her for a week. Someone once told him that some women get prettier the longer you know them, and others just uglied up. Hank had to admit that he'd really never stayed around long enough to test the theory until now. The shy librarian was getting more beautiful each day. He loved the graceful way she moved, even while injured, and the slender lines of her body and the way she never complained.

Hank spent his time trying to make everything easier for her. He'd put dead bolts on her doors, built a ramp. Erected a long line of bookshelves on one side of the hallway so most of her books had a place. Hell, he'd even changed the oil in her car and put security lights above her outside doors.

Now he realized she didn't need him anymore. She could get around the house in the wheelchair and even on her crutches. It killed him to see her in pain, but he knew if he'd been the one hurt, he'd be fighting just as hard to be independent.

"Do you have to go into work, Millie? It's Sunday and we already went in for a few hours yesterday. I worry that you're pushing it. Can't you wait a few more days?"

She smiled at him. "Dr. Monroe is expecting the research. It won't take me more than a few hours." She moved slowly toward him. "If you'll help, I'll take you out to dinner. Someplace we can go into and sit down, not just pick up a bag."

"You got it, pretty lady." He slowly moved his hand around her waist and guided her as she limped along on one crutch. "Only, I'm paying."

Millie shook her head. "But you have to pay to fix your bike, and I've kept you from working this week."

"Don't worry about it." It was past time he told her about his job, but it meant something to him that she liked him, even though she thought he was a bum.

"And while you're lining up all the papers you want me to copy for the professor, I'm going to go have coffee with that friend of mine."

"I'll call you when I'm ready to leave." She moved toward the door. "But if you need more time to talk to your friend, I won't mind waiting."

Sometimes Hank just wanted to hug Millie. Any other woman would be giving him a timeline or warning him that he'd better not be late.

But not the librarian.

In his rodeo days there had been a revolving door of women. At some point he'd just started calling them all "honey." It was easier than trying to keep up with names. Millie would never be a "honey."

When he started working on oil rigs, most of which were offshore out in the Gulf, he'd decided to take a few online classes. Before long he'd picked up a degree. When the chance came to get into fire control and explosives with the oil company, Hank jumped at it. He'd found something exciting and dangerous with twice the pay. When he'd learned the Houston Police Department had an opening in the bomb squad, he went for it. It took him a few years to learn, but finally he felt he was where he belonged.

He loved his job, but it wasn't something he could talk about to people outside of law enforcement. People wanted to hear the exciting parts but didn't care about the science that went into the work, or the times when the good guys didn't win.

He couldn't imagine Millie, gentle as she was, being interested or understanding what it meant to him.

Hank picked up Millie's bag. Rambo was smart enough to know they were leaving and started whining.

Hank lifted Rambo and tucked him into the bag. There was just enough room for the pup to spread out over the books and journals. "Keep quiet till we get there, then you can run all over the closed library."

Rambo looked up at him, and Hank could have sworn the little ball of fuzz nodded.

As Hank loaded the bag and wheelchair into the Lincoln, he thought he might tell Millie about what he did for a living. Just the facts, nothing more. One more trip to carry her out and lock the door, and they were on their way.

He'd miss taking care of this sweet lady when he headed back to Houston. They'd worked out every detail of her day. She was comfortable around him. As he buckled in her seat belt, she kissed his cheek.

"You missed." He grinned.

She kissed him again lightly on the lips, then smiled as if she'd done something wicked. "Is it about time for the wild and scandalous things to come out in you, Hank?"

"Any minute. You might consider being afraid, Millie."

"Oh, I am." She grinned.

When Hank drove Millie to the back of the library, there were cars and students everywhere. Spring break was over.

Colby McBride pulled up in the oldest van Hank had ever seen running.

"You lose a bet?" Hank yelled to Colby as he carried Millie up to the back door.

"No, my bride says this old piece of junk sounded funny, so I have to drive it until I figure out what's wrong. Why is it women think all men know about cars and lawn mowers and broken toilets?" Colby patted the steering wheel. "I'm going to tell her that it's dying and I'm going to have to put the old van down."

Hank lowered Millie carefully into her wheelchair as she kissed him on the cheek again.

When he lifted Rambo onto her lap, Millie squealed. "He can't come in."

"Sure he can. The library is closed, plus he's your guard dog. I'll fill him out a library card." Hank patted Rambo's head as he opened the library door. "Take care of my lady while I'm gone."

The tiny ball of hair stood at attention.

As Hank pushed her chair to her office, he whispered, "Are you sure that dog doesn't understand everything we say?"

"No, I'm not."

Hank got her settled in, made sure the back door was locked as he left, then took the back stairs two at a time and climbed into Colby's old van. "I'd rather ride with you than drive the Lincoln around."

Colby backed out. "Your dad know you're driving it?"

Hank laughed. "He wouldn't let me drive it when I was

eighteen, why would he change his mind? I think he thinks I'm his greatest failure."

"You could set him straight. Just read off all those commendations you've got on your office wall. Last time I was in Houston on a case I walked past your office."

"I couldn't do that. Sometimes I think trying to save me from a wicked life is the only thing that keeps the old guy alive."

They pulled in front of a coffee shop. "Fill me in on your progress with the pipe bomber before my mind turns to mush. Millie wants to watch the Hallmark Channel every night. All the sweetness is killing me."

Colby laughed. "I like the 'fall in love over a weekend' movies. Piper and I curl up on the couch and watch one or two a week. Of course, we're usually naked before it ends, so, to me, I don't really think of them as G-rated."

Once the men took a corner table, Colby got down to business. "I'm not sure what's going on. We've found four more pipe bombs. The guy started with rural mail boxes, but now he's moved into town. The guy is getting better. If this keeps up someone is going to get hurt."

"Do we need gear?"

"They are far more dangerous." Hank whispered the obvious.

Colby nodded and continued, "No telling how many are out there that no one's stumbled across. Two were found at vacant houses, another in one of those 'tiny libraries' people put in the front of their houses. And get this. One was at the house next to where you grew up. The only one that looked like it was made with any skill was that one."

Hank's brain began to try and find a pattern. "Someone who hates 'little libraries'? Or empty houses? Or the whole town. Where was the pattern?"

"The day you pulled into town was the starting point.

The sheriff asked me the same question. That is the pattern. Plus you are the only one the sheriff knows of who hates Clifton Bend. If he knew you worked with explosives, you'd be in jail right now."

"The sheriff's right," Hank admitted as he stood and tossed his coffee in the trash. "It has to be me. I'm the bomber. And I must be really smart, 'cause I'm doing this while driving a huge old red Lincoln that everyone knows belongs to the preacher. How is it possible I haven't been caught?"

Colby grinned and followed Hank out. "Is this some kid just playing with us, or someone trying to make a point? Should we circle around every location where a bomb was dropped one more time?"

"No use. Drop me here at the library."

Hank's cell beeped. He checked the ID and picked up. "Are you all right? Did you fall?" Both men climbed in the van as Hank switched the cell to speaker.

"No," Millie whispered. "I didn't fall, but I'm not all right. I heard the drop box top fall, so I rolled in the back to retrieve the books. I've found a pipe in the return slot and . . ."

Colby gunned the van.

Two blocks later Hank jumped from the car before Colby had time to stop. "Don't touch it," he kept telling her. "Move away from it and put a wall between you and the slot. Then head for the front door."

The Ranger tried to keep up with Hank. "What's happening? I couldn't hear her."

"My librarian just found the next bomb." He returned the phone to his ear. "Millie, we're at the front door. Let us in."

The ranger was calling in the sheriff while Hank swore.

As they ran up the steps, Colby said, "When this is over, I plan to ask you why your librarian kisses you goodbye.

She's never kissed me goodbye." Colby knew his job. He headed toward the back door.

Hank didn't reply. His mind was packed with scenarios of what might happen. A little library in someone's front yard had been a target, now the college library. Not a pattern, but a clue. His dad's house had just been a coincidence, and the vacant houses were just practice. The targets the bomber picked made no sense.

Hank took a deep breath as Millie opened the front door.

He pulled her outside and away from the glass doors. "Stay here. I'll go take a look."

She must have seen the worry in his eyes. "Don't go close to it. You could get hurt."

He gently pulled her finger free of his shirt. "I know what I'm doing. I've done this kind of thing a few times."

A tall, bone-thin deputy showed up at the front door before Hank could move away from Millie. He looked like he'd run the half block from the office. "Sheriff's officer Pecos Smith." The kid was loaded down with equipment.

He couldn't have been more than a year into his twenties, but he was on duty.

"Step back, sir. Let a professional handle this. We don't want any people getting hurt. I've been trained. Just point me toward the bomb's location."

Hank grinned, knowing that any training the kid had was probably done over coffee and donuts. He'd already made a half-dozen mistakes, but he got an A for effort.

"All clear of people inside the library. I did not go near the drop box." Colby stepped from the storage room. "Deputy Smith, I'd like you to meet Captain Norton of the Houston police." Colby hesitated, then added, "He's with the bomb squad."

Pecos Smith looked skeptical, but he obviously respected Colby too much to argue.

Hank took the shield and the helmet from the deputy. The equipment was at least ten years out of date, but it was better than nothing. "I'm depending on you to be my backup, Deputy Smith. Keep everyone at a safe distance. That includes the ranger."

"Will do," Pecos Smith answered.

Hank moved toward the drop box in the storage room by the back door. As soon as he lifted the lid a few inches, he recognized the same poor attempt at making a bomb, exactly like the one he'd seen a few days ago.

With gloved hands he reached in and pulled the fuse out before pulling the pipe from the metal box. It was poorly made, but all the parts were there. It occurred to Hank that it was made to look like a bomb more than made to explode.

"All clear." Hank's words hadn't been loud, but they seemed to echo around the room.

Colby was by his side in a minute, ready to bag the evidence.

Pecos stood just behind the two men, but Millie remained outside.

"We've got trouble," Hank whispered. "Either he's getting better with each attempt or he's playing with us. Maybe he's putting out samples to let us know he's coming. Looks to me like he's got his target in mind and he's just circling around before he strikes."

Colby nodded. "You in on this with me, Hank? I could use your help."

"I'm in," Hank answered.

"I'm in too," the deputy echoed.

Hank glanced at Colby, and the ranger nodded slightly.

Hank heard the front door open and close. "Don't worry," Millie called. "It's only me and Ketch coming in to pick up some papers now that I heard 'all clear.'"

* * *

Half an hour later, Hank was laying Millie down on her bed. "You sure you'll be all right?"

"I'll be fine. I'm just tired."

He brushed her chestnut-colored hair back and kissed her forehead. "You were great, Millie. You did everything right. You called in help and you waited."

"I called you," she whispered. "I knew you'd know what to do."

Hank grinned. He needed to add one thing to Colby's list of things every woman thinks every man knows how to do. "I wanted to tell you what I did for a living, but it just didn't come up. I do know about bombs."

Sleepy eyes watched him. "I was eliminating the occupations down, one by one. I knew you weren't a cook and you looked at the vacuum like you'd never seen one, so I guessed you weren't a janitor. But, to be honest, being a policeman was way down on the list of guesses."

"What was the last on your list?"

She smiled her little smile. "Preacher."

He couldn't resist. Hank leaned closer and kissed her. Not a light, polite kiss but a tender kiss.

For a moment, she didn't move, then she opened her mouth and let out a little sound of pleasure.

Hank kissed her again. A bit deeper but just as tenderly. When he finally pulled away, she closed her eyes and went to sleep with a smile on her lips.

He couldn't stop staring at her as he fought the urge to kiss her again. He'd given up fear a long time ago, but when he'd known she was in danger, his whole body shook. He cared about her.

As he lightly moved his finger down her neck, he whispered, "When I get back . . ."

He couldn't promise anything. He didn't know how to be with a woman like her. He'd decided he'd go very slowly, but now he was the one newborn to her world. He wanted to make love to her one day. He didn't want just a roll in the covers and a goodbye in the morning.

Hank had worried he'd frighten her if he went too fast, but going slow scared him like nothing ever had.

"Watch over her," Hank whispered as he lifted Rambo atop the bed. "She's precious to me."

As he made sure all the doors were locked and headed out, he looked back at her one last time and thought, *When I get back you're going to teach me how to love.*

Monday

Chapter 22

Jenny

Professor Virginia Clark sat at her cluttered desk pretending to be hard at work on the survey. She didn't miss the fact that Benjamin had left the door between their offices ajar.

They were almost working together. After their night of loving last week, she wasn't sure he'd ever speak to her again. He didn't call or talk to her more than necessary. She'd thought about asking him to come over for another house call, but they both needed time to think.

He was a loving man who'd pressed all emotions inside. Her midnight lover who needed to step out into the light.

She fought down a chuckle. She'd never tell Benjamin that she cared little about the chemistry-of-mating research or winning the award. From the day she'd accepted the teaching assignment at Clifton College, all she'd wanted was her Benjamin back.

All fall she swore that only the shell of him was left, but last Wednesday he'd proved her wrong.

She'd given him up long ago in favor of adventures. Then she'd traveled the world, but in her mind, Benjamin had always traveled with her in those dark, predawn hours when she'd held her pillow and thought of how they had made love.

Touching him, holding him that first night had been like coming home. If possible, he'd become more shy, more reserved, but he still made love in that gentle way, as if all he wanted to do in the world was please her.

Then he'd told her their relationship would not exist on campus. Those few words hurt. She hesitated. She didn't want to make another mistake. Years ago she'd run too fast. This time she didn't want to run. She wanted to think.

At noon, he was at her door again. "Would you like some lunch?"

"No, thanks." She pretended to be busy.

He stood in the doorway for several moments. "I could bring you back something if you're working."

"No, thanks."

Benjamin retreated back into his orderly office.

An hour later, she was snacking on her second Snickers when he began to pace.

After ten minutes, she went to the connecting door. "Dr. Monroe, do you have time to look over the first draft of the thesis of our study?"

"Of course." He moved around her, careful not to touch her as he removed a half-dozen books and took the extra chair in her office.

They worked together on the first draft, their heads almost touching as they edited. The need to touch him distracted her, but she didn't dare make the first move. She'd follow his rules.

When they finished, she gathered up papers and stood. "We've got a good start."

He stood too. "May I suggest we take a walk to refresh our brains? The weather is quite nice. Once around the campus and then back to work. I have prep to do before class tomorrow."

She hesitated, then looked up at him and said, "A walk might be nice."

When they walked past the drugstore, he offered to buy her a malt.

When she smiled, he vanished on his mission. He hadn't held her hand or walked too close. He was polite, and nervous for some reason.

When he returned with one chocolate malt and one vanilla he apologized for not asking what flavor.

"You live above here, right?" she asked as she picked the closest malt.

"I do. Would you like to see my quarters?"

She nodded, as he looked both directions to make sure no one was watching them. She followed him up a side stairs attached to the drugstore and into a nicely equipped two-room apartment. Everything had its place and all the furnishings matched, like he'd bought them all at the same time as a set. The room almost looked staged to sell and not where someone lived.

Jenny set her purse on one of the kitchen chairs and took a long drink of her malt, hoping it might cool her down. "You have a nice place. Everything is in order, just as I would guess it would be."

"Thank you." He studied her for a moment and added, "We're not on campus anymore, Jenny."

She set her malt down. "No, we're not. Does that mean you'd like to kiss me, Benjamin?" She might as well say what had been on her mind all morning.

He smiled. "I would, if you have no objection."

"None at all, dear."

Leaning down he kissed her lightly, then straightened. "I think I love the taste of chocolate on your lips."

She thought of adding that she could rub the malt all over her, but she guessed that would panic him. She settled for, "Would you like to touch my breasts?"

Benjamin frowned.

She was disappointed that the question hadn't worked a second time.

He straightened, as if about to lecture her, but instead his words were low, almost a whisper. "I want a great deal more than that."

"Me too." She grinned.

Before she could close the space between them, he took her hand and led her into his bedroom. For a man of few words, Benjamin was making it clear what he wanted. She might have liked a few endearments, but it had been so long since she'd slept with a man, communicating with touch might work out just fine.

She pulled down the covers while he locked the door and closed the blinds. Then she stood perfectly still as he unbuttoned her blouse. As flesh began to show, he slowly moved his hand over her. Piece by piece he removed her clothes and folded them over a chair.

They were not college kids; they were old enough to know just what they wanted. They made love, and then he held her close to him as she drifted to sleep. Just as she knew he would, as she relaxed, his hands made long strokes along her side, slowing at every curve. When his fingers crossed over her breasts, which she'd always thought were too big, she heard him whisper, "I love touching you, dear."

An hour of afternoon passed in peace, then the low buzz of his cell woke them both. Ben slipped from the bed and dug in his trousers for his phone. He was walking out of the room when she heard him say, "What's up, Dad?"

Jenny scrambled off the bed and started dressing as

she heard Ben repeating over and over, "Calm down, Dad. Calm down."

She was in the bathroom brushing her hair when she heard Ben getting dressed. "Is something wrong?" she asked.

Ben didn't look up as he tied his shoes. "You might say that. My dad sounds like he's having a heart attack."

"Oh no. Do you want me to go with you or call an ambulance?"

"No," he snapped. "Not that kind of heart attack. He's not dying. At least, I don't think he is."

She moved closer, trying to understand or offer comfort to a man who suddenly looked angry.

Ben dug his fingers through his hair and stared at her. "He says my mother is en route. She called to tell him. She'll be at the farm within the hour."

Jenny saw the hurt of a little boy and the anger of a man suddenly staring at her.

"I have to go." His hand brushed her shoulder as if he suddenly remembered what he was leaving. "I . . . this was . . ."

She saw it in his eyes. He didn't want to leave her. "I know, Ben."

"No," he answered. "You don't know how much it means to me that you're here. I feel . . . I feel dead inside when you're out of reach."

Jenny smiled, finally able to read him. "I'll go with you, if you like. We'll have time to talk about us later." She brushed his hair back. "And there will be an us." She held him for only a moment as she whispered, "I feel the same as you feel."

He slowly pulled away and nodded once, then took her hand. "I'd like you to come with me. I don't know what we're stepping into with my parents, but whatever it is, I'll handle it with you near."

Three minutes later they were running downstairs. He slowed as he stepped on the street.

"I'll stay by your side, Ben, for as long as you want me to."

To her shock, he leaned down and kissed her on the mouth. A quick, hard kiss in the sunshine. In the street for everyone to see.

Ten minutes later when they drove toward his father's farm, Ben had finally calmed. "There are things that need to be said between us, Jenny."

"It can wait." She grinned, expecting him to have more rules. "We'll figure it out in time."

"No." He glanced over to her.

He couldn't seem to find the words, so she helped. "Sleeping together, or maybe having afternoon delight, is nice."

"Stop." His one word came low, almost like he didn't realize he'd said it aloud. "Don't make light of this. You have to tell me where you stand . . . I don't want to put it off . . . not again. I don't know if I could survive you walking away again. I . . ."

For a man who lectured all day, Benjamin seemed to be losing his words.

She leaned her head sideways, making her soft red curls bounce. He didn't even know how to ask for what he wanted. She guessed. "You want to know what I bought at the drugstore?"

Ben frowned like she wasn't making any sense. "What?" he snapped as if angry once more.

"I bought you a toothbrush to keep at my house."

She stared at the professor as she watched his face relax and a smile spread across his face.

Jenny folded her arms to keep from touching him. "Is that enough talk for now, Benjamin?"

"That's enough." For a moment he slowed the Jeep, then suddenly stopped in the middle of the dusty road. His hand cupped one side of her face. "You do know, Jenny, that I'll have to spend the night to use my new toothbrush."

She closed her eyes, already feeling his touch all over her in her mind. She'd had sex several times in her life, but making love was very rare, and from the looks of it, she'd just hit the mother lode.

"Let's go check on your father and stay as long as it takes to see what is going on, then I'd like you to undress me again and hold me all night. It seems I've become addicted to your touch."

"I will do exactly that, dear," he said formally, as if she'd given him an assignment.

His hands were gripping the steering wheel.

She couldn't look into his eyes, but she could read him clearly now. Her shy professor was fighting the need for her, and if she had anything to do with it, he wouldn't have to wait long.

Chapter 23

Benjamin

When Ben pulled onto his father's farm, he saw his dad standing in the wide yard beneath a grove of pecan trees. He had his work clothes on and his boots, but he'd shaved and his clothes were clean.

He hadn't dressed up to greet his wandering wife. If she finally came to see him, he must have thought she should see him exactly as he was. Joseph Monroe was a farmer. He had been all his life. He loved his land.

Ben parked the Jeep in the shade by the barn, as he always did, and walked across to his father. Jenny climbed out but waited in the shade. She was giving them time. Ben had no idea how much he'd need.

As he approached, Ben thought of how the farm had changed over the years since his mom had been here. Apple trees, ten feet high, ran the fence line out front for half a mile. There was a new windmill in the pasture a few hundred yards behind the house, and a hay barn as well as a pole barn at the turnoff to his dad's place.

The house was still small, four rooms downstairs and three upstairs, but his dad had added on a wide porch.

With the pecan trees close to the house, the yard almost looked like a park, with paths leading every direction over uneven ground spotted with wildflowers and natural vegetation.

Years ago his dad had planted a rose garden; he'd even built a gazebo where Ben used to do his homework. It wasn't fancy, but when the days were warm the vines wrapped around the latticework, making the place cool and colorful.

It suddenly struck Ben his old man had made the place beautiful for when she came back. He'd painted the trim of the house red every spring and made sure the flowers got plenty of water. Beside the picnic table he'd set out benches, and a swing made for two that faced the sunset.

He nodded once at his father. Twenty years separated them, but they were the same build. Tall, just over six feet, slender, but both were hard-work strong. His father's hair was white, no longer peppered like Ben's. His hands wrinkled and scarred.

"You sure you want me here, Dad?"

"I do. She'll want to see you."

For a time, they didn't say any more; they simply waited. The air was still, as if waiting along with them. His father had never said a mean word about his wife, just that she'd left to paint. After a few years, Ben gave up on the idea that she would ever return, but now he wasn't sure his dad ever had.

Eventually, his dad noticed Jenny by the barn. "You brought your girl. You still like her?"

"I do. I think I'm growing on her. I'm hoping she'll stay around."

"If she ever runs, son . . . follow her, and keep following her until she threatens to shoot you. Even then, don't leave until she buys the gun."

Ben fought down a laugh. "That's your advice on women, Dad?"

"That's about it. Monroe men aren't that easy to look at, and that little redhead is looking right at you and smiling. I think you got a good chance with that one."

He was glad he was past the age of having children. Thanks to his dad, he had no wise advice to pass down to the next generation.

A red spot of a car turned off the county road and headed toward their place. Dust began to fly behind her, but she didn't slow down.

Ben and his father straightened slightly as they watched.

The sports car still didn't look big enough to be a real car when it turned off at the gate.

Neither of them moved as the woman drove straight toward them. When she got to the edge of the yard, she came to a stop and cut the engine.

For a few minutes all she did was stare at them. Dad could have skipped painting the trim. All she saw was the two of them.

Finally, she stepped out of the car and pulled off her sunglasses.

He saw a woman with a long braid of hair so light it looked silver. His mother was still tall and slender. Willowy, his dad used to say. She wasn't pretty so much as striking. The faded memory Ben had of her blended with her today as she slowly moved toward them.

She'd been gone all except the first four years of his life, but her timid smile seemed familiar.

A wisp of a memory floated into his mind of dancing with her in the kitchen. Her hair had been dark and swaying to her waist then, and she'd been singing. His dad came in through the back door and saw them. He'd lifted Ben up on the counter and danced with his wife while Ben laughed. They'd twirled to a country song.

The woman walking toward them had lived a completely different life than she would have had here, Ben thought. She was thinner maybe, and her skin was no longer tanned from the sun. Her clothes were different somehow. She looked a bit boho in her sandals that were laced almost to her knees, and with a colorful scarf flowing around her. She reminded him of the artists who sometimes displayed their work at the college, not a woman born and raised in the valley.

She moved with a grace he hadn't noticed as a child. And as she neared, Ben saw fine wrinkles on her face that somehow blended with her beauty.

She walked toward his dad.

"Joseph, I've come home," she said.

Ben heard a hint of a foreign accent flavoring her words.

He turned to his father. The man who'd stayed and raised him alone. The man who never expressed love in words, but who Ben had never doubted loved him. No matter what was said here today, no matter what happened, Ben would stand with his father. If the old guy wanted her to go, Ben would open her car door for her and wave goodbye.

She took another step toward them. "I'm home."

A dozen things ran through Ben's mind. Fiery words his dad might yell. Maybe he'd order her off his land. Maybe all the words he'd held in over the years would explode out of him.

But his father just stood there, his back straight, almost rigid. His words came low. "It's about time."

Ten minutes later Ben was in his Jeep flying back to town, feeling like he'd been struck by lightning and no one noticed.

"Did you see that, Jenny?" he said for the tenth time.

"She didn't even look at me, her only son. Her only child—that I know of. Did you see that? She just looked at my dad like I was invisible."

Ben glanced at Jenny and wasn't surprised she was laughing. The scene he'd just witnessed should go in some drunk-weekend scene in a movie called *Seniors Go Wild*. His dad had smiled like he'd never seen his dad smile. Like he was having a stroke and welcomed it.

"Dad hadn't seen her for years and she drives up and says she's home and he says three words. Then he takes her hand and they walk into the house. The house I grew up in, by the way. Without a mother, by the way.

"Before I could even think about following, Dad closes the door, and I swear I heard the dead bolt click."

Jenny couldn't hold laughter in any longer. "This is not about you, Ben."

"Obviously!" He was not ready to settle down. "For all I know they've forgotten they had me years ago and are upstairs making another kid right now."

She was still laughing, but she managed to say, "Again, this isn't about you, Ben. Give them some time."

He pulled up in front of her cabin but didn't cut the engine.

"You coming in?" she asked.

"I can't. Then we'd be doing what they're doing right now. I can't handle it. They're both sixty. They're in their heart attack years. What they are doing is dangerous."

"Maybe they are not having sex. Maybe they are talking. They've got lots of catching up to do."

"Don't say that word."

"What word?"

"Sex."

She was giggling again. "You do know where you come

from, Ben. I know it's biology and not chemistry, but you do know the concept."

He turned off the engine. "You're right. I'm cracking up. I'm never like this."

"Come inside and I'll make you an egg sandwich. It'll go great with a shot of whiskey."

He followed her in and let her pamper him. There was reason in her voice. He downed the whiskey in one toss and didn't even remember eating the sandwich until she asked him if he'd like another one.

She was the flighty one. He was the rock-solid one. But here she stood as he sat at her bar and she was patting on him like he was a lunatic.

Finally, after another drink, they ate cookies and talked about growing up. She had three sisters and swore her father never got their names right, and he laughed about asking his dad the facts of the birds and the bees, and his dad took him out to watch cows.

Both were tired. When they tried to watch the late news, they fell asleep on the couch. He liked cuddling into her. She was a woman who knew how to melt into a man.

"Stay the night," she whispered to wake him.

"All right, but no sex."

"I agree. We've already had our month's ration."

He slept in his T-shirt and underwear and she slept in her panties and bra. He decided he looked like a nerd and she looked sexy as hell.

Late in the night they both forgot their agreement to not have sex. They didn't just have sex; they made love. He couldn't resist the way her soft body tried to push out of her underwear.

The first time they made love, he decided he'd been distracted by how grand she'd felt—so after an hour of worrying about it, he woke Jenny and tried again.

He got it just right the second time.

Chapter 24

Ketch

Though he'd been up most of the night, Ketch felt good about what he'd done on the survey. The study was progressing and Professor Clark had a way with words that made the research fascinating to read. The more he read, the more he learned that people are attracted to one another not just by looks but a hundred other things.

Another week, maybe two, and the project would be ready to send in. If he went into teaching or applied for grad school, the part he did on this project would look good on his résumé. Might even help him find a job.

But more and more lately, it was the blueprints on his wall that drew him. He was even starting to dream about building homes. Not the ones like the Randall brothers built—all in a row using only three floor plans—but the kind of unique houses like Primrose Hill. The beauty of a house was not just in its bones but in its originality.

As he reached for his cell to call Tuesday, the phone rang. Without looking at the ID, he answered.

"Kincaid here."

"Don't hang up, Ketch!" Crystal's voice shouted.

He might be able to not pick up when she called, but he

couldn't hang up on her. "What do you need, Crystal? Didn't you say it all in your letter?"

"We need to talk about a few things. I thought I'd fly down . . ."

"Don't bother. I'm working and have to study for finals."

"Ketch, we can't just toss away all we have." She had that little hiccup in her voice that she always got when she was about to cry.

He'd heard the sound several times, but he'd never seen a tear.

"I'll keep the good memories, but your letter put an end to the future we might have had." He took a breath, trying to calm down. Maybe he could even be kind. Part of him would always love her, but he knew they'd been trying to make something work that had rusted away a long time ago. "I'm over being mad, Crystal. I'll even wish you well."

"But, Ketch, we're engaged. I have the ring."

"You never wore it, remember? You said it didn't go with the uniform. Keep it."

"You can't just break off, we . . ."

"I didn't. You did. You ended it, Crystal." Ketch closed his eyes and remembered how broken he'd been that first night. If it hadn't been for Tuesday, he might have done something crazy like quit school or jump into the river just to see if he could swim. "Don't fly to Texas. Don't call me again."

He ended the call. There was nothing else to say. If she'd loved him, she wouldn't have hurt him like that.

The phone rang again. He stared at the ID before answering. A scam voice would be better than hearing Crystal act like she was about to cry.

He hesitated, then answered, "Kincaid here."

"Ketch, this is Hank Norton. Remember you met me at the library Sunday? I didn't introduce myself completely . . ."

"Are my books already in? That was fast."

"I don't know." Hank barked a laugh. "I don't officially work at the library, but I do want to ask for your help. Ranger McBride told me you're ex-military. I have a feeling you can handle what I need you for. You'd be working with Ranger McBride and me. In my real life I'm Captain Harrison Norton of the Houston police, and we have a situation here. I should add the job might get dangerous and there is no pay."

Ketch frowned. He already had two jobs, and it seemed the librarian's nurse-turned-cop was offering him another. "How can I help you, Hank? The offer seems too bad to turn down."

The man on the other end hesitated a few heartbeats, then said calmly, "What do you know about bombs, soldier?"

Bombs. Ketch felt his body go on high alert. "Not much, but more than most. I'm at your service, sir."

"Meet me at noon outside the library. We're going to try and stop something from happening before someone gets killed."

"I'll be there if this is about the pipe bombs folks have been finding around town."

"It is." How could Hank have thought the problem wouldn't get out? This was a small town. Everyone on campus was talking about it. The Ag boys were thinking of organizing a search party.

"Noon. The library," Hank said in more of an order than a request.

Ketch hung up. He'd worry about forgetting Crystal another day. Right now, he was too busy.

Wednesday

Chapter 25

Hank

Millie sat in her office chair with her back straight and her hands shaking in her lap. The librarian was so nervous her words echoed as if in a canyon. "You can't do this, Harrison. This is not your job. I'm fine. I don't need your help anymore. Go back to Houston and let Ranger McBride and the sheriff take care of this bomb problem. It's probably some kid wanting attention."

Hank was strapping Deputy Smith's too-small bullet-proof vest around his chest. "I can't go anywhere, Millie. This is my job. It's what I do. And this is personal; the bomber put a pipe bomb in my lady's way. You could have been hurt. How could I not get involved?"

"I'm not your lady, Harrison. You were just helping me. We're friends, remember. I've never been anyone's lady."

She took a breath and tried again. "In Houston you'd have a team and trucks and equipment. I've seen you guys work on TV." A tear rolled down her cheek. "If I hadn't stepped off that curb without looking, our wreck wouldn't have happened and you would have already been back home. If you get killed, this is all going to be my fault."

Hank wanted to yell that none of this was her fault, but he could never raise his voice at Millie. The librarian was fine china and he was a tin beer mug. He'd run toward danger all his life, and Millie had run away.

He knelt in front of her wheelchair. "This is what I do. I'm not going to get hurt. I'm maybe the one person in town who knows how not to get hurt."

With two fingers he brushed away her tear. This one tear said it all. It was the reason he never got involved with anyone, why he didn't tell his father what he did, why he'd rather people think he was a biker than know what he really did for a living. How could he explain that this wasn't just his job? It was his life, his calling his dad might say.

Hank craved adventure—no, danger. He needed that rush to keep his heart beating. He'd discovered the thrill of driving fast in high school, rode it through years in his rodeo days. No matter how many times he got hurt, he'd found he could have the excitement running through his veins forever if he balanced it with knowledge and precaution.

People might say he was trying to kill himself, but in truth, Hank was keeping himself alive. Most folks walk around mostly dead inside, not ever knowing their heart is beating, but not him.

It seemed the only thing that could hurt him was the fearful look in people he cared about.

He cupped Millie's face and kissed her, loving and hating that she cared. "I'll be fine. I have to do this. I want to do this. Colby said they found three more bombs yesterday and two of them were live. That means they could have gone off and hurt someone. A little kid pulling out the mail, or a person just walking by."

When she looked like she was going to argue, he kissed

her again. This time the kiss was sweeter, longer, than ever before.

When he pulled away, she whispered, "Why are you kissing me, Harrison?"

He smiled. He'd figured out that she always called him Harrison when she was mad or wanted to push him away. "It's the only way I can think of to stop the argument. Is it working?"

She laughed. "That's thoughtful of you. I feared it might be because you were attracted to me."

Hank held her face so she couldn't look away. "I am attracted to you, Millie. How could you not know that? In fact, when you get well I wouldn't mind doing a great deal more with you than just kissing."

Her eyes widened as she tried to pull away. Apparently the possibility of him being blown up wasn't as frightening as him making love to her.

Hank stood and almost ran for the door. Maybe he should have asked if she was attracted to him before he deepened the kiss. "I'll be back as soon as I can. If you need me, just call."

He was at the Lincoln when he realized his heart was pounding like it did when he stood in front of a live bomb or just before the gate swung open.

Fear. An emotion as old as mankind. The one emotion that saved the cavemen from extinction. Fear. You run or you fight.

He sat behind the wheel and started the engine.

He'd run from the library . . . from Millie, as if she could somehow hurt him. He'd run! The first action when danger appeared.

But he wasn't facing a bomb. He wasn't on a thousand-pound bull or driving way too fast. He was not in peril.

He faced the fact that he might care for Millie. Hell, he might even be falling in love.

For the first time in his life, Hank feared he might die of fright.

Chapter 26

Hank

When Hank looked up, Ketch was on the library steps waiting. The tall guy still had the look of a soldier about him. He stood at attention and seemed to be deep in thought.

Hank waved him over.

As Ketch climbed into the Lincoln, Ketch asked, "You all right, man?"

"Sure, I just had something else on my mind." Hank smiled, hiding all feelings. If he told how he felt about the librarian, Ketch would think he'd gone mad, yet for the first time ever, Hank knew he was falling for someone he might not be able to walk away from.

"Must be intense if it outranked a bomb." Ketch faced forward, showing no interest at what it might be.

"Forget it. You're right. We've got a wannabe bomber to find. I never would have thought I'd end up in the center of America, in my small hometown, chasing a bomber."

Ketch looked straight ahead as if on surveillance. "Me either. I might not have been born here, but this place is as near to home as I've ever felt."

Hank knew Kincaid was a top student, but he'd turned from a student to a soldier in a blink when called.

"How long have you been out of the service?" Hank pulled away from the campus.

"I was in for four years. I served two tours in places where sweeping for bombs was a daily duty. I've been out for almost three years. Thanks to summer classes and a few online courses, I'll graduate this May."

Hank thought Ketch seemed nervous, or maybe just excited. He also seemed young, but he was older than most students. "I looked you up, Kincaid. Glad you agreed to help. Fine record in the army and here."

Hank drove out of town, heading for the first known drop of a pipe bomb. "We're going to circle all the known sites. Try to find a pattern. Somewhere there's one location or person who links them all together. But first, the number one rule. Follow everything I tell you to do. No questions. No discussion. Got it?"

"Got it." Ketch looked more interested now than worried. "I can follow orders. I looked you up too. Impressive. I guess bull riding got too boring and you had to switch to bombs."

"Something like that." Hank relaxed a bit. Between Ketch and the young deputy he had a team, and Hank would do his best to see they stayed out of harm's way.

After a few minutes, Hank tried conversation. "Got a girlfriend, Kincaid?"

Ketch raised an eyebrow but played along with small talk. "I do, but she don't know it yet."

Hank grinned. "I got one of those too. I'm not sure, but I think she's afraid of me."

"You're one scary guy, Captain. Pecos told me the Texas Rangers call you sir. He also said the sheriff in Honey Creek claims you hit a hundred on Main when you were a kid riding a Harley."

"When did you talk to the deputy from Honey Creek? And it was only eighty, not a hundred." Hank always stuck to the facts.

"We had a class together this morning. He may still look like a kid playing cop, but he's a hero around here. He usually shows up to class in uniform so he can step into his job the minute he's finished."

Ketch added, "He's also got the best-looking wife in the valley, and for some reason she's crazy about him. I heard that a few years ago he saved McBride and the mayor of Honey Creek from a fire. Pecos will probably be sheriff the next time you drive through this community."

"I read about what he did. I may not live in the valley, but I keep up with the news. I guess your hometown is always going to be a part of you." Hank slowed at a line of rural mailboxes.

Ketch shook his head. "I wouldn't know. I was moved from one foster home to another so many times that to this day I have trouble remembering my zip code."

"So you enlisted as soon as you were old enough?"

"Right. Only kin I had was Uncle Sam. But I heard about this valley from a drill sergeant and decided this place would be nice to visit when I got out. Came and never wanted to leave. Sergeant Randall lets me work construction when I have free time." Ketch laughed. "Only problem is, on the job, he still sounds like a drill sergeant."

Ketch's phone pinged, and he picked it up. "I'll tell him. We'll be there as soon as we can."

When he slipped his phone back in his pocket, Ketch said calmly, "Pecos says we've had our first bomb go off. Clifton's hospital. Did some damage. No one hurt."

"Where in the hospital?"

"Between the front doors. Shattered glass in both directions. Sheriff is en route to determine damage and secure the location."

Hank swung the Lincoln around, running off the road on both sides, and headed back to town.

"Our little hospital is off—" Ketch started.

Hank snapped, "I know where it is. I was there a week ago after I ran over Millie."

"Remind me to slug you later for that, sir. You couldn't have run over a nicer woman."

"I know." Hank nodded. "I will remind you to swing when this is over. I deserve it."

Ketch stared at Hank as he said slowly, "One bomb next door to your father's house, one planted in the library that your car was parked behind. Now the hospital you've visited."

"Coincidence . . ." But one more fact rolled around in his brain. They found the first bomb the day he arrived. "Coincidence?" he said again and let the echo roll around the car.

As they came in sight of town, Ketch answered another call.

This time he didn't say anything.

Hank could make out the caller screaming but not the words.

"Where?" Hank asked as Ketch ended the call.

"You been to the pharmacy lately?" Ketch whispered. "They just called in, one pipe bomb found beside the building. The ranger's headed to the second site. He said it is thought to be armed but hasn't gone off. He wants us to meet him there first. The hospital doors are roped off. That crime scene is being guarded by security."

Hank frowned. "I hung out at the hospital for hours one

night and I didn't see any security." He pressed down on the accelerator.

The old Lincoln bucked once and then took off. "I had nothing to do with the drugstore. I used the drive-through to pick up Millie's pills. I didn't go in, so that blows your theory of the bombs being connected to me."

Ketch braced his hand against the dash, but his voice was calm. "You didn't see security because Bull sleeps in the break room most of his shift. The nurses' aides claim he eats their lunches."

"How do you know?"

"About the lunches or about Bull?"

"About Bull!" Hank yelled as the pharmacy came into sight.

Ketch laughed. "Captain, you're sounding more like a cop every minute I'm around you. I can't believe I thought you were a nurse to the librarian when we first met."

Hank turned a corner on three wheels.

"You must be a time traveler, Hank, or living multiple lives, because you don't seem to be putting much care in this one."

"Tell me about Bull Wills."

"I didn't say his name was Wills, but you guessed right. My lab partner is his little brother. Wynn claims his dad keeps threatening to saw off Bull's branch of the family tree. Says Bull is too dumb to remember to breathe."

"It's been years, but I remember him from high school." Hank slowed. "Bull was a year or two younger than me, but he was big and played football. He'd get high before a game and start tackling his own teammates." Hank barked a laugh. "If he's still doing drugs, what brain he had is probably mush."

Ketch nodded. "That pretty much describes Bull. His

dad gets him a job and Bull loses it before the year's out. Being security for a ten-bed hospital is going great, I hear. Four months and he's not fired yet."

Hank swore as he pulled to a stop. "And he's the one watching the hospital crime scene?"

"Yep."

They climbed out of the Lincoln across the street from the pharmacy. Pecos's cruiser was already there. "If this bomb isn't live we'll bag it as fast as we can, then head for the hospital."

Ketch nodded. "You want me to keep the crowd back?" Four people were standing at the corner. One was peeking into the alley as if making sure the bomb was still there.

"Tell Pecos to make notes of everyone standing around. Our bomber may be watching nearby."

Pecos was already keeping everyone away from a pipe bomb resting on the third step of the stairway to what looked like an apartment entrance above the drugstore.

After clearing the perimeter, Hank stood alone just outside the alleyway and finished suiting up to do his job. He'd had Houston overnight him his gear, but it hadn't arrived yet. Even before he touched the pipe he knew the bomb wasn't live. The bomber was playing a game, but the standard protocol was, every bomb, every call-in was treated as a live bomb.

Fully armed, Hank walked slowly toward the bomb. A pipe and a fuse taped to one end. He could see the other end was open. He took a long breath. Part of him would always be the cowboy waiting for the eighth second to come.

Hank gave the OK to Ketch and Pecos as he tugged off his headgear and studied the surroundings. Then he turned to the deputy. "There has to be a reason he put it here. It's a place he could step in and leave it unseen, but the chances of it being seen by someone walking by are high, so the bomber wanted us to find it. Maybe he thought we'd find it first and not take the hospital bomb seriously. Or maybe he thought we'd panic."

Neither Pecos or Ketch had an answer, and the crowd was growing, moving closer as if hoping to hear what Hank was saying.

Hank tried another angle. "Who lives upstairs?"

"The pharmacist said Dr. Benjamin Monroe does, but he is not up there," Pecos answered.

"How does he know?"

Pecos nodded and pulled out his notepad. "The pharmacist said Dr. Monroe's Jeep would be parked where we're standing if he was home. Plus, he called Dr. Monroe a few minutes after his employee spotted the bomb and the professor said he'd gone out to his farm last night and hadn't made it back home yet."

Pecos straightened. "I asked everyone who works here questions. No one saw anyone go close to the stairs. The bomb could have been placed on the step sometime last night. One of the girls who works at the soda fountain stepped between the buildings to smoke and saw it about 12:10. She said she would have noticed if it had been there on her five o'clock break yesterday." Pecos looked up from his notes. "She usually sits on the steps."

"I want to speak to the professor when he shows up." Hank felt frustrated.

A low voice from the growing crowd answered. "I'm standing right here."

Hank watched a thin man with graying hair step out of the crowd. He offered his hand, then noticed Hank still had on his gloves.

"Can you spread any light on this situation, Professor?"

"I'm Benjamin Monroe and, if you'll allow me, I'd like to make a few observations. The man who placed the pipe on my step was short. Under five-five, I'd say, and right-handed."

Ketch moved beside the man and nodded at the doctor. "Why do you think that, sir?"

"Well." The professor pulled out a pen to use as a pointer. "If I were setting a pipe down, the nearest step at my height would be the fourth. For you, I'd guess you'd leave it on the fifth. The last thing anyone holding a bomb would want to do is let the bomb drop from his hand. Plus, a right-handed person would naturally place something a bit to the right, just as a lefthanded person would place it to the left. Whoever did this was probably in a hurry and would not take the time to center the pipe on the step."

Hank gave up being irritated at the civilian butting in and started being interested. "Anything else?"

"Well, yes, there is. Whoever placed the bomb raised his foot to the first step as he leaned forward. See the mud."

"How do you know it was our bomber?"

The professor straightened. "I would have noticed the mud on the step when I left yesterday, and it's very unlikely anyone would go up my steps. The girl who smokes would not have mud on her shoes."

Hank thought of asking what kind of freak notices a bit of mud, but both Ketch and Pecos were leaning down to look at the evidence.

Hank grudgingly added, "Anything else, Professor?"

The thin man looked shy, as if he was uncomfortable being the smartest one in the room. "The mud is brownish red. River mud. And it is still damp, not dry, so the bomb was placed less than an hour ago. It is likely the man walked up from the river behind the pharmacy."

"One last question, Dr. Monroe. Is there anyone you know who would wish to harm you?" Hank asked.

To his surprise, the doctor hesitated. "No," he finally answered.

Hank thought of himself as great at his job, but this teacher, with probably no police training, had proved him wrong. He hadn't been looking close enough. "Chemistry teacher, right?"

"Right."

"You ever work in a lab? Do forensics, maybe?"

"No, but I do read about it. Before I made tenure and hit forty, I dreamed of investigating crimes."

"You'd be good at it, but this wasn't a bomb. It was just set up to look like one. My guess is the bomber was just trying to distract us, or maybe someone wanted to have some fun playing copycat. The real bomber was at the hospital. The copycat here."

Hank handed Benjamin the bag into which he'd put the fake bomb. "Professor, could I interest you in taking a look at this? We've sent five just like this one to the lab and gotten no clues. It's a long shot, but somehow I wouldn't be surprised if you notice something we missed."

The professor took the bag. "I'd be honored to help. I'll do my best."

"I have no doubt. If you're free, I'd like you to ride with Pecos to the hospital. A live bomb went off over there. I could use another set of eyes."

Benjamin glanced at the sheriff's cruiser parked across the street. "Can I ride in the front seat?"

Pecos laughed. "You can drive, for all I care. OK with you, Captain Norton?"

"Sure. I'll ask the sheriff to deputize him. Dr. Monroe is officially part of our team."

As Ketch and Hank climbed back into the old Lincoln, Ketch said, "You made the professor's day."

"No," Hank answered. "He made mine. We now have a few clues."

Ketch laughed to himself. "I noticed something strange that has nothing to do with the bombs. The professor had the same clothes on today as he did yesterday. I probably wouldn't have noticed, but I also had on a navy-blue shirt and tan pants yesterday and worried that someone might notice that we were dressed alike.

"You'd think a man who noticed mud would change clothes. If he was in college I'd think his date lasted till dawn or he'd studied all night."

"I can solve that mystery. The professor didn't come home last night. Pecos said he went to his farm yesterday."

Ketch leaned back in the seat. "Yeah, but you'd think the man would have a change of clothes there. He goes out there a few times a week."

"Maybe they were all dirty?" Hank would bet a month's pay that the professor was a good guy, but there was that moment he'd hesitated when Hank had asked if anyone wished him harm. Add the fact that a man who noticed a bit of mud would probably notice if his clothes were all dirty.

They pulled up at the hospital and forgot all about the doctor's wardrobe. Sheriff LeRoy was out in front of what had been the hospital's main entrance.

Hank knew he'd have to face the lawman at some point. He couldn't just go through Colby for information and assistance. McBride might be a Texas Ranger, but Leroy was still the sheriff of this county. The ranger and Hank were both in his territory.

"Sheriff," Hank said as he walked up.

"Captain Norton." LeRoy said the name slowly and without smiling. "Damn, if I didn't know you'd end up doing something dangerous. What I never guessed was you'd be on the right side of the law."

"Sorry to disappoint you, Sheriff."

"Does your father know?"

"Nope. He'd just worry."

"Hell, Harrison, did it ever occur to you that he might pray for you?" The sheriff shook his head. "I'm a man who can admit I'm wrong on the rare occasion that I am. I was wrong about you. You're not just good at your job; you're a living legend. I looked you up on my computer."

"Apparently I'm trending." Hank grinned. "I had to put up with you growing up, Sheriff. I knew the make of a legend."

Hank went to work, afraid if he talked to the old guy another minute they'd be hugging.

Professor Monroe stood to the side, watching. He must have watched enough cop shows to know not to interfere. Hank wished security guard Bull Wills had. The leftover high school football star and druggie had contaminated everything.

While they were finishing, Ranger McBride showed up and suggested they all meet and talk. The campus cops had offered him their conference room.

Sheriff LeRoy said he had to be in court in an hour, but the rest of the team headed toward the campus.

Hank noticed all three men, including the professor, pulled out their cell phones to make a call. So Hank pulled out his phone and called Millie.

"You all right to stay a little longer at the library?"

"Of course." He could hear the smile in her voice. "I'm fine, Harrison. I work here, you know, and all three of my staff are mothering me. It is time I got back to work."

"Since you got your one shoe on, how about we go out to eat when I pick you up? This may take a few hours."

"I'd like that."

For a few moments after the call ended, Hank was smiling. He'd never met a woman like Millie.

Chapter 27

Benjamin

The day had turned cloudy by the time Ben drove his Jeep to the campus security building behind the gym. He had to go into the small box of offices every year to get his parking permit. Twice over the twelve years he'd been teaching, Ben had forgotten his faculty ID. Not surprisingly, the clerk would not give him a faculty sticker without proper identification.

Now and then he'd stay overtime at the library and a ticket was always waiting on his windshield. Ben considered it his opportunity to support the college.

But now he was a part of an elite team. The Clifton Bend Bomb Squad. Ben couldn't wait to tell Jenny all about it. He'd give her the facts calmly and watch her explode with excitement, then she'd probably hug him tight and worry about him.

Of course he wasn't worried, but he didn't mind if she did, just a bit.

He loved the way Jenny loved life. Last night she'd woken him to tell him she thought she'd heard a mouse. He might have complained, but he'd had too much fun comforting her.

He knew this bomb squad was just living a fantasy, no more than a kid playing Spider-Man on Halloween, but Ben planned to enjoy it as long as possible. He'd be serious about his responsibility, but he'd have fun telling Jenny all about it.

Putting all the clues together was pure chemistry theory. Figure out the facts you know, then what you don't know, add in the variables, and come up with the final solution after eliminating all other possibilities.

Hank did most of the talking once they got to the conference room, which looked more like a break room no one ever cleaned. Ben followed the talk, mentally logging everyone's comments. Ketch added a few suggestions. Pecos seemed to have lots of theories. The sheriff didn't say a word except to ask for more coffee and remind everyone he had to leave in five minutes.

When Ben suggested they check the drugstore's camera, everyone jumped up shouting the same thing. "The store has a camera?"

Ben explained that it was behind the pharmacy window facing out. It showed anyone collecting medicine and also the window behind the customer, looking out to the street. It was a long shot, but maybe they'd find something.

Colby said he'd go by and get the footage. Ben would examine the pipe found on his stairs. Beyond that, all they could do was wait for the next sighting.

As a group they tried to come up with a list of suspects. They decided Bull Wills would be at the top of the list if he had a few more brain cells working. Pecos suggested the two plumbers in town because they'd have pipe. Hank asked for the names of any unbalanced people in town, but the sheriff said there were too many to fit on the page.

Colby seemed convinced it was just kids wanting to stir up excitement.

Finally the team broke up. Ben walked out with Hank and Colby. Ketch and Pecos both had classes.

Colby and Hank were making dinner plans and asked if Ben would like to join them. Both men looked tired. Ben had a feeling they needed a bit of normal for a few hours.

"Mind if I bring someone?" Ben asked.

Ben ignored their surprise. All three headed out, planning to meet at the café on the square in Honey Creek at dusk.

As soon as Ben climbed into his Jeep, he called Jenny. "I've got lots to tell you, dear. Will you go out to eat with me tonight with some law enforcement friends I'm working with on a problem? I'll tell you all about it on the way to Honey Creek."

"I'd love to but, Professor, we'll be seen together."

Ben was silent for a moment, then said, "It's about time, Red."

"Then come get me, farmer."

When he dropped his phone in his pocket he felt young for the first time in years. He had a date that would probably last all night. She'd called him "farmer." It felt like he was twenty-one again.

He dropped by the apartment to shower and change clothes. He arrived at her cabin early, so he walked to the water's edge, thinking about the mud he'd seen on his steps. One question kept rolling around in his head. Why would the bomber pick that exact space to leave a bomb? If it was left last night, the bomber couldn't have known that Ben would not come in late, or leave before dawn. Then what if he'd stepped on the bomb in the dark and it had been real? He might be dead right now.

Ben was a teacher. He wasn't used to thinking about scenarios that ended up with him dead.

Logic told him the drop was just convenient, not intentional. The street was quiet, but people often walked past the pharmacy. Maybe the bomber had placed it to make a point. Maybe he wanted to scare the entire town.

Ben would try to find a few minutes at dinner to talk about his theory. Maybe the bomber was playing a game with those looking for him. He wasn't wanting to frighten the community. His game was with the lawmen.

Ben was beginning to feel like the no-name rider in an Old West posse movie who gets shot out of his saddle by the bad guys. The hero never died, only the extras.

Another theory crossed his mind. What if the bomber had gotten the two bombs mixed up, and the one on the steps had been meant to go off and the one between the hospital doors had only been meant to frighten people? If so, Ben might have been the first casualty.

One more question haunted Ben. That hospital bomb must have gone off quickly because, otherwise, people would have spotted the pipe on their way in or out.

A few minutes later, when he saw Jenny, Ben forgot all about his worries. She wore a very modest black dress with just enough cleavage to make it interesting and a colorful shawl that brought out the blue in her eyes. He loved the way the dress showed off her curves.

He wanted to tell her how beautiful she looked, but he couldn't find the words. He just smiled as his hand slid along her side, and that seemed to please her.

She was a woman who liked to be handled and he was addicted to touching her.

"How are your dad and mother doing?" she asked before he found words.

Ben had forgotten about his parents. "I have no idea. Maybe they're fighting or making love. Either way, I don't know why they haven't called me."

She chuckled. "You're such an only child, Ben."

He didn't hear her say "This isn't about you, Ben," but the echo of those words was still circling in his mind. "Give them time." He voiced her thought. "If they are catching up, it'll take a while."

She nodded. "I don't want to talk about them. I want to hear about your day."

As they walked out she patted him on the bottom.

"You can't keep doing that. Someone might notice," he said with a smile.

"Yes, dear," she agreed as she patted him again.

On the thirty-mile drive to Honey Creek he told what had happened and she listened, taking it all in.

When they parked at the café, Ben saw Hank lifting the librarian out of his ugly Lincoln. The bomb expert held the librarian as if she were glass.

Her shy smile greeted them as Ben held the door.

As they joined Honey Creek's mayor, Piper McBride, and her husband, Colby, in a small dining area for six, everyone was talking like old friends. It was cozy as they ate in the space where shoulders almost touched and the lights were low so the town square sparkled in the light rain.

Ben couldn't remember when he'd felt so content. He had Jenny by his side and interesting people to talk to. Part of the reason he'd gone into chemistry was that he loved puzzles, and now everyone at the table was working together to solve one.

Colby laughed about how all four of their guests had two names. "My wife thought we were having ten for dinner from the way I was talking, until she figured out Harrison was Hank, Benjamin was Ben, Amelia was Millie, and Virginia was Jenny."

Hank took over the introductions. He pointed to the professors. "Mayor, please meet Ben and Jenny, and we are Hank and Millie. Tonight, we'll keep one name and be pals. No titles or proper names."

Piper McBride, a classic beauty, nodded politely to her husband and said, "It is a pleasure for Colby and me to welcome you all to our little town." Her dark green eyes shined with intelligence and kindness.

As Ben always did, he mentally sat back a bit and observed. He noticed the ranger's gaze kept returning to his wife. They'd only been married a year, but anyone could see they were madly in love.

Ben couldn't help but wonder if the fact that Colby had a dangerous job made their love stronger in some way. Like they had to love deeper just in case their time was short.

But he also noticed the other couple. Hank and his librarian looked like they were on their first date. Millie was shy and a bit nervous. Hank was protective.

Ben figured he and Jenny were somewhere in-between. No words had been said between them, but he was losing count on how many times they'd made love. He could say he'd known her since college, but in truth he didn't know her at all. They talked about the survey. They made love in silence, but he didn't know much about her childhood, her politics, her likes and dislikes.

That wasn't true. He knew her body. Every curve. He loved the soft way she felt. He loved the way they made love. He even loved the little sounds she made. He loved holding her until she fell asleep.

Feeling brave, Ben put his hand beneath the table and touched her knee. She touched his leg just above his knee and the game was on. While the others talked of the weather and the three towns in the valley, Ben was trying to slow his breathing as Jenny's hand moved higher up his leg.

Jenny was winning whatever game he'd started, and Ben hoped he made it through dessert without moaning with pleasure.

Chapter 28

Benjamin

Ben meant to have a talk with Jenny when they got to her cabin. They were both over forty and did not need to be doing what they'd been doing under the table. What if they'd been noticed? Maybe he should start a list of things not to do in public places. No, he decided. That would just give her ideas.

What next, sex in the restroom? They were not two teenagers going wild. She seemed to take any rule as a challenge.

As they walked through the darkness, she held his hand. It was official. They were a couple. He liked the thought. Things would settle into a routine. They'd have nights they'd meet for dinner, maybe get away for a weekend between semesters. Maybe they'd take turns staying at each other's places when they didn't have classes the next morning. Maybe she'd come out with him to the farm and spend the night . . . in separate rooms, of course. If his dad didn't mind, and she liked the country, he'd fix up the spare bedroom for her, assuming his mother wasn't sleeping in it.

But when they stepped in her cabin, he didn't have time to start a lecture.

She unbuttoned the top few buttons of her blouse, and her breasts seemed to pop out like bread dough from a can. Ben swore a few thousand brain cells died and he reverted to a primitive man who only wanted his woman.

"You are staying tonight?" she asked.

"I am. It's probably safer," he answered. "After all, my place, or at least the stairs to my place, is now a crime scene."

She opened another button and Ben lost all ability to speak.

Suddenly, she was pulling him to her bedroom as they both tried to take off their clothes first. They were laughing and kissing, and Ben's last thought before passion took over his brain was that he didn't have to worry about blowing up in a bombing. He'd die of a heart attack from having too much sex. Her body was some kind of drug that he couldn't get enough of.

And he didn't care.

Long after midnight she got up to go to the bathroom and came back wearing just her shawl.

Ben smiled. Yep, he was going to die right here in her bed. An hour later he reminded her that people didn't have sex twice a night. Without a word she talked him into doing it anyway.

After number three they finally settled into sleep. Tomorrow he'd remind her that beds were for sleeping.

Well, maybe. Maybe not.

Chapter 29

Ketch

Friday

Dawn beyond Ketch's wall of windows was just beginning to break into sunshine after two days of clouds. He scrubbed his dirty sand-colored hair and stood up from his big desk. His long legs, trapped under the table, seemed to still be asleep, so Ketch staggered like Frankenstein learning to walk.

Between surveying the town looking for pipe bombs, going to classes, and conducting research for the two professors, he felt like he'd given up sleep completely. But after feeling the imprint of a pen on his forehead, he knew he must have dozed off at his desk for the third night in a row.

Climbing over a pile of dirty clothes, he finally made it to the shower. A hot quick shower and breakfast would wake him up. As warm water ran over him, Ketch smiled. He was human again. Though he hadn't seen Tuesday all week, they'd talked every day. She was working in her garden and trying to turn the upstairs into her space.

He'd told her about the continuing progress on the

survey. The professors were hopefully finishing it up this week. He'd also told her how nothing had happened with the bomb squad. Ranger Colby had to go to Austin and wasn't sure he could make it back for the weekend. The sheriff's theory was that the bomber was a kid and it was pure luck he'd made one bomb that actually went off.

Everyone in town was on the lookout for a pipe bomb. Well, every person but one. The bomber.

No one had heard from Hank. Word was that he took care of the librarian all day and walked the streets and the river's edge at night, looking for clues. No fingerprints had shown up near any bomb site except for Bull Wills's prints all over the hospital crime scene.

Ketch shut off the water, wrapped a towel around his waist, and called Tuesday, even though it was early. If he woke her up, it would be fun to hear her complain.

"Morning, old man." She sounded wide-awake.

"Morning, kid. It's Friday, any chance we could have a date?"

"A date? What's that?"

"Pizza and beer. Maybe talking face-to-face, if you don't have to work."

She laughed. "I quit the bar. I was only part-time anyway. One of the other girls needed more hours. And, thanks to you pushing me, I've decided to make this place mine."

"Oh, I almost forgot to tell you. I mailed a few of Eva's ink sketches off to an address I found taped to her desk. The name on the card was a man who died twenty years ago, but his son still owns the small gallery. He said they might be worth something."

Tuesday hesitated, then whispered like her words were a secret. "I also enrolled in the first summer semester,

Ketch. I'm going after that nursing degree." She laughed.
"I figured with you as a friend I might need it."

"Thanks for thinking of me. That's great." He'd be finishing up and she'd be starting. "I'm glad."

"Me too. Thanks to you, I see that it's time I start making a life and not just hiding from one."

"Thanks for what? I didn't do anything."

"You saw me, Ketch. No one has done that in a long, long time. It's my life; I better step into it. This house is my house, not Eva's anymore. You'll never know how much you did for me."

"It sounds like you're saying goodbye." He fought to keep his voice calm.

She was silent for a moment. "I don't want to hold you back. You are graduating. But don't worry, we'll keep in touch."

Just friends, Ketch reminded himself. *Keep it light and easy.* "How about we talk more about this tonight on our date?"

"Sounds good. I'll be ready when you come by."

"Seven?"

"Seven." She hung up without saying goodbye.

Now and then Ketch almost felt he had a memory of being adrift on the sea. Maybe it was a core memory of the day he was born. He could almost see two young people birthing him on a sailboat and then drifting up to civilization in the dark a week later and leaving him on the dock.

They'd written *His name is Ketch Kincaid. Tell him his parents loved him but we weren't born with roots.*

When he'd been a kid he'd dreamed up all kinds of adventures they were having. Reasons why they couldn't come back for him. They were fighting in a civil war in Africa. They were saving children from harm in the Mediterranean. They were searching for gold off the coast of Finland.

By the time he was in his teens he decided they must be dead. Why else would they not come back for him?

Ketch dressed and pushed his feelings aside. He had one class he had to attend, then he planned to drop by Dr. Monroe's office to make sure the survey was being mailed. Maybe he'd work in the Randall brothers' office until it was time for his date.

The theme song of his life played in the back of his head as he walked to class. "Alone Again." Maybe if he played it cool with Tuesday they would remain friends.

After all his dreams and plans, all he wanted to do was stay here in Clifton Bend. This was the one place he'd ever lived where he felt almost at home.

As he walked onto the campus, a weasel-size of a man stepped up beside him. "Hi, Ketch."

"Hello, Wynn." Ketch hadn't talked to WW much since he'd seen him at the pizza place. But he figured the guy didn't hold a grudge over them leaving him, or he'd have no one on campus to talk to.

"I hear you're helping the sheriff to find out who is making those bombs."

"I helped one day. I think it may have settled down. None found for forty-eight hours."

"Good." Wynn's head bobbed as they walked. "I hope so. I really do. Someone could have gotten killed. My big brother says he's afraid to go to work at the hospital since it is the only location that was actually bombed. He claims he's working in the danger zone."

Ketch didn't say what he was thinking—that Bull was more than likely the bomber than the victim. After all, Bull was family to Wynn and family is family, even if they are crazy.

Ketch just kept walking and Wynn, for some reason, was almost running to keep up.

"I was thinking, Ketch, with us being friends and all, you might put in a word for my brother to be on the bomb squad with you guys. After all, he's trained to be a guard."

Ketch thought about screaming "Hell, no," but then decided against it.

Wynn took Ketch's silence as a good sign. "It would make Bull feel good. He's not a bad guy, he just hasn't found his place in the world."

"You don't think being a guard at the hospital is it?"

"Nope." Wynn thought for a moment and whispered, "Look, he might be a great help, he knows most of the druggies and nuts in the valley. He might be able to work undercover."

Ketch thought this was the dumbest idea he'd ever heard of, but Wynn could start a lot of trouble for everyone if Ketch made the little guy mad. He liked spreading rumors. He might not be able to hurt Ketch, but he could cause trouble for Tuesday.

The sheriff would never go for this idea of Wynn's; neither would anyone else on the team. Professor Monroe had mentioned that he'd almost gotten fired the first year he taught because he'd banned Bull from the chemistry lab. The family supported the college.

And Hank had said that Bull tried to fight him every chance he got because he thought Hank took his place on the high school football team.

Half the folks in town had crossed Bull's path. He'd caused so much trouble in the bar one night that there was a raffle going on for who got to kill him first.

It crossed Ketch's mind that letting Bull guard a place might be a way to keep Bull away from the bomb squad. He'd suggest it to the team.

"How's Tuesday doing?" Wynn tightened the game. "She

looked nice the other night. Maybe the rumors about her aren't all true."

Ketch nodded as they slowed in front of the science building. In the shadows, Ketch whispered, "You know, WW, you're right. There may be a place for Bull. Tell him to lay low. Keep an eye on folks going in and out of the hospital. I'll be in touch soon with details."

Wynn started hopping around. "I'll do that. I knew Bull would be an asset. I'll suggest he keep a log. Time, date, reason for walking through the hospital doors. The hospital is probably the center of this fight and Bull doesn't even know it."

"Make sure he stays off drugs and sober. When we move, we'll move fast, and he'll need to be ready. Don't try to contact any of us. We'll contact him. He'll be our secret agent working undercover. The fewer people who know he's working with us, the better."

Wynn slapped Ketch on the back. "Smart. I got to skip class and go tell Bull."

"Remember. Tell him to keep his eyes open and be ready to help when the time comes. And make him swear he will not do anything until I call. I'm his shadow contact." Ketch had no idea what that meant, but it sounded official.

Wynn hurried away.

That night as Ketch and Tuesday ate their veggie pizza, Wynn stopped by to say hello to Tuesday. The little guy was so nice, Tuesday was convinced his brain had been occupied by aliens.

They were still laughing when Ketch walked her to her steps. Tuesday thought he should buy Bull a hat to wear. After all, all spies have a fedora.

She made it two steps before she turned to kiss him good night. As he pulled her closer, the kiss deepened. Then she pulled away and touched his shoulders. "Good night." She smiled. "You do know I love you, Ketch."

Before he could react she was gone.

He stood, staring at the closed door.

She loved him? But her kiss had been just a friend kiss . . . hadn't it?

When the light went out downstairs he knew Tuesday was climbing the stairs. Without him.

Friend kiss, definitely.

Ketch walked to his truck with swear words bouncing around in his mind. Part of him wanted to rush in and make love to her, and part of him wasn't sure he could take the fall if he guessed wrong about loving again.

"Damn," he said as he started the truck. "I might as well buy the guard hat and stumble around the hospital foyer like I know what I'm doing." Life was no more real to him than it was to Bull.

Chapter 30

Hank

Saturday

In his craziest days Harrison Norton, the preacher's son, the champion bull rider, the roughneck, and a well-known bomb expert, never thought he'd be sitting in Clifton Bend, Texas, counting cars go by.

"Was that eight or nine, Rambo?"

The dog opened his eyes and looked up at Hank. He was obviously not interested in counting.

"You're right, Rambo. I'm cracking up." Hank picked up the dog in one arm and headed in to check on Millie. The order of supplies and gear he'd called in wouldn't get to town any sooner just because Hank was waiting.

He'd been in Clifton Bend for two weeks and still hadn't visited his dad. Millie didn't really need him anymore. She was getting around fine. No one had seen a bomb for three days, so that crisis had settled down as well.

So, what was he still doing here?

Hank told himself he was worried about the bomber, but he knew the real reason was simply that something wasn't finished between Millie and him. Maybe it was just saying goodbye, but he wasn't ready to say the words.

The kind lady had become his obsession somehow. Half of his brain seemed to have taken up worrying about her. He worried about how she was doing, if she was in pain, if she liked him. Part of him wanted her as a man wants a woman. Another part swore he'd break his own arm if he hurt her.

Hell, his actions were digressing all the way back to middle school while his thoughts were dreaming of midnight rodeo.

Getting to know her was a gift he didn't want to give back. He would have never met a woman like her without running over her. Good women like her don't speak to bad boys like him. They didn't hang out where he did.

When he walked back into her little house, Millie was reading in her favorite chair by the window. She smiled at him. They'd grown comfortable with one another. They liked talking and laughing, but the quiet times when they were just near one another were special too. He'd even kissed her a dozen times. They'd become friends, and Hank figured that was all they would ever be.

Car lights flashed across the window. Hank winked at her. "I knew they'd come as soon I came in."

"Your protective gear has finally arrived," she whispered, as if it were still a secret that he was a Houston specialist.

Hank walked out, not surprised the rangers had sent a highway patrolman to relay the box to him. Colby said they'd get it to him fast, but it seemed forever since he'd requested the equipment. Hank hoped he didn't have to use it, but if he needed the protection at least it would fit.

"Evening, Trooper. Thanks for driving this up."

"Captain Norton, it's an honor." The trooper looked tired, and Hank wondered if he had made the drive after his shift.

The lawman helped him lug the huge box into the house.

Hank tried to thank him again, but the man stopped him. "Before you thank me, you'd best pick up the other cargo, Captain."

"But I didn't order any . . ." Hank looked out and saw a little boy dragging a duffel bag out of the back seat of the cruiser. Eight years old and more trouble than a bar fight. Hank and the boy's dad had been best friends when Simon's father died in the line of duty.

"You do know him, Captain?" The trooper looked worried.

"Simon?" Hank said. "I signed on to be his guardian uncle two years ago. I didn't know how hard a job it'd be."

The trooper had the nerve to look sorry for Hank. "I watched a detective and two sergeants try to talk the kid out of coming to you, but the kid wouldn't budge. He told me he was at the station being passed from one of his uncles to another. He claimed you four were his almost uncles. When you called in and asked for your gear, the kid said if the gear goes, he goes."

Hank walked toward the chubby ball of trouble. "What do you think you are doing here, Simon? I said I'd be back. You shouldn't be here."

"Uncle Ray said it was your turn to watch over me, and Uncle Andy said he had to work overtime, and Uncle Dan claimed he had a hot date he couldn't miss." The kid took a few steps toward Hank and clobbered two sunflowers when his bag fell over. "Sorry, sorry," he mumbled to the broken flowers.

Then Simon faced Hank like he was on the last step of the gallows. "When I broke Uncle Ray's computer and accidentally dropped Andy's cell, they all three agreed to let me ride with your box."

The patrolman shook his head. "I texted his mom and she said it would be all right. Just get him back before she gets home next week."

Simon tried again. "I missed you, Uncle Hank."

"Sure you did," Hank answered. The kid had fought going with him every time he'd come by. "You are getting back in that car and heading back to Houston right now."

The patrolman interrupted. "I'm not going back, Captain. I was just in Houston dropping off a prisoner for questioning. I'm headed back to Midland."

Simon smiled, knowing he'd won, at least for tonight. "Well, Uncle Hank, it looks like it's your turn to babysit me. I'm starving." He pointed at the trooper. "This guy tried to feed me a little box of cereal he picked up at a breakfast bar somewhere and a carton of warm milk. He told me if I put them both in my mouth at the same time it would taste just like breakfast."

The trooper shrugged. "Bad idea, I know. He threw up in my back seat."

Hank gave up. None of this mess was the trooper's fault. "Thanks for driving him. If you hear from the three other guardian uncles, tell them I plan to kill them when I get back to Houston. I've got my hands full here."

"I'll help," Simon offered as he tried to pull his bag out of the flowerbed and managed to behead a few more sunflowers.

The trooper smiled for the first time. "Will do. Good night, Captain, and good luck."

As Hank picked up Simon's bag the kid frowned at the row of dead flowers. "I don't like them flowers, Uncle Hank. You ever get the feeling that they are looking at you? They turn their heads first one way, then the other."

"They are following the sun. That's why they're called sunflowers."

Simon frowned. "That is downright creepy if you ask me. You think they think about what they're doing?"

"I hadn't worried about that until now." Hank opened the door and waited for the kid to pass. "Come on in, Simon. We'll try to figure out what to do with you in the morning."

After Hank introduced Simon to Millie, she agreed he should stay the night. She talked to Simon, asking questions and smiling.

While the kid put on his Batman pajamas, Hank made him a sandwich. No milk, just a Sprite and two Oreos to go with it. "You all right about this, Millie?"

"I'm happy to have him. What a sweet little boy."

Hank wondered if she was losing her sight, and maybe hearing, too! The kid had killed half her sunflowers, tracked mud in, and asked if Rambo was contagious.

Ten minutes later, the boy was sitting cross-legged at the end table and eating without spilling anything for a change.

"You going to be all right with him, Millie, for a while? I need to call a few guys and issue death threats."

She smiled. "We'll be fine."

As he called from the kitchen, Hank heard Simon ask Millie what happened to her leg. When she told him that Hank ran over her, the kid moved closer to her and gave her a hug, and then said that Hank had tried to kill him several times. Once when they played football, once when he tried to teach him to row a boat, and another time when Hank threatened to throw him down the bowling lane if he didn't hit at least one pin. Simon whispered, "I'll watch out for you, miss."

"And I'll watch out for you, Simon." She glanced in Hank's direction. "We'll both be safer if we stick together."

By the time Hank finished trying every number for the *flown-the-coop angels*, Simon had fallen asleep beneath her protective arm.

Hank kneeled beside her chair. "I'll find someplace to take him."

"No," she said softly. "This little guy belongs with you. He needed you, Hank, or he wouldn't have fought so hard to get here. He told me his mother had to take this assignment or lose her job. He's worried about her, but he says you're the only one who always tells him the truth. If you say she'll be back, she will."

Hank put his hand over Simon's head. "I'm the one who had to tell him his dad was dead. He was only six then, but he knew all the other things people were saying weren't true." Hank looked up at Millie without bothering to hide a tear threatening to fall. "I didn't know what else to say. I just held him until he cried himself to sleep."

Millie smiled. "You are his rock."

"But I can't take care of him right now. I have the bomb threat and you to watch over."

"No, you can't handle him right now, but we can. We have no choice. He's too little to put on a bus alone, and you can't pass him off to strangers. All he's got is a mother and she's out of the country. It's time you step up to your guardian angel reputation. If a time comes that you can't keep him with you, then ask him to take care of me. I'll keep him safe."

An hour later Hank had made Simon a bed on the small couch, but the boy woke when Hank lifted him from Millie's side.

Millie offered to read to him until the boy fell asleep so Hank could finally go visit his dad. "It's time I made it over there," Hank said. "In fact, time is running out. I don't know what tomorrow will be like, but I need to make it to the nursing home before lights out."

She stared at him for a moment, then said softly, "You're leaving town soon, aren't you?"

It wasn't a question. They'd talked about it a few times and both knew their days together were counting down.

"I thought I'd rent a truck to carry the bike and this box back home. If all goes well, and there are no more bombs turning up, Simon and I will leave Monday. My bike's fixed and I've got to get Simon back. You're on the mend, and with Simon here it complicates everything. I'll make sure the kid enjoys our road trip."

Her smile didn't reach her beautiful blue eyes. "Of course I want you to stay. You've been a true friend, but I know it's time."

"I'll call to check on you, Millie. I promise I'll stop by to see you every time I'm in town." He lowered Rambo to her lap. "I'll be back soon. If I hurry, I'll catch my father before he goes to bed."

She nodded but looked away. "When you get back from seeing your dad, I'd like to talk to you for a minute."

"Sure." He leaned down and kissed her cheek. For some reason they'd started kissing each other like old friends, never lovers.

He almost ran from the house. Now it was time to leave, he wanted to hurry, not drag it out. He hated goodbyes. Most of the time he left a woman it was before dawn, while she was still asleep.

The only thing that slowed him now was the fact he was headed toward his father. He never remembered just talking to his father. It was always listening to a lecture, or worse, a sermon.

Maybe that was what he'd been doing to Simon. Telling him what to do, not just talking. He probably drove the kid crazy. So why had he fought to get to him?

When they headed home, Hank decided he'd let Simon pick where they stopped and what they ate. They'd talk about what Simon liked. No more lectures.

A few minutes later when Hank walked into what everyone in town called "the home," a sleepy desk clerk waved him through. It was after eight and most of the "guests" were in their rooms. Supper was over. The guests, as the staff called all patients, would watch an hour of TV before they drifted off to sleep. Hank had seen the routine before. A rounds nurse would take off the residents' glasses, tuck them in, and turn down the lights at nine.

He wasn't surprised to see his father already in bed, but no TV. His father always read his Bible before sleep.

"Hello, Dad." Hank stood at the door as if waiting for permission to step in.

The old man smiled. "The prodigal son returns."

"I've been in town for a few weeks helping out a friend who was hurt. Sorry it took me so long to come by."

"I don't mind. I've heard of your good deeds. Helping a woman who was hurt. Fixed up her house, I heard. And got my old car running. Thanks for that. The Andrew sisters told me you were solving crimes. Someone said you even helped a Texas Ranger out."

Hank moved closer. His father looked frail, but his eyes were as sharp as ever. "Dad, I'm a cop now. Have been for years. Some folks around here don't believe it, but that's what I do for a living."

"I know all about you, son. I've got an old friend in Houston. He sends me the newspapers when you're in it. I figured you didn't want me to worry and you'd tell me in due time. There are many ways to serve, son."

Hank took his father's wrinkled hand. Part of him wanted to tell the old man all about his life. He thought of confessing everything he'd done wrong or any time he'd walked away when he could have helped someone. But Hank wasn't sure his dad could take the whole truth.

His dad patted Hank's hand. "I used to wonder why God

gave me such an adventurer, a fighter, a risk taker for a son. Finally, I figured it out. I needed to build a base for you to come back to. Maybe you'll never need it, but if you do, it'll be there."

Hank pulled up a chair and for the first time in his life he just talked to his father. There were no lectures. No sermons. Just talk.

His dad admitted he'd made a mistake by not letting Hank talk about his mother. "I thought I was doing the right thing, but I've heard every time you leave town you stop by your mother's grave. I'm thinking she's looking down and smiling."

"I do," Hank answered.

The old preacher pushed a tear away with a twisted hand. "Next time you come, boy, I'd like to go out with you."

"You sure?"

"I'm sure."

An hour later when his father dozed off, Hank smiled. His father might never understand him, but he accepted him.

When Hank got back to Millie's house, she was sleeping in her chair with Rambo on guard. Hank silently slipped inside. Simon was on the couch, rolled up like a burrito in one of Millie's fuzzy blankets.

He gently lifted her up and carried her to bed. As he covered her, she whispered, "I need to ask you something."

"All right, ask away." He kissed her forehead as he sat beside her.

"Will you sleep with me these last few nights? Would you hold me all night long? I think I can make it through the winter of my life if I have this one memory."

Hank stood and pulled off his shoes and socks and his sweater. Then, with only his jeans on, he slid beneath the covers. She asked so little of him and he wished he could give her more.

She turned to face him and smiled. When he raised his arm she slid closer, the cast on her leg between them and the sling resting atop her left side.

An hour later he didn't think she was asleep and he was still very much awake. Her strange request had simply seemed a favor. An answer to where he would sleep since Simon had the couch, but he'd thought about how much courage it must have taken for her to ask.

But now, after being so close for an hour, he thought again about why she'd asked.

Hank took a deep breath. He loved the way Millie always smelled. Of flowers and linen sheets and woman. He also liked being so close he could feel the warmth of her against him.

In the stillness, he whispered his thought: "You asleep?"

"No," she answered just as softly. "I don't want to miss a moment."

"Would you mind if I kissed you? I'll be careful not to bump your leg or arm." When she didn't move, he rolled to his side and brushed her lips with his. The kiss had meant to be tender, but it deepened as if they were both needing more.

As his fingers moved over her, Hank knew he was handling fine china. One touch too many or too hard and she'd shatter into pain. Somehow the danger made it all that more priceless.

He moved his hand along her unharmed side, feeling the long, slim line of her body. Finally he was feeling the beauty of her, not just seeing. He could have offered passion with his touch, but he turned it to cherishing.

When she began to touch him, she was hesitant and shy, but in the midnight shadows she grew bolder. Her hand moved over him, learning his body and slowly driving him mad with the knowledge that what they were starting could not be completed.

Finally her hand spread out over his heart and rested there as she drifted to sleep.

"Millie," he whispered her name as he moved into sleep. "Millie, my love."

Sunday

Chapter 31

Ben

Benjamin got up early, as was his habit. He thought of touching Jenny before he left the warm covers, but he didn't want to wake her. He liked watching her sleep.

She wasn't young or beautiful in a classic kind of way, but she was precious to him. If they lived another forty years and slept together until they died, he'd always see the girl in her. Life doesn't give many second chances, but Ben had found his. Everything he thought she did wrong didn't matter. In an odd way Jenny was perfect just as she was. He couldn't love her less and, he realized, he couldn't love her more. She had all the love he had to give.

Closing his hand, he wished he could remember the feel of her a moment longer than his heart would beat. He wanted her soft skin to be the last thing he remembered in this life.

Ben slipped from the bed and pulled on his slacks as he walked to her tiny kitchen. Rummaging through her cabinets he found coffee and made a pot. Part of him felt like he was invading her space, but he guessed since he'd kissed pretty much everywhere on her body, she wouldn't mind him opening drawers.

While he waited on the coffee he pulled on his shirt and picked up a legal pad on her desk.

With coffee and paper in hand he moved beside the bed. For a moment he just watched her hugging her pillow as if it were a lifeline keeping her afloat in dreams. Her dark ginger hair covered half her face. He had to fight to not straighten it back behind her ear. It had been lighter twenty years ago, but he liked it just the way it was now.

Forcing himself not to touch her, he began to make his list. He was on the third page of the legal tablet when he looked up and saw her watching him with those big blue eyes full of laughter.

Pulling the sheet over her chest, she used her cuddle pillow to prop her head up. "You making a list, Benjamin?"

"I am." He smiled at her.

"Of what I did wrong in public last night?"

"No, dear. I rather enjoyed what you did, but of course we should never do it again."

"Of course." Jenny winked.

She moved her head from side to side with hair sticking up in every direction. "Let me guess, you're organizing my day."

"No, dear." Ben tried not to notice that the sheet had slipped down away from one breast.

She laughed. "Don't tell me you're writing why you are attracted to me."

"No." He smiled as her other breast peeked out from the covers. "I'm writing all the reasons why we should move in together."

"Your place is too small for two, Benjamin. My stuff would never blend into your organized world. And this cabin is too small for me; I'd never get you in here."

"I agree," he said, looking at his list. "But there are advantages for us cohabiting. We would save time traveling and save gas by carpooling to work. We could take turns cooking. It would save money on living expenses if we lived together."

She folded her arms over her bare body and shook her head. "I'm not that interested in saving time or expenses or shortening the commute. We're both set in our ways. Benjamin, are you trying to convince me, or yourself? If we lived together, I'd have to put up with you not only at school but also at home. I can barely tolerate your habits at the office."

"What about in bed? Do you tolerate me there?"

She grinned. "That's definitely a plus. For such a flawed man you do make a perfect lover. Though, you could use a bit more practice." She pushed the covers away. "I'm willing to help you polish your skills."

He dropped the tablet and pen and climbed on top of her, his arms bracing her face. "Don't move, dear. I have to finish my thought before we begin. I want to wake up with you every morning. I don't want to have to get dressed and go home the next morning."

Of course, she wiggled.

He was so close she touched her nose to his. "I wouldn't mind sleeping with you every night, but we don't have to move in together for that. Tell me how you feel about me, Benjamin, because we are *not* moving in together to save time."

He kissed her. "You drive me crazy. You're not organized. You don't seem to own a watch. You don't have boundaries. You treat my body as your own personal play toy, even when we're in public. You drive me crazy."

"You already said that."

Ben kissed her again. "See. That proves my point. I'm

insane about you and because of you." He kissed her deeper. When he finally broke the kiss it took him a moment to remember what they'd been talking about. "I'm sure I have a few traits that bother you." He couldn't think of any but he needed to be fair. "How do you feel about me, dear?"

He moved his lips to her throat so he could nibble while she answered.

"Sure." She laughed. "I'd probably need three, maybe four tablets to get them all written down, but Ben, you have one thing you do that is perfect."

"What?"

"I love the way you make love to me." She wrapped her arms around him and they stopped talking for a while.

When their breathing finally slowed, he whispered, "Move in with me, sleep with me, marry me for one reason."

"What's that?" she asked, almost asleep.

"Because I don't want to live without you in my life."

Patting his jaw, she whispered, "You think you could say you love me a few more times before you start changing our lives, Ben?"

He rolled off her and onto his back. "Decisions should be backed with logic, not feeling. We fit together. We share careers and interests in common."

"No. Love is a feeling. It is not logical. None of your reasons of saving time and money can be measured in feelings."

Ben closed his eyes. He could feel her pulling away. A memory buried deep in his thoughts floated up. They'd had this same conversation at the lake all those years ago. He wanted to think logically, and Jenny wanted to talk about feelings. She hadn't just disappeared. She'd walked away from him that morning. She'd left because of what he hadn't said.

He remembered swearing that morning that he'd never let emotion rule his actions. He'd seen his father break because of them.

Ben was barely aware of Jenny moving out of bed. He knew she'd only gone into the bathroom, but he felt her loss as if she were an ocean away. The knowledge that he'd pushed her away all those years ago hit him like a blow.

He felt her loss even though she was almost within his reach.

Chapter 32

Ketch

The whole world seemed to be resting in still, silent air as Ketch stretched his long, lean muscles at the bottom of his loft stairs. He needed to run to clear his head and think.

His part in the professors' project was finished, and he felt most of his studies were winding down. He could almost feel his life shifting again, changing, morphing into another foreign land he'd have to cross. Before long he'd be moving, and he didn't even need to pack. Starting over. Rebuilding his life, remaking himself.

Sometimes he felt like he was an astronaut flying from one planet to another, having to adjust to the climate as he learned the terrain and the language. In a month he'd have to learn to breathe in different air.

Without much thought, Ketch turned to the river for his run. Like a wild animal he needed to turn away from civilization to inhale deeply.

Near town a walking path followed along the water's edge, but a mile downstream the bank turned rugged and unpredictable. He liked that part of the run best. Going over uneven ground, weaving in between trees and climbing up embankments.

As he pounded out a few miles he could feel his mind clearing. His body was strong and powerful, like it had been in the army when he could run for miles. Then he'd had to be on full alert. Ready for anything. Always prepared to fight. Thinking fast. In survival mode. For a while he wanted to feel that way again.

Today the run was easy. The fight was in his mind as he tackled one problem. The bomber. Nothing but a few sliding doors had been damaged, but Ketch felt that something more was coming. The sheriff seemed to think the threat, if there really was one, had passed. But Ketch could sense the shadow of trouble still hanging around, waiting.

Another mile and the problem still played out in his mind like a puzzle with random pieces floating before him. The locations. The lack of skill. Even the mud that Dr. Monroe pointed out on the steps was somehow a clue.

Figuring out the puzzle was like building a house. Get the foundation solid first. What did he know for sure? The placement of the bombs must mean something. Then the amateur errors seemed more planned than accidental. The bomber seemed to be getting better, then worse. He was sloppy and reckless one moment and the next skilled enough to blow up the entrance to the hospital.

At first he thought the bomber was learning, experimenting, but the skill wasn't growing in what Ketch thought would be a predictable line.

Alone, two miles from town, pieces of the puzzle began to fit together. Somehow the people in the town, the students, maybe even the lawmen, were involved.

One fact slowly formed. One explanation. There had to be more than one person building bombs. Two or maybe three. That would make it easier to buy supplies without arousing suspicion. Easier to move around town without too many people noticing.

The first bombs, mostly in abandoned mailboxes, were practice shots. Random targets. But what if one of the bombers had figured out how to make the bomb explode? Then they'd left the bomb at the hospital because it would attract the most attention. One member of the team had learned how to build a bomb that worked while his partners in crime were still trying. Only others were still leaving their efforts around for others to find.

That might explain why, after the hospital bomb, the next bomb didn't work. The one left on the professor's steps had been made by another bomber.

Ketch turned around and began to walk toward home.

Another factor: Why? No one on the squad could think of anyone who hated Clifton Bend enough to destroy it. But a group? Even a gang of three or four could push each other along. That's why gangs damage property that none of the members would have gone after alone. From lynch mobs to rioters, one brain forms.

The only thing they needed to have in common was that they hated something about the town or the people. Maybe they saw themselves as making a point. Somehow making the world a better place by blowing up something made sense to them.

If there were two or three bombers, they'd have to meet somewhere to plan. Then they'd probably touch base with one another. Make bombs in one place.

Ketch would bet the gang would meet somewhere public to plan, and somewhere very private to work.

A coffee shop. A café. A bar would be a good place to meet.

With spring break, most of the crowds were gone from the coffee shops bordering the campus. Cafés were mostly families, so they wouldn't go there to talk. That left two places. The town's only bar and the pizza place.

Ketch took off running. There were only two people that Ketch could think of who hung out at both places and stayed in town during the spring break. Wynn Wills and his brother, Bull. If there were others who might be willing to play with trouble, he'd bet the Wills boys would know them.

The question was, were the Wills brothers the bombers or were they their intelligence source? Both brothers had ways of learning what was happening in town.

Ketch almost tripped at the thought that WW and his brother might be the help he needed to solve the case.

As he stormed the stairs to his loft, he started planning. First, he'd get Tuesday to talk to the other barmaids and the bartenders who worked during spring break. Maybe one of them had seen a small group of men with their heads together planning, and Ketch would guess they'd also been together the night of the hospital bombing, probably celebrating that one bomb finally worked.

Crazy as it seemed he was about to put Bull to work solving the crimes, even if he was one of the criminals.

By tonight he'd get the bomb squad, minus Bull, together and go hunting. Hank had said that the reason all was quiet the past few days might be because the bombers were planning something big.

Ketch ran the facts one more time. One lone bomber, not likely. Three or more made sense. These guys were not smart, but they were locals. They knew the town.

Monday morning the college would be wide-open. There was even a ceremony planned to congratulate the college for winning an award. People, even the press, would be everywhere. A few working bombs on campus could cause chaos.

Chapter 33

Hank

Hank was busy burning breakfast when Simon woke up.

The kid crawled out from under his covers and looked in Hank's direction. "You can cook?"

"Nope, but I try. I do great on toast and fruit, but I can't seem to make the eggs look right. But don't worry, I've figured out if you put ketchup on them they're edible."

Simon yawned a yawn that seemed to take his whole body to complete as he walked to the kitchen. He climbed up on one of the stools and stared at Hank. "Mom says I got to learn to cook because it's a fifty-fifty chance my wife won't know how. I think it might just be easier to find a woman who likes fast food. No cooking. No dishes."

Hank grinned. "You thought about this, haven't you?"

The little boy looked exhausted from the effort. "We can turn our kitchen into an aquarium if we never cook anything. The shelves could hold cages for all the bugs and spiders I find. I thought about having birds, too, but they'd probably eat the bugs and spiders." He looked at Rambo. "I know what I don't want. I don't want him. That dog woke me up twice last night licking my face. It's too little to be a dog, too hairy to be a mouse, and too noisy to be a fish."

Simon picked up Rambo and put him on the bar.

Rambo walked to the edge, looked down, and must have reasoned it was too far a fall, so he started barking.

The kid poked him. "Is this a dog or a big nosy bug? It looks like a wind-up toy."

Hank lifted Rambo off the counter and stuffed him in the pouch of his sweatshirt. If the kid kept talking he'd hurt Rambo's feelings.

The dog popped his head out the other end of the pouch. He gave Hank a look that seemed to ask, "Why didn't you leave the kid outside?"

Hank went back to cooking. He could hear Millie moving around in the bedroom, but she hadn't called for him. He thought it might be good to give her a bit of privacy since he'd spent most of the night cuddling with her.

He grinned. What they'd done was only slightly over the line of innocent, but it was like getting drunk on sweet wine. Every kiss, every brush, every taste felt so good.

As he poured her a half cup of coffee, she rolled into the room. Her hair was combed and her housecoat buttoned to her neck, but the woman he knew by touch was still there. He saw laughter in her eyes and satisfaction in her smile. She had a quiet kind of beauty that settled against his heart.

All he'd done last night was kiss her tenderly and touch her, but he'd given her what she'd asked for. What she'd wanted. In an odd way he felt he'd never so completely satisfied a woman.

"Morning," he said as he knelt down to her level. "Did you sleep all right?"

She blushed. "I did."

When she turned her attention to Simon, Hank answered his cell. "Captain Norton," Hank said when he noticed the area code.

"Look, Captain." Simon's uncle Andy's voice came through loud and clear. "We didn't have a choice."

"About what?" Hank grinned, realizing the sergeant must have drawn the short straw and had to be the one to call. "Thanks for sending Simon. It'll be nice to have him here."

"You're not mad."

"Nope. I'll bring him back in a few days."

If Simon hadn't taken his place on the couch last night, he wouldn't have been in Millie's bed.

"All worked out well. Simon is going to help me take care of the lady I ran over, then we're going to take our time driving back. See you guys soon if another bomb doesn't go off."

Andy was yelling, "Wait! What woman? What bomb?"

Hank hung up and turned to Simon. "Would you mind putting the plates on the table so Millie and you can eat breakfast? Remember, you're the waiter, so make sure she has a drink and a napkin. I'm going to take a shower."

Simon jumped off the stool. "I'll take care of it, Captain."

"Thanks."

He watched Simon carefully pour the juice as Hank leaned over and kissed Millie before he disappeared for a shower. When he returned ten minutes later, Millie and Simon were laughing at names they'd thought of for the eggs he'd cooked.

While Simon took his shower, Hank helped Millie dress. For once she wasn't so shy and he saw a hint of the perfection that he'd touched last night.

"Do you have to go in today?" he whispered as he buttoned her dress.

"I'll only be a few hours. Simon can pick out some books and you can go to the store. We'll need food a kid would eat."

"He eats pretty much the same things I eat. Cereal, cookies and sandwiches."

"I'm not surprised but toss in fruits, vegetables, and milk. When you pick us up, I thought we might eat lunch out."

"I'd like that." Hank didn't add that it would be a nice thing to do on their last day together.

As he heard the shower go off, Hank brushed his lips against her ear and whispered, "Did you like last night?"

"I did."

"Mind if we do it again tonight? I'll be careful."

She pressed her face against his chest and didn't answer. He'd embarrassed her, talking of night things in the light. But the way she held him tight and smiled told him all he wanted to know.

He wished he could stay around until she healed and he'd teach her about loving. Although Hank felt like he was the one learning, not her.

Half an hour later, Simon was in heaven when he discovered Millie's library had a whole bookshelf of biographies on famous people. He'd read most of the children's books on presidents, but this library had several mid-grade books on scientists. He'd been reading since he was five. He was ready for something with chapters and less pictures.

After he'd asked Hank, "Did you read this one?" for the third time, the kid took his questions to Millie. She seemed to have read them all.

She pulled a book about Horace Mann from the shelf. "Monday the governor of Texas will be on campus giving an award named after this man. Horace Mann lived a long time ago. He's known as the 'father of American public education.' When he was your age, he only got to go to school three months a year."

Simon laughed. "Sounds lucky to me, but I'll read the book."

Hank didn't comment, but he guessed he'd probably learn something every day if he hung around Millie.

As they settled into Millie's office, Hank waved a silent goodbye. He checked to make sure the library was locked, then headed to the Lincoln to buy enough groceries for Millie to last a month. She'd be walking with only a boot by then. Maybe he'd drive up and help her out for a weekend or two.

As he glanced toward the street, he wasn't surprised to see the sheriff leaning against his father's old car. LeRoy looked bothered on a good day and something told Hank that this wasn't a good day.

When Hank was within three feet of LeRoy, Rambo pushed his head out of Hank's pouch and barked at the lawman.

"What is that?" The sheriff swore.

"It's a service dog. I'm training him to be a bomb sniffer."

"A fire cracker would blow him away. Toss the pup. I've got something I want to show you."

Hank wasn't stationed under the sheriff so he ignored the command. "You'll have me back in an hour?"

"I promise."

"And you'll buy me a cup of coffee? I had to make my own this morning and it was terrible. I think Millie must wash the pot."

LeRoy sneered. "My first wife used to do that. Drove me to start drinking hot Dr Peppers for breakfast. I swear it was better than her coffee."

"You've had a hard life, Sheriff."

As LeRoy started the cruiser, he tossed Hank a stack of reports on the pipes sent to the lab, and the talking was over.

Hank had seen enough of these reports to skip the rambling and get down to the facts. Not one fingerprint found. Most were not bombs. Not all the parts were there. Whoever was making them was sloppy. The pipe was ordinary. Parts could have been bought from any hardware store.

"Nothing new," Hank said as he glanced at the last page.

LeRoy pulled through the Sonic and ordered two large coffees by screaming at the speaker.

"You remember that guy you had with you? Ketch was his name." LeRoy paused as if he'd delivered a complete thought.

"What about Ketch? He's a student of Dr. Monroe's and he's a former Army Ranger. Two tours in action."

LeRoy seemed to wake up. He spent a good ten seconds nodding his head, as if all was starting to fit together. "Well, Ketch called me this morning and wants to meet with all of us at Primrose Hill for supper. Says his girlfriend will cook while we'll plan. He claims that her house is the only place where we can disappear in the county without someone noticing."

"You have any idea where Primrose Hill is?" Hank asked.

"I've heard of it, but never had any need to go out there. Besides, you're a captain. You should be bright enough to find it. I'll give you a hint, it's probably on a hill.

When Hank just frowned at the sheriff, LeRoy added, "Ketch says to bring a plus-one. Whatever in hell that means. Ketch says he wants this to look like just a dinner party on the off chance someone sees us. Except for one thing: Come armed. We may do some reconnaissance after dark."

Hank nodded. "Since when are we not armed? You probably sleep armed."

"I did until I married. Just passing along what Ketch said."

LeRoy paid for the coffee and blocked the drive-through line while he added sugar to his cup. He cussed when he stirred his coffee and the line of cars behind him honked. "When in the hell did I start taking orders from a student in college? Damn, next thing I know, I'll be carrying around a fluff ball and calling it a dog."

Hank decided the old guy was growing on him. "I'll be there, but it'll be a plus-two for me."

"I'm not eating at the table with that dog."

"No. I'm bringing the librarian and a kid."

LeRoy didn't seem surprised. "You and the librarian are moving fast. You might want to talk your father into marrying the two of you if you've already got a kid."

"I'll do that." Hank laughed, figuring that LeRoy probably knew about the boy's arrival last night. The old guy might be slowing with arthritis, but he still knew what was happening in his county. "So, what are we doing out here this morning, Sheriff?"

"We are mapping the spots where all the bombs have been found. I've already made marks for the hospital, the library, and the professor's stairs."

Hank opened the map and marked off the house next to his dad's place.

LeRoy drove, and Hank marked locations as they drank their coffee. Then, as promised, the sheriff dropped him and his dog off at the library.

"See you tonight before dark. Ketch told me twice that if I didn't turn into the drive before the sun went down I might not be able to find the house."

When Hank told Millie about the meeting, she started worrying about what to bring. When he got back from buying groceries, they all went home for a nap, then Millie and Simon made gingersnaps and he checked his email.

Hank's mind was already leaving Clifton Bend and headed back to work.

He'd be fine in the days to come, he thought. He could forget about all the problems in his hometown and sink into Houston's crime.

But during the nights he had a feeling he'd be thinking about Millie and would wonder how she was doing. Of all the women he'd known, she was the only one he thought of as "his lady."

Chapter 34

Ketch

Tuesday shook her head. "I've never had company. Never." She stared at him as if he was asking the impossible. "I can't."

He bent and kissed her cheek. "It's not a party. It's a meeting, and we need to get together without anyone knowing." He circled her waist and raised her up. "You can do this, Tuesday. You can do whatever you want to do. Be whatever you want to be." He kissed her on the mouth. "You're my girlfriend and I believe in you." He kissed her again, a bit deeper. "Besides, I'll help."

"No, you will not. If I'm going to do this for you, I need to do it alone. You'll only be a distraction." She held his face in her hands. "I'll do it to help you, Ketch. Because we're friends, understand. I don't want to be your girlfriend. You plan the meeting in the study. I'll get the dinner ready and set the big table."

He lowered her to the floor and began laying out papers as if he was about to give a report. "Thanks for offering to help." He tried to keep his words calm, but the knowledge that she didn't want to be his girlfriend hurt a bit.

Not that he was surprised. Apparently no one wanted that

job. He should have gotten the hint when she didn't kiss him back.

She walked out of the room, talking to herself. "Cooking is the easy part. The hard part is talking to them."

"You've got a house that is a treasure. How about showing it off tonight?"

"Sure. I'll give them all a tour after dinner."

A half hour later Ketch had everything in order, even a map of the town pinned to one of the blank canvases that had probably hung on the wall since Frank died forty years ago.

When his cell sounded, Ketch was ready to go. "Where?" was all he said when he answered. "Then give me ten minutes."

Ketch passed through the kitchen. "I'll be back before anyone gets here. Do you need anything from town?"

She shook her head but didn't look at him.

On his way into town he couldn't stop thinking about Tuesday not wanting to be his girlfriend. He'd thought they were making progress, but obviously not. He was lost in the translation. The Rosetta stone might as well fall on his head.

By the time he arrived near campus, he'd forced his mind into what had to be done. He was about to talk to Bull and Wynn and ask them for help.

They'd made the first step easy. They'd picked the pizza place to meet. One, it had beer; and two, it was one of the two places that Ketch had thought might be the bombers' hangout.

The memory of a few weeks ago when Ketch had slammed Wynn's face to the table came back. Wynn had been drunk. Ketch began to put the pieces together from that night. Wynn and Bull had been with a couple of guys who fit the profile of the bomber. Drunks, dropouts, mad at the world. One wore dirty jeans, like he'd been kneeling in mud all day. Ketch had noticed that the drinking buddies seemed more Bull's friends than Wynn's.

Ketch walked into the pizza place with all his senses on full alert.

At three in the afternoon the crowd was small. One old couple was splitting a pizza, and half a dozen middle-schoolers were playing video games in the back.

Ketch stopped by the counter and ordered a large pizza.

Bull and his little brother were already at a corner table. Before Ketch could get settled in his seat, WW started talking. "I told Bull you said he was on the team to solve this problem we got in Clifton Bend. He knows the rules. We talk to no one but you."

"Thanks, Wynn. You did me a favor for recommending him." Ketch turned to Bull. "Another rule. You stay clean and sober? You keep your eyes open."

Bull straightened slightly. "I'm sober. I know this is important. I've always thought I should be in law enforcement. Do I get a badge? I should have already had one at the hospital, but they said they didn't have one."

Ketch swallowed down a scream. "No, you wouldn't wear a badge; you're undercover. That's the most dangerous job on the force. No one, besides your brother and me, is to know you're going deep."

Bull's head seemed to be loose. It just kept nodding.

When three beers arrived, Ketch said, "Drink up, boys. This is the last drink until we're on the other side of trouble."

Ketch didn't even make sense to himself, but the Wills boys were eating up the talk. "Swear on your life that not one thing we're about to discuss will go beyond this table. All our lives depend on it."

Now Wynn's head started nodding. He raised his hand. "I swear if I ever let one word out I'll eat a bullet."

"Me too," Bull said.

Ketch wasn't sure Bull understood what his brother was promising. He wouldn't have been surprised if Bull asked if he got ketchup with the bullet.

"Now first, boys, I'd like you to tell me if either of you have heard about anyone wanting to cause trouble here in Clifton Bend."

After twenty minutes of worthless stories of students wanting to beat up a teacher, or kill an admissions clerk, or fights over women, Ketch still had nothing.

Bull said he heard all about two women fighting over one man. It turned out the guy was lying to both of the girls, so they got together and decided to beat him up. Bull also said he heard a nurse say she was going to kill the neighbor who started his mower behind her house at dawn.

Ketch had to listen to several stories about spouses wanting to end their marriages fast. Wynn said the girl in his English class was plotting the death of her parents, but she planned to wait until they finished paying off her college bills.

Finally, Bull mentioned a couple of dropouts like him who were talking about causing such chaos that no one would want to send their kids to Clifton.

Ketch started to ask questions without appearing too interested. After a few minutes it was obvious that the dropouts were trying to recruit Bull.

"I told them I had to work nights at the hospital and couldn't make the meetings. When they found out that I was security for the hospital they wondered if I had a gun and could pick up drug samples." Bull looked sad. "After I said no, they stopped being friendly."

"They were using you, Bull," Wynn said.

"I know, but it was nice to listen to them talk. It was like I was a part of a big plan. Exciting. It was like I belonged to a club."

"Any idea where the clubhouse was?" Ketch asked as he began to mentally log into his brain everything Bull said.

He described a place past the tracks. Said they called it the "supply stash."

As the brothers ate the pizza, Ketch made mental notes of the descriptions of the men, the cars they drove, even the girlfriend of one, who Bull said looked meaner than any of the guys.

Bull rubbed his face. "I just smiled at her and she slapped me so hard on this side that my teeth are still loose."

"Was she pretty, Bull?"

"No, bulldog ugly and had a prison tattoo on her throat, but I'd still do her as long as she didn't slap me again."

Wynn slapped him for being an idiot. "Don't talk like that. We're talking official-like. Remember, we've been asked to do our duty. This is our town, brother, and no one messes with our town."

"I know." Bull started bobbing his head again.

Ketch knew he'd gotten all he could. He leaned in close. "All right, soldiers, here is the plan. Keep your eyes open. Wynn, as a favor to me, watch the campus for anything unusual and report to me if you see anything. A stranger that doesn't look like he belongs. Someone sneaking around."

"I'll cut all classes tomorrow and be on patrol."

Ketch turned to Bull. "You stay on guard at the hospital. That's a hot spot for trouble. We already know that."

"Right. Right," Bull answered.

"These friends of yours may have simply been talking, but we have to be prepared. This is dangerous, men. If you see anything that's not in place, call in. Don't do anything. Your life is on the line." Ketch was laying it on thick.

Wynn looked afraid, but his brother was full into playing the undercover agent.

"I'll even watch the nurses. A few are so homely they

might be in disguise." Bull leaned closer. "And I'll keep one eye on the groundskeepers. One came in the hospital and tracked mud all over the lobby. After the janitor cussed him out, the guy probably hates us all."

Ketch shook hands with the Wills brothers. He had no idea if he had even a hint of a suspect, but he did have a few places to check out.

On the way home the guy tracking in mud kept playing through his mind.

Ketch got back to Primrose Hill in time to help Tuesday do the dishes. By the time the professors arrived, all was clean and ready.

Professor Clark made a big deal of loving the house. She had a sunshine way of making everyone feel good, and Tuesday fell under her spell.

When Hank and the librarian arrived with a little boy in tow, everyone went out of their way to make the kid feel a part of the gang.

Pecos and the sheriff showed up without spouses. LeRoy explained that tonight was his wife's Bunco night, and she never missed. Pecos just said the baby was fussy and no one asked more.

When they sat down to dinner, everyone bragged so much about the meal and the presentation that Tuesday blushed.

They all seemed to be struggling not to talk about work, but when Ketch suggested the squad step into the study, all chairs scraped back. To Ketch's surprise, all but Simon moved toward the study.

Simon asked if he could play on Millie's phone while they talked.

She handed him her phone and smiled. "When I get back will you teach me?"

"I will, pretty lady," the little boy answered.

Chapter 35

Ketch

Ketch began with his theory that the bomber was not one man, but a gang, and they'd been practicing for a big event. With the governor coming to present the Horace Mann Award tomorrow, that might be the chance they were waiting for to make a big bang.

"If I'm right, the men involved were all kicked out of the college. I don't think they are trying to kill anyone, just make the college less attractive to anyone coming. They want to hurt the college, and what better way to get publicity than blow something up while the governor is near."

Hank agreed and wanted to check out the place Bull said was called the supply shack. If they could find their workshop, they'd find enough evidence to stop them from doing any more harm.

Ketch said he'd go with Hank. If the men were there, Hank would need backup.

Pecos and Benjamin decided to go to the top floor of the science building and stake out points where they could see the ground where a stage had been set up for the event in the morning.

To no one's surprise, Professor Clark said she was going

with Benjamin. Ketch liked the biology teacher. She might not be in shape exactly, but she was a fighter. All three knew the campus well.

Ketch's low tone was that of the soldier who'd led many missions. "We go in quietly tonight. And we go in armed. Meet back here in an hour." Like muscle-memory, Ketch knew what to do.

Everyone nodded in agreement and all checked their weapons except Benjamin. He simply took Professor Clark by her hand and asked if he could speak with her for a moment.

As the professors stepped onto the porch, Hank knelt in front of Millie's wheelchair. "You'll be safe here. Will you watch over Simon?"

Ketch noticed tears falling from her eyes. Evidently this whole thing frightened the librarian.

"I will," she whispered.

"I'll be fine." Hank played down any danger. "Don't worry, Millie. This is what I do for a living, and besides, I'll have Ketch with me."

She smiled. "Then I won't worry," she said as she straightened. "I plan to learn Simon's game while you're gone."

The sheriff rose from an old chair in the corner of the room. "I'm staying here, boys. I'm too old to run around after dark, chasing ghosts. If any of you get into trouble, dial 911 and they'll patch you through to me. I'll have a few highway patrolmen at the edge of town and anything else you need. I think I'll be your backup tonight. If any one of you don't make it back in one hour, I'll be on my way."

The others all nodded.

Chapter 36

Ben

Ben could barely make out Jenny's big blue eyes in the moonlight as it spread over the porch. "You can't go with me, dear one. You need to stay here. I'll be back, I promise. All I'm doing is mapping out where the speech will be."

"But you'll be in danger. I have to go with you." She put her fists on her waist as if puffing up to make herself fierce. "Benjamin, I know you. If someone stood in front of you with a gun pointed straight at your head, you'd be thinking about what the man planned to do. Would he really shoot me? Or was he just trying to make a point? You'd think about it. Should I run? Should I stay? I need to be there to tell you to duck."

He shook his head. "I'm not going to get shot." He almost smiled as he saw the fire in her eyes. The fire of the fighting Irish was in her blood as well as her hair.

"You don't understand, Benjamin. I can't lose you. I don't care if you don't believe in love—I do, and I flat out, no doubt in my mind, love you. I don't care if you don't love me. That doesn't stop me from loving." Both hands gripped his shirt. "I go where you go."

Benjamin frowned, knowing he'd gotten everything wrong

and it was time he straightened it out. "Don't you know, Jenny, that I love you too? I have since that first time we made love at the lake when we were in college. I love you with my brain and my heart and a few other body parts."

She laughed. "I'm glad you finally remembered, but now I know I really have to go with you. I cannot lose the man I love, the father of my baby."

"We're too old to have a baby, but we'll have a good life."

She puffed up again, ready to fight, only this time he was the opponent. "That's just it, we're not too old, apparently. I bought all four brands of pregnancy tests at the drugstore and they all said the same thing. I'm pregnant. Correction, we're pregnant. You're the only man I've been intimate with for years, so I have no doubt you're going to be a father."

"How did that happen?" he demanded, but he couldn't stop his smile.

"Benjamin, you really do have to take my biology class."

He sat down on the porch railing and breathed like the world was running out of air. "Making up a pregnancy won't work, Jenny. You have to stay and I have to go. I swear, I'll be back in an hour. We'll talk later."

For a moment he'd believed her. "You must know I'm not the least bit afraid of a bomb. But just thinking about the possibility of a child made me feel like a bomb went off in my chest. So stop pretending."

"Listen to me, Benjamin. We are having a baby in about eight months, whether you believe it or not."

He stared at her.

She held him up. "You know, Ben, I have a feeling this pregnancy is going to be lot harder on you than it is on me."

For a moment he pulled her close, realizing his world was in his arms.

"You be careful while I'm gone, dear."

Jenny smiled up at him. "All right, Benjamin, if it means

that much to you, I'll stay. I plan to eat another slice of pie and put my feet up. Maybe I'll consider writing a paper on the effects of pregnancy on the father over forty."

"Thank you, dear," he whispered against her neck as the other men came outside. "Stay off your feet, morning sickness can come any time of day. You might want to make a list of books I'll need to read. Breast-feeding. Choking hazards. Car seats, we can't forget that and . . ."

Pecos looked at the two professors and shook his head. "You got to be kidding. I'm surprised at you two."

Ben looked at the deputy. "I'm trying to analyze the possibility of me having a heart attack. I've had some rather surprising news. Stay ready in case we have to make a run to the hospital, Deputy."

"Come on with me, Doc." The twenty-one-year-old pulled him along. "I've had a kid for a year. I'm an expert."

Ben kissed Jenny on the cheek. "We will discuss this later, dear."

Ben climbed in the deputy's cruiser and they pulled away. Hank and Ketch followed in Ketch's pickup.

LeRoy stood on the porch like a general left behind.

Jenny watched as the man seemed to be aging in the moonlight. This time, maybe for the first time, he wasn't joining the fight. She felt like she needed to change the subject before the man crumbled. "I should have waited to tell Benjamin that I'm pregnant. This wasn't the right time."

Sheriff LeRoy glanced at her as if she'd just said she was a serial killer. "I don't know about that, Jenny. The professor seems like a man who'll need all nine months to figure it out. You want me to help you inside, little momma?"

"Oh please, LeRoy," she snapped as if she'd known the

sheriff for years. "Pregnancy is not an illness. Reproduction does not cannibalize the host's brain."

They both laughed as he offered his arm anyway. "As the father of four daughters who have given me eleven grand-children, I'm an expert on pregnancy, childbearing, and babies." He shrugged. "I had to threaten to arrest my Allie if she didn't stop talking about her sore boobs, and my Sadie ate her way into blimp size in nine months."

She linked her arm in his. "We'll forget about worrying about the bomber. Let's talk birthing." The sheriff had just said more to her right now than he'd said in a year.

LeRoy nodded. "I watched the birthing four times and listened to every detail of eleven more. I even had to drag my son-in-law out of the delivery room twice after he fainted. The nurse said no one had time to worry about him, so I took on the job."

Jenny patted his arm. "Tell me all about it, Sheriff. We've got an hour to wait."

Chapter 37

Hank

Hank and Ketch moved through the old abandoned train yard. Shacks and piles of forgotten track were scattered between rusting railroad cars and the river. At one time there had been a small depot and a train that stopped every day, but as roads improved, the freight was transferred to trucks. Long trains still ran through Clifton Bend, but they no longer slowed.

Hank felt alive as he moved in the night, and Ketch was right beside him. They were both cut from the same cloth. Men of action.

Once in the center of the yard, Ketch whispered, "Do we split up?"

Hank nodded once and blinked his flashlight at the three sheds on the right as he moved off to the left.

They searched, both men in sight of the other. Both traveled as silently as the breeze off the water.

Hank waited until Ketch's flashlight blinked once, and then his shadow moved toward the next building on his side of the yard. Hank turned toward the little box of a building that had once been a depot.

The windows had been boarded up, but the door sagged open. Years of wind had swept a carpet of leaves and tumble-weeds inside.

Two blinks toward Ketch and the soldier was at his side. "Nothing here," Hank said.

Neither man talked more than necessary as they moved to addresses LeRoy had given them. If Hank had been in Houston, he'd have experts with him and dogs to sniff out explosives.

They checked the homes of the two guys Bull had talked to in the pizza place. Nothing. No car at one house, and the other address had a van left unlocked. Again nothing. Either the men weren't involved or they'd made a real effort to cover their tracks.

Just to make sure, they checked out the Wills boys' un-locked garage. Again nothing.

If the pipe bombs were not in the work shed or the cars, Hank feared the worst. They were already in place. But where?

The stage that had been built on campus over the week-end was his first thought. Hank had checked it the past two nights, and he'd bet Ketch had also. The stage seemed the most likely place to put a bomb if you wanted to stir up trouble. Too obvious, Hank decided.

If a bomb was beneath the boards, one explosion would only cause a racket and smoke. If they put it above the platform, the bomb might injure anyone within ten feet.

"Should we check the stage?" Ketch asked, obviously reading Hank's mind.

"Yes, but it's too obvious."

"I agree, but if they planted a bomb to upset the ceremony, it would have to be close to get the attention."

Hank pulled out his cell and dialed Dr. Monroe. When

the professor picked up, Hank asked, "You up on the top floor?"

"Yes," Benjamin answered.

"Tell me what a person standing on the platform could see." Logic told Hank the bomber would want the governor to see the blast. Since all the bombs had been small, this last one would have to be close to the stage.

Ben's voice was lecture steady. "The clock tower. The front of the science building. Faculty parking. The front of the library, and across the street from the north entrance is the back of the hospital."

"Anything else?"

"A circle walk twenty feet from the platform with six trees surrounding it and a rose garden in the center with flags."

"Thanks, Ben, see you back at Primrose Hill."

Chapter 38

Benjamin

Pecos and Benjamin headed down the steps of the science building. Ben had spent his life blocking everything but work as soon as he stepped on campus. Tonight, work was the last thing on his mind. He'd concentrated on finding a place where someone might hide a bomb. He saw nothing.

As they walked away, Jenny filled his mind. She'd told him she was pregnant so calmly, as if it wouldn't change their lives forever.

Before he could think of the future, Ben had to deal with the present.

Ben had helped Pecos find the best locations to post lookouts at dawn. Every inch had to be checked. Then if anyone got close to the speaker stand before the presentation or the path leading to it from the street, they would be questioned. He had to help.

Hank had told them that the governor wouldn't call off his appearance without a real threat, and they had no proof and no real evidence. The pipe bombs that were poorly made were of different interest to the Texas Rangers, but the governor had seen it as only a possible threat. He refused to cancel his speech.

"Do you think we're all making something out of nothing?" Ben asked Pecos.

"Yep. The way I see it is that it's better to chase a hundred nothings and come up empty than stand by and let one something happen."

"You're a wise man, Deputy." Benjamin felt like their roles had switched. The student was getting smarter than the teacher. "Let's finish up. I'm kind of in a hurry to get back. I need to make a list of what to worry about as soon as this bomb threat is over. I'm going to be a dad, you know."

"I heard. I'd like to give you advice, but to tell the truth your troubles are just starting. Maybe we should set up a weekly talk. My baby girl is only one and I stayed up worrying half the night last week thinking what I'd do if she wanted to marry a bum.

"Then I looked over at Kerrie's dad, my father-in-law, and realized he's still worrying about me.

"I fear this parenting job never stops. No sleep, worrying, money always tight. It's like running a gauntlet. And I'm still young. I don't know if you have a chance of making it."

"Thanks, Pecos. Now I have to worry about dying before I finish worrying."

"Any time, Professor."

Ben fought down a laugh as he considered the news would spread that the chemistry professor had just knocked up the biology professor.

Bomb or no bomb, Jenny was always on his mind, so Ben needed to concentrate on finishing and getting back to her.

He smiled. He didn't care what anyone said. He was going to be a father. Ben couldn't wait to see his dad's reaction. For the past twenty years, Dad hadn't bothered to put up a Christmas tree. "After all," he'd say, "trees are for the kids."

This year the big tree would be going up.

But first he had to get Jenny to marry him. That might not be easy; she didn't even want to move in with him. But for some reason she loved him, and women in love do strange things.

She loved him. He had almost said it aloud. *She loved him.*

"Doc, you ready to go?" Pecos asked.

"Sure. I was"—Ben needed to think fast—"was just thinking we should have the lookouts in place by dawn."

"Good idea. How about we walk past the stage and make double sure no surprise is waiting? An hour before the ceremony I'll sweep the place again. I have a feeling we'll all be doing the same thing."

On the way back to Primrose Hill, Ben asked the deputy a few questions about pregnancy. Pecos explained that emotions fly around like bullets, and half the time the mother-to-be will be aiming at the father-to-be. "For the next eight months, if she's upset, it's your fault. Remember that and you'll be fine."

Ben nodded as if he understood.

As they pulled up to Tuesday's house, Ben wasn't surprised to see Jenny and the sheriff sitting on the porch.

A few minutes later he stood behind Jenny with his arms wrapped around her. The others talked about the plan for tomorrow and how everyone would be watching, checking, on alert. Ben thought about only one thing. He was holding his family in his arms.

Ketch suggested that the brain-dead gang may have given up on their prank, but LeRoy said he still wanted to catch them. A crime had been committed at the hospital, and he planned to see that they paid for frightening sick people.

Hank said he'd already called in and told his Houston

office that he planned to stay a few more days. The cop agreed with the sheriff. These guys needed to be caught and they'd need more evidence than Bull's account of a conversation.

Pecos and the sheriff headed home, but the other three couples settled on wicker chairs scattered around the porch. Simon had fallen asleep on the couch with Rambo cuddled against the top of his head.

Ben didn't say much as the others talked. He knew he needed to worry about a bomb going off, but he also wanted to map out the rest of his life.

When he finally drove Jenny home they were silent during the ride, but her hand never stopped brushing his leg.

Once they were in the darkness of her cabin, she whispered, "Tell me what you feel, Benjamin. I need to know where your mind is tonight."

He kissed her lightly and said simply, "I love you. I have since we met. I want to spend the rest of my life with you. A baby is going to complicate our lives and I plan to enjoy all of it. But, Red, I got to tell you right now; I'm a marrying kind of man. I want to go to bed with you every night and wake up with you every morning."

She looked up at him and answered, "Well, I'm not a marrying kind of woman. I've always thought of myself as a free spirit. I've never believed in growing roots."

She frowned at him and he dropped his head as if he was broken before the fight began.

Finally he leaned down and kissed her softly as he tried to think of what to say.

She kissed him back and he felt warm tears running down her cheeks.

"I love you too, Benjamin. I really do."

He braced for the blow.

"And"—she pressed her forehead into his chest—"I guess this once I'll make an exception to my rules."

"You'll marry me?" Ben didn't breathe.

"Sure, but you have to promise to give me space."

He took her hand and tugged her toward the bedroom. "We'll talk about building a house tomorrow. I've been thinking I may not have time for making wine. We can use the land I planned to have a little vineyard on to build a house on. That way my dad can walk over and tell us how to raise his grandkids."

"Kids?"

"Why not?"

As he unbuttoned her clothes, he talked about how they could organize their schedules so they wouldn't have to worry about a sitter. Then he worried about his dad buying the kid a horse. That is, if his dad ever again returned his calls.

Ben grinned. Maybe his folks were making up for lost years. By the time they came up for air the kid would be calling them Grandpa and Grandma.

Jenny finally stopped his thinking when she stood naked in front of him. Her fists were planted on her nicely rounded hips and she looked so beautiful.

"Benjamin, you have a great many habits that will drive me crazy before we lie beside one another in the ground. I have no doubt we'll fight about them all, so we might think about numbering them. But, you should know right now, from the beginning, not one thing you do is ever going to make me stop loving you."

She tugged off his shirt as he dropped his pants. "But with all your faults you've got one grand gift. You do a great, complete, perfect job of loving me."

Ben got the point. He climbed into bed with Jenny and didn't say a word as he showed her just how much he loved her.

When he was sure she was asleep, Ben slid his hand over her middle and smiled.

Chapter 39

Ketch

Ketch helped Tuesday get her house back in order after everyone left. "Thanks for doing this. If this group had met anywhere in town we wouldn't have been able to talk freely."

"I enjoyed it much more than I thought I would. Millie is shy like me, but we talked. She even offered me a job at the library if I wanted it. She said I could work my classes around my hours."

"Sounds great," Ketch said as he thought about how he'd not be there to help her if she kept the bar job. He was graduating. He was leaving soon. The library would be safer for her.

"I think I'd like to work in the library. You and I could maybe meet at the coffee shop for lunch."

For a month, he thought. Then he'd be packing up for parts unknown. For a moment he'd thought maybe he'd apply to teach in the valley, but the chance of finding a job in a small district wouldn't be good. And roofing houses all day, every day, didn't appeal to him. It was time he found a place where he could build a new life. He'd traveled the world. He'd lived adventure. Now he wanted peace. Honey Creek had almost felt like home.

If she'd agreed to be his girlfriend, he might have tried to make something work, but she didn't want that, so he was going to have to move on. He wanted more and she wanted to stay just friends. If he stayed, he had a feeling she'd break his heart.

"You want to go to the attic and look at the stars?" She opened the secret panel they'd found.

Ketch knew he needed to get some sleep. He needed to keep his mind on the bomb threat. On the governor coming. But he followed her up the tiny stairs anyway, to the third floor where windows were slanted to let in the sky.

They lay down on the quilted pillow almost the size of a mattress. His legs hung off from the knees down but he didn't mind. Tuesday was beside him.

Ketch had always faced any problem straight on, and he faced it now. "Kid, you willing to tell me why you don't want to be my girlfriend?"

"No," she answered.

He waited for more of an answer, but none came. The night sky was so beautiful they seemed to just drift among the stars for a while.

Finally he tried again. "I sorta thought we were getting along fine. Friends, you know, maybe heading to a little more than friends. Is there something about me that bothers you?"

"No," she answered as she pulled his arm over a few inches so she could use it as a pillow. "You're great."

Ketch knew he should drop the subject, but this time he couldn't. She was too important to him. "Then why don't you like me?"

She laughed. "I do like you."

"Tell me the truth, Tuesday."

She rose on her elbow. "All right, but it's not something

I'm proud of, and the person I was is not the person I want to be."

She stared up at the stars, then added, "When I was fifteen, after Grannie Eva died, I was so alone. There were days that no one talked to me, or even said hello.

"Boys started talking to me at school. They were usually older than me and had cars. They'd ask me if I wanted to go for a ride or to meet them somewhere so we could be alone to talk. Only they didn't want to just talk. When I did go with them, they'd call me their girlfriend. But we never went anywhere but parking or making out behind the bleachers, and the next day in school they wouldn't speak to me."

Ketch didn't ask more. He didn't want to know what a kid alone did to be liked.

He pulled her closer. "You're a long way from that little girl, Tuesday."

"I know, but now and then a man comes up and asks if I'd like to be his girlfriend for a night. He'll even point out that I've done it before so it's nothing new." She added after a long silence, "Even when I started saying no, they still told stories about me. Some even gave details about what we did, and no one believed me when I said it wasn't true."

Ketch lay beside her trying to think of what to say. He could put all he knew about women in a walnut. Maybe all she wanted from him was friendship, but he wanted more.

She pointed out a few constellations in the night sky.

He thought of asking her for a list of the guys. Ketch could beat up two or three a week until he got down the list.

He'd rather ask nothing of her than frighten her.

When they finally went downstairs to eat the last of the pies she'd made, he asked, "How about going out to eat with me tomorrow and we can rehash all that happens, if anything does?"

"If you're still alive, I want steak." Ketch smiled. "It's a date, then."

Chapter 40

Benjamin

Monday

Benjamin and Jenny stood on the top floor of the science building looking down. They'd both brought binoculars but all seemed calm below. But the "what could happen" made his heart pound.

People were walking past the stage erected for the governor's speech. One more hour and there would be dozens of students and faculty below, listening to a ten-minute presentation, then all would be over. If nothing happened in that ten-minutes Ben swore he'd stop worrying.

As he watched the groundskeepers were placing flowers on either side of the podium.

Ben and Jenny saw Ketch stationed just behind the trees the governor would be traveling through from his car to the platform. Three sheriff's deputies were on the other side of the open area. Two campus cops were already on the steps making sure some stranger didn't get close to the stage from behind.

Ben had no idea where Hank was, but he had no doubt the cop was close. The sheriff would be in his cruiser ahead of the governor's car. And, of course, another car would follow with two Texas Rangers traveling with the governor.

"We've got more people watching over the site than will be listening to the speech," Jenny whispered.

She stood like a soldier next to Benjamin.

The minutes ticked by. No stranger came near the podium. Ben knew Ketch, Pecos, and Hank had checked all buildings surrounding the stage. If the bomber wanted to make a scene he'd have to set off a bomb near enough for the cameramen hanging around to see it. If he wanted to harm people, he'd have to place the bomb close to the stage.

To do that, he'd have to get past the growing crowd.

Ben tried to figure the odds that the incompetent gang could actually make a bomb that worked. One in five, Ben determined. Then the chances of getting it within a hundred feet of the presentation were almost zero.

"Thirty minutes." Jenny checked her watch.

The grounds workers were finally putting up folding chairs for the guests and several of the faculty.

A few students were starting to gather.

Ten minutes to wait.

Ben saw Wynn Wills and his brother, Bull, move up in front of the walkway. They were both close enough to see the guest of honor, the governor, arrive and hear the speech but not close enough to be noticed if they decided to cut out of the speech early.

Ben checked the wall clock and wished his heart would slow to the second hand's pace.

A long black limo pulled up with a county sheriff's cruiser in front and a highway patrolman following behind. Before any door of the limo opened, the sheriff stepped out just ahead of the limo and two Texas Rangers climbed out of the back of the patrol car.

Just as the limo door opened, Benjamin saw Bull Wills

take off in a dead run through the rose garden. Everyone had turned their attention to the governor's arrival.

Ben was three stories up. He could do nothing but watch. Jenny let out a cry as people below cheered the governor.

But those on guard shuffled and guns were drawn as Bull plowed into one of the groundskeepers at full speed.

A silver pipe flew out of the guy's hand and rolled beneath the podium as Bull flattened the groundskeeper to the ground and planted almost three hundred pounds on top of him.

Benjamin and Jenny had a front seat to all the action as the crowd's attention shifted.

The limo door closed. Texas Rangers stepped to either side. Sheriff LeRoy rushed toward the limo from the other direction. Hank seemed to come out of nowhere as he ran toward Bull.

The campus cops herded all the people on the platform off and into the science building's lobby. Students standing around on the grass scattered. The whisper of a bomb became a roar.

It seemed to Benjamin that in a blink the landscape had completely changed. A celebration had flipped to a crime scene.

No one near the stage or Bull Wills seemed to notice that both of the rangers climbed into the limo with the governor and drove off, with the highway patrol car following close behind.

Ben forced out the breath he'd been holding. The governor was safe. Bull was still on top of the groundskeeper, but no one was moving toward the rose garden.

Ben watched Hank pull his gear from the side of the building and walk alone toward the stage. He seemed calm, focused.

As deputies kept the few reporters back, Hank knelt and

pulled out a pipe bomb from under an arrangement of flowers by the podium. Slowly, he placed the pipe in a box and moved away. No one moved.

It was over. Ben reached for Jenny and they both relaxed as the frozen scene below began to melt and people started moving around.

He took Jenny's hand and they walked down the stairs. A group of university staff was huddled in the foyer but Ben walked right past them. When one of the deputies started to stop him, Hank yelled that the two professors were part of his team.

Ben stood a bit taller but he didn't turn loose of Jenny's hand. One day he'd tell his son, or daughter, of this adventure. Maybe he'd even admit to being more worried than brave.

Amid the rose bushes, Ketch lifted Bull off the bomber, who looked like a deflated Halloween blowup. The guy was covered in dirt, and from the smell, half drunk. He started yelling that he didn't do anything. "This is police harassment," he said between complaints.

Bull doubled up his fist and yelled, "I ain't the police. I'm the hospital security and you're about to end up there if you don't stop bellowing at me."

After cussing for a while, Bull turned to Ketch. "When I saw him, I remembered he'd been mowing the grass outside the hospital a few minutes before the bomb blew the glass. It took me a while, but I recognized him as the silent drunk with the two losers in the bar that night. He was dirty, smelled like shit and kept telling the college had crushed his dreams. When I saw him put the flowers down and walk away, I remembered him so I decided my job was to do nothing but watch him."

Ketch motioned for Pecos to cuff the man, then he patted

Bull on the back. "You did good, Bull. Best tackle I've ever seen. You're a hero."

The drunk in handcuffs yelled. "Bull, you should be on my side of this. The college flunked you too. Place needs to blow up or burn to the ground."

Bull chest-bumped the guy. "The college didn't flunk me. I did that to myself." He fisted his fist. "You could have hurt someone. We got enough folks in the hospital already."

The drunk yelled he was being harassed again. He claimed his friends backed out on him when they realized people might get hurt.

He yelled, "Pain is the price of change."

No one commented, but when they put on the cuffs, the drunk started crying.

In what seemed like minutes everything was cleaned up and all went back to normal. A reporter got a few great shots of Bull tackling the bomber and the sheriff took charge of the groundskeeper. As he was being shoved toward the cruiser, he claimed he had hearing damage from being yelled at.

The sheriff didn't mind posing for a few pictures. Hank told the press LeRoy was the head of the operation.

The next morning Bull's picture made the campus paper and LeRoy gave him a badge to wear.

Ketch and Hank and the professors seemed to vanish from the operation, but that was all right. The locals learned the details.

Chapter 41

Ketch

As the sun set on one hell of a day, Ketch drove out to Primrose Hill to pick up Tuesday for their first real date. He felt nervous. He hadn't really dated before he joined the army, and then Crystal was just there. They ate meals together, worked together, and slept together, but they'd never dated.

Tuesday must have been looking forward to dinner because she was waiting on her beautiful porch. They drove out to a steak house halfway between Honey Creek and Clifton Bend. For the first time she wore a dress and he wore a tie. He held her chair for her.

Tuesday wanted to hear every detail of what had happened. Ketch had already given the account of all he saw a half dozen times, and wasn't all that interested in doing it again, but he loved watching her face as she learned the whole story.

The low lights in the restaurant made the night romantic as they held hands between courses.

When they moved outside on a patio to have dessert under the stars, she asked him about his plans for graduation.

"I'll move on after finals, I guess. I'm not sure where

I'll end up. I've got enough money to spend the summer traveling, then I'll look for a job."

"Aren't you going to walk at graduation?"

"No, don't see much point in it. I have no family to watch."

"I'd come and watch."

Ketch stared at her. How could a woman like him and be afraid of him at the same time? She'd hold his hand on a date, but she didn't want to be his girlfriend. "Then I'll walk. If you'll watch."

She smiled and thanked him for the date as he drove her home.

When he followed her to her porch, she stood on the second step and kissed him good night.

He wished he could know if she'd ever be able to love him. Sometimes he felt like his heart hung under the lost sign on a telephone pole and no one ever noticed.

As the kiss ended, he said his thoughts. "I don't want to let you go."

She laughed. "You have to, Ketch. We can't stand here all night. Besides, if you have time for lunch tomorrow, drop by the library. I'll be starting my training."

Tiny moments, he thought, nothing more. He wasn't sure he could live on small bits of her, but he knew he didn't want to step away.

"I'll drop by. Dr. Monroe wants to see me tomorrow after his one o'clock class."

"I thought the survey was over. The 'Chemistry of Mating' will soon be an article and maybe a winner."

"It has been turned in, even with all the excitement going on. They barely got the article and research findings in on time.

"Who knows what Monroe wants to talk to me about. The Randall brothers also want to meet about something.

They probably want to know if I'll stay around and work for them this summer."

She kissed his nose. "Will you?"

"I don't know."

"Well, don't even think about standing me up tomorrow. I'm not ready to give you up."

"You don't need me, kid." Ketch turned around before he said too much. "See you tomorrow."

The clock tower was clanking out the noon hour when Ketch picked up Tuesday from the library. She chattered on about how she loved her job and how wonderful Miss Remington was.

He was halfway through his sandwich when she asked about his morning.

"Fine." He smiled. "Perfect, in fact. Monroe asked me if I wanted to design and build a house for him out on a piece of land near his dad's place. When I asked what kind of house, he just said it needs to be a one of a kind, like Primrose Hill is. He and Jenny are getting married as soon as the semester's over. They want to be settled in their new house before the baby comes."

When Tuesday didn't ask any questions, he continued. "I talked with the Randall brothers about supplying the lumber, and they'll let me be in charge."

"That's wonderful."

"Benjamin—that's what he told me to call me now— only had one request on the house. The rest, he said, is up to Jenny. 'Make it big,' he said."

"I asked if she had any questions and he said he was sure she would.

"Then he told me the strangest thing. He said he'd bought one of the fishing shacks down by the river and as soon as they move in, he wants the shack she lived in moved to the trees behind where the house will stand. He says he promised Jenny her own space."

"He's a wise man, your Dr. Monroe."

"Yeah. It'll be fun building them a home."

Tuesday laughed. "You'll get to design houses, Ketch. Your dream."

"I think I'd try it for a while. Maybe take a few architectural classes online. My dreams haven't been turning out so well so far. Randall told me I have to move out of the loft. They've got another student coming in."

"You'll need a bigger place to live. Someplace to spread out. Like the big workplace at my house where my Grannie once painted. It's got great light, and your house plans will cover the walls and you can use the downstairs bedroom as an office. I can see you bounding up the stairs three at a time."

Ketch frowned. "You want me to move in? I thought we are just friends."

She met his eyes. "We are, Ketch, but I thought we could be friends with benefits."

"What benefits?"

"Meals from me. Free repairs from you. Free rides to work on rainy days. And dates to eat out now and then. I wouldn't be afraid at night and you'd have someone to carry you to bed when you get drunk."

"And . . ." Ketch waited.

"And great kisses every night. We'll start there."

"Fair enough, kid. I think I could handle that as a foundation to build on."

Ketch had no idea where his career was going or his life was going, or which way his love life was headed, but as long as Tuesday was in it he'd be fine.

She was offering him a home and a promise of someday.

Chapter 42

Hank

Wednesday

The U-Haul was loaded and ready as Hank sat down with Simon for their last breakfast with Millie. She'd progressed to one crutch and a boot that came to her knee.

Today would be her first full day at work and she'd dressed as the very proper librarian she was.

He couldn't take his eyes off her. He'd gotten used to dressing her, carrying her, holding her at night. She was the gentlest person he'd ever known and she deserved to be with a gentle man. Words of love, or even affection, had never passed between them, but he loved her and he knew a part of her loved him.

"We'll come back to see you in a month," Hank said. "Simon will be out of school by then and his mother won't mind."

"You don't have to. I'll be fine."

He wished he could load her in the truck and take her with him. From the tears in Simon's eyes he felt the same way. But his little librarian belonged here. And his career was in Houston. They'd started out a world apart and they'd end a world apart.

As Simon ran around chasing Rambo so he could give the dog one more hug, Hank moved closer to Millie.

"I'm going to miss you."

"Me too, but in my experience, I've learned that I'm a woman people can walk away from." She held her head high. "I'll be fine."

He'd learned to be careful not to move too fast around Millie. "One last hug, pretty lady?"

"I'd like that."

For the first time she was standing as he moved close, and he realized she was taller than she'd seemed. As their bodies touched, he felt how lean she was as he slid his hands down the lines that he'd loved seeing and feeling.

Hank knew he was too wild a man for a woman like her. They'd never fit. But right now, in this one moment, she felt like his mate. He'd love her and miss her in all the quiet moments of his life, but she'd never be his.

"Goodbye, my lady," he whispered as he kissed her softly one last time.

"Goodbye, cowboy."

Slowly they pulled apart and moved outside. Simon was excited to be riding in a truck. Hank talked about the route he'd be taking. Millie remained silent.

One quick hug and they were gone.

In the rearview mirror, Hank watched her standing outside, standing tall, waving. He kept her in his sight until he had to turn the corner. Then felt a pain in his chest all the way to Houston.

After he was home and settled, Hank still couldn't sleep.

Finally, after midnight, he pushed her number.

Millie answered on the second ring and she didn't sound like she'd been asleep.

"You all right, Millie?" was all he could think to say.

"I'm fine," she answered.

"I just had to be sure." He felt like a fool, so he might as well fall off the cliff. "You do know I love you."

Silence. Then in a tiny whisper, she answered, "I love you too."

Hank wasn't sure he said goodbye. He just fell asleep almost believing she was beside him, and he had a feeling she was doing the same.

Epilogue

Christmas on Primrose Hill

Ketch watched Tuesday run around the house for two days. Christmas had exploded everywhere.

Their home, he almost said aloud. In November, when she'd finally agreed to marry him, she'd put his name on the deed as a gift to him.

When he'd told her the gift was too much, she just laughed and said she was giving him her heart and that was much more valuable than an old house.

They married over Thanksgiving and spent their honeymoon at home. There was nowhere else either wanted to be.

His business was growing. He now had four unique houses in production, and Tuesday had talked him into knocking a wall out and incorporating the space from his bedroom into his office. His future house plans and designs lined the walls and he had to knock out a wall to enlarge the upstairs bedroom to be their room, not just hers.

Tuesday had been cooking for two days. She'd invited a long tableful of guests. When he told her there was no room for a Christmas tree in the dining room, she put it up as the table's centerpiece.

The first to arrive were Deputy Pecos with his beautiful wife and their little girl. The child looked just like her mother except she had her father's brown eyes.

The next to rush in from the cold were the Monroes, with a screaming newborn in Benjamin's arms. His parents followed, both telling their son to hold the baby's head.

The whole town claimed Benjamin's mother might not have been a great mom, but she was a great grandmother. Benjamin's father, who never talked much anyway, seemed to have given it up completely with a wife and a daughter-in-law around. He'd made one comment about getting his grandson a horse, and the objections were still being voiced.

When Tuesday asked Jenny if she'd heard about the results of her study, "The Chemistry of Mating," Benjamin said simply, "We didn't win the grand prize."

Jenny winked at him. "Oh, yes we did."

The last vehicle to pull up was a red Land Rover. No one was surprised when Hank swung Millie up in his arms and carried her to the porch. No one knew exactly what their relationship was. His Rover was parked outside her door a few weekends a month, and she flew out to meet him for a few days of skiing or mountain climbing or visiting museums.

As everyone hugged and laughed, Ketch put his arm around Tuesday and lifted her up to eye level, then turned to the crowd.

"Welcome all!" he shouted. "Welcome to our home."

Ketch closed his eyes and breathed in the smells of Christmas. He'd found his home, not in a place, but in a person, and he owned a house he planned to live in the rest of his life.

Read on for a special preview of Jodi Thomas's next heartwarming Honey Creek novel, forthcoming in spring 2023 . . .

A VALLEY CALLED HOME

In a valley where most families go back generations
and have relatives scattered for miles,
four strangers meet and unite
as they bury a father none of them has ever seen.
Slowly they piece together a bond that will not only
change them, but the community for the better.

One by one the children of Joey Morrell come back to
Honey Creek. A father they never met left them not only
money, but what each one needs to build a life.
One will learn to love, one learns to trust,
one learns to fight, and the last learns to forgive . . .

The Will

"The bed is too hard. I thought hospital beds were supposed to be comfortable," Joey Morrell complained to Jackson Willington in a half-drunk whine.

"Mr. Morrell, I'm not involved in hospital furnishing. I'm your lawyer." Jackson lifted his briefcase as if showing proof of his new title. "Now, we need to get down to the topic of your will. You may not have much time left."

Jackson kept his voice low, hoping to sound older.

Joey reached for his cigarettes. Camels, no filter.

"I didn't know they still made Camels. Never mind. Irrelevant. You can't smoke in here, Mr. Morrell. I don't think Dr. Hinton would approve, and I saw the no smoking sign when I ran through the emergency entrance."

"Jackson, you're no more fun than your dad. The S.O.B. up and died on me before I got my affairs organized. I'd just finished listing my heirs from a few of those affairs years ago, when they tossed me in the ambulance, and now I find out I've got a wet-behind-the-ears lawyer."

"You were having a heart attack, Mr. Morrell. The bartender called 911, then you told him to call me." Jackson noticed the old guy wasn't listening. If sins showed on a man's face, Joey Morrell was the bad side of Dorian Grey.

Joey coughed. "I did love those women I found in my younger days, but I never wanted to do the paperwork. Every darling I slept with cussed me out for not marrying her. They all said I didn't have a heart, so that's proof I can't die of a heart attack. But you, being my lawyer, are going to make it right, Jackson, just in case? I'm keeping my word to your old man to sign a will. I plan to pay for my folly."

"I'll do my best to help you, sir." Jackson thought of cussing. He should have been an accountant. His dad left him every crazy old goat in the valley to deal with. Joey Morrell was as bad as the lady who came in every Monday to change her will. Every time one of her cats died or peed on the rug, the feline was disinherited.

"Good. Make it fast, boy. I'm not feeling so good." Morrell coughed again. "About time to roll the dice on whether I walk out of this place one more time. The women I attract nowadays are drunks, mean and ugly even with my glasses off. Might as well head down to Hell. The pickings couldn't be much worse."

Jackson leaned over the bed. "That why you're refusing the heart surgery, Morrell? You want to leave it to chance?"

Joey smiled. "I may have done a hell of a lot of bad things, but I swear I'm not a liar. I've spent sixty years gambling and I ain't stopping now. I like women, but I wasn't born with enough heart to love one. Strange little creatures if you ask me. Nesters. And me, I was born to ride the open roads." He stopped long enough to push the call button again.

"I've already cheated death three times. I got out of that hospital in New Orleans after I was left for dead in an alley for two days. Ten years ago, I was in a bad wreck they said no one could walk away from, and at twenty a medic took four bullets out of my chest.

"Jackson, it'll be another thirty years and another dozen women before I wear out, but I promised your daddy I'd make a will if I ever ended up in a hospital again."

"Then, let's get started. How about we begin with your assets, Mr. Morrell. I know you have an old Camaro, a little piece of land along the north rim, and an eighteen-wheeler truck. You never married. No living relatives."

Waving the lawyer away, Joey leaned back on a stack of pillows. "I'm tired, boy, and I'll miss the news if you stay any longer. I wrote down all you need to know." Joey handed him a folded piece of paper. Draw it up all legal like. Don't come back until after breakfast. The nurse said she has to spoon-feed me if I'm weak come morning." A wicked smiled crossed his pasty face. "There ain't nothing nicer that a big-busted woman with short arms feeding a man."

Jackson had enough of Joey Morrell. The drunk was as worthless as his father used to say he was. "I'll take care of everything, Mr. Morrell." Just for spite, he added, "Anyone you want to notify to come to your funeral?"

"No. I'll go it alone. Cremate my body and spread my ashes out on Eagle's Peak."

Jackson put the folded paper in his empty briefcase and walked out of Joey's room. As he passed Dr. Paul Henton, Jackson shook his head. "The old man thinks you're too young to be a doc and I'm too dumb to be his lawyer."

Paul took the time to look up from a chart. The doc nodded. "He won't let me operate or move him to a big hospital for surgery. Claimed he'd chosen option number three. Get over it. He told me he plans to be out of this place before happy hour tomorrow."

"What are his chances?" Jackson asked.

The doctor Jackson had played football with through high school was honest as always. "Not good. You might want to get that will done."

"I'm heading home before the rain gets worse. I'll work on it tonight and have it ready by morning." Jackson hesitated, then added, "Call if you need me."

The doctor turned back to his charts as he added, "I will. Same for you."

Jackson turned his collar up and ran for his pickup, thinking if he ever made any money in this small town, he'd buy a proper car. Maybe a Lincoln, or a BMW. Lawyers should drive something better than a twenty-year-old, handed-down beat-up farm truck.

Half an hour later Jackson was holding the square of paper Joey had given him in his hand when the hospital called. As the nurse explained how Mr. Morrell died yelling for his supper, the lawyer read the note below four names with birthdays beside each. It read: *Give it all to my offspring.*

Morrell's signature was clear. Dated an hour ago. Witnessed by a nurse and some guy who wrote *janitor* under his name.

"Damn," Jackson said as he stared at the names. "The old guy knew he was dying. Probably didn't mention it just to irritate the hell out of me."

Joey died leaving all he owned to four names on a piece of paper.

Four sons he'd probably never met. All with different last names and none of them Morrell.

ANDY DELANE—30—FORT SILL

RUSTY MACAMISH—34—SOMEDAY VALLEY

ZACHARY HOLMES—25—AUSTIN

GRIFFITH LAURENT—27—FRENCH QUARTER
 NEW ORLEANS

Joey lived within a day's drive of one of his sons. Another son lived thirty miles away on the other side of the valley, but Jackson would bet not one of them had ever seen Joey. That could be a good thing. Joey wasn't much of a man or a father. That not one carried his name was proof.

Jackson had taken over his father's practice in Honey Creek two months ago and his first client left this world without paying.

But Jackson would do his duty and hope none of Joey's boys took after their sperm donor. He'd find the boys, now men, but he doubted they'd be glad to see him.

Chapter 1

Someday Valley

Midnight

Rusty MacAmish gunned the old Ford's engine just before he swung left and headed up the hill toward Someday Valley. There was always a chance the car wouldn't make the incline on the dirt road, but he'd had a hell of a day and figured bad luck had to run out sometime.

Mud moved downhill like lava on his left. A ten-foot drop was on his right. Bald tires didn't put up much of a fight to hold on to the two-lane road.

In the midnight rain Rusty felt the Fairlane began to slide sideways. Then like a slow-mo rerun, the Ford tilted left as the road disappeared and three thousand pounds of steel began to roll. Rusty tightened his grip on the steering wheel as if he still had some control of the car . . . or his life.

He didn't bother to scream or cuss. He simply braced for a crash.

The ground slammed into the passenger side shattering glass and metal. Then, as the roof hit the incline, he felt the cut of his seatbelt and it seemed to be snowing glass.

The Ford rolled again and the driver's door pushed against Rusty's shoulder. He clenched as it rolled again and the inside of what had once been a car was now a coffin of flying glass and metal.

Something hit his head and the night went completely black but, for a moment, the sounds remained in his head as if echoing what had been his life.

One last echo whispered through the bedlam. One word he'd heard for as long as he could remember.

Worthless.

Chapter 2

Starri Knight lay on the hardwood floor of her aunt's hundred-year-old cabin as she watched rain slide down the huge picture window. If she didn't move, maybe she'd feel closer to nature as she had when she was a child. Maybe the moon would play peek-a-boo with her in the storm clouds. She was almost positive the man in the moon had once when she was small.

When she was a kid, stars winked at her and the moon smiled. She'd tell her Aunt Ona-May and they'd laugh.

But tonight, all Starri saw was car lights making their way up the hill and lightning running across the sky like a tidal wave igniting.

All her life pretty much everyone who took the back trail in rain got stuck. Her aunt Ona-May would wait until morning to back the tracker out of the barn and go pull them out of the mud. For thirty bucks, of course.

Starri watched the rain as she remembered the story of the night her aunt took her in as if she were really kin. Her aunt said one dark night a young couple, not out of their teens, took the road to Someday Valley way too fast. They collided with a pickup coming down hauling hay. The crash killed both the teenagers instantly, but the baby in the back didn't have a scratch.

While the two farmers to the north heard the crash and came running to help the driver pinned inside his truck, Ona-May crawled in the window and pulled out a baby in the back seat of the young couple's car. She said the minute she pushed the blanket away the baby reached up trying to touch the stars.

No one came to take the baby that night. Ona-May decided to call the tiny child Starri until kin came. But, no one came. No one wanted the tiny baby.

Since Ona-May Jones was a nurse in her younger days, the county let her foster the child.

Starri smiled remembering the beginning of her story. She couldn't miss parents she'd never known, but she was thankful Aunt Ona-May found her. Auntie might never have had a family of her own, but she poured all her love on a tiny baby.

Starri watched as the car on the incline began to roll sideways down the hill. For a moment it seemed no more than an awkward falling star.

Then she heard the sounds of breaking glass and snapping metal blending with the rain, and Starri screamed.

Someone was dying in the same spot her parents had twenty years ago. She closed her eyes, reliving a memory that had formed before words.

As always Auntie's arms surrounded her. "Starri, it's all right." As the old woman saw the car rolling, she added calmly. "Get on your boots. We've work to do."

Auntie's old body straightened into the nurse she'd been in Vietnam fifty years ago.

As she collected supplies, Starri dialed 911 and was told the road between Honey Creek and Someday Valley was closed. One of the bridges was out. The only ambulance in the valley was on the other side of the bridge.

"We'll take care of it, Starri. Don't worry. Doctoring

humans is pretty much like doctoring the other animals around here."

Starri nodded but she wasn't sure she believed her aunt.

As they marched up the hill, the lights on the car went out but the rattling continued as if the auto was dying a slow death. The engine was still sputtering when they reached the wreck. Their flashlights swept the ground like lightning bugs hopping in the night.

"Here," Ona-May yelled as she moved a few feet below the car.

Starri ventured closer making out the outline of a body. A tall man dressed all in black. Rain seemed to be pounding on the body as if determined to push him in the ground.

Auntie pulled off her raincoat and covered him. "I can't see where he's hurt, but he's breathing. We'll roll him on your raincoat and pull him to the cabin. If he makes the journey back to the house, I'd say he's got a chance."

Starri followed orders. She'd seen her aunt set a broken leg and stitch up a cowboy who refused to go to the doctor. Auntie delivered babies before the doctor could come out. The people in the valley were mostly poor and didn't go to a doctor unless they had to. They knew Ona-May would take care of what she could and often loan them money if she recommended the doctor.

As they pulled the unconscious stranger over the wet grass, Starri thought of another talent her aunt had. She loved people. Not just the good ones or the righteous ones like the preacher counted. She loved them all, even the sinners and the drunks.

Starri figured Ona-May overlooked folks' shortcomings because she had a few herself. She wasn't beyond stealing the neighbor's apples or corn, and she cussed when she was frustrated. And, every New Year's Eve she'd drink and tell stories of her days in the army.

As they reached the cabin, her aunt started issuing orders as if she had troops and not just Starri.

"We'll put him on the floor by the fireplace. Get me towels and warm water. Start cleaning him up while I collect supplies and call the doctor over in Honey Creek. I can already see our patient has an arm broke, so cut off his shirt. I'm guessing he's got internal injuries. Oh, add logs to the fire, girl."

Starri stared down at the muddy man with hard times showing in worry lines. "You'll have to help me, mister. I can't even remember all the orders. Ona-May gets like that sometimes when she's excited but my ears still listen slow. She was an emergency nurse for thirty years. You're in good hands."

"Starri, get moving," Ona-May yelled from the kitchen. "We got to keep him alive until the ambulance gets here."

She handed her aunt the phone as she ran for towels and a pan of hot water. When she returned, the stranger's eyes were open. She saw pain, but not fear.

"You an angel, sweetheart?" he whispered.

"No," she answered. "I'm a star that fell out of the sky twenty years ago. Kids at school said I'm as strange as they come, but I'm not. I'm just different."

"Me too," he said. "I'm Rusty MacAmish. Folks say I'm worthless. You're wasting your time fixing me up. I'll just scatter again."

He closed his eyes as she gently washed his face. She didn't know if he fell asleep or passed out, but the worry lines faded on his face. She barely heard him whisper, "Watch over me, little star."

"I will. You just rest. Don't worry about that windshield wiper sticking out of your side. My aunt can fix that."

Chapter 3

Jackson ran through his parents' house stripping off his clothes as fast as he could with one hand as he held his cell in the other.

"Slow down, Paul. I can meet you at the bridge with two mounts. I've got Raymond saddling two horses and loading them in the trailer now. I can be there by the time you can drive from the hospital to that old bridge heading into Someday Valley." Jackson hit speaker as he pulled on jeans. "Any idea who the injured man is?"

"Yeah," Paul answered. "He's your client's son. He's Joey Morrell's oldest son."

Visit our website at
KensingtonBooks.com
to sign up for our newsletters, read
more from your favorite authors, see
books by series, view reading group
guides, and more!

BOOK CLUB
BETWEEN THE CHAPTERS

Become a Part of Our
Between the Chapters Book Club
Community and Join the Conversation

Betweenthechapters.net

Submit your book review for a chance to win exclusive
Between the Chapters swag you can't get anywhere else!
https://www.kensingtonbooks.com/pages/review/